Brotherly

Love

&

BETRAYAL

By Daphine Glenn Robinson

12/2011

Truthful Press Publishing

Brotherly Love & Betrayal

Truthful Press Publishing
A Glenn Sisters' Creation Company

PO Box 240
Statesville, NC 28687

ISBN   978-0-9799707-0-2

Library of Congress Control Number: 2007906900

All poems in this book are the original works of
Daphine Glenn Robinson and Dana M. Glenn

Visit www.DaphineRobinson.com

For Richard, Victoria, and Andrew

Acknowledgements

Lord, this is the work that I prayed would put me on the map. Thanks for ordering my steps and making my dream a reality. You're an awesome God!

Thanks to my family, especially my husband, for supporting me through another endeavor. Victoria and Andrew's mantra, "Mommy is a published author!" finally paid off. I'll always believe in the mustard seed faith.

I want to especially thank my friend, Sibyl Goode-Bines for being the first person to read this from beginning to end in record time. I thank God for allowing us to meet many years ago. You know we're kindred spirits.

Dana and Melvin, ya'll know how much you mean to me. Thanks for letting me pick your brain, and your enthusiasm about what was going to happen next kept me going. Thanks for continually asking me what the status was. Some days I felt like giving up, but when I'd think of you three, I felt obligated to move on towards the end!

Lenethia Wells, my assistant at Tube Specialties, thanks for listening to me unload almost everyday about getting this book out. You believed in me while others stood back to see what I was going to do. Thanks, Miss Lady!

To the employees at Tube Specialties, thank you so much for supporting me.

A big thank you goes out to my buddy, Dr. Napoleon Burt. Thanks doc for helping to make sure the medical lingo was on the up and up! You are a true friend.

And as always, my church family at Greater Salem at the Lake in NC, and Macedonia Church in Pittsburgh, PA, you have been life preservers for this southern girl. You never cease to amaze me. Thank you for your support and encouragement.

Finally, to my readers, I know I've kept you waiting long enough after years of talking about this novel. I wouldn't be successful without you. You're the best! It is my prayer that I continue to write what you want to read. Be blessed.

Daphine Glenn Robinson

Prologue

Before Spring

"Woman! Do you want to enjoy the fruits of my labor or not?" Crystal knew her husband was being sarcastic by trying to sound as if he were speaking in Biblical terms. His voice resonated through the telephone.

Donnie slammed his pen down on the desktop, and then lowered his voice. He kicked his office door shut while still sitting in his high back leather desk chair. "If I didn't work, you'd be complaining, and…" He took a deep breath then paused. "I can't win. I just can't win."

Who does he think he's talking to like this, and did he just say 'woman' to me?

"What do you want from me, Crystal? This is getting to be too much. Every night, you call hounding me about what time I'm coming home. I'm not a schoolteacher like you with set hours. You know that. I'm telling you, I don't know how much more I can take! I'm already stressed and work is off the chain. My clients are getting more demanding, and when I am home, I need some peace. If I didn't work as hard as I do, you wouldn't be able to have the type of life you have. No, we don't have a palace, but we're comfortable, and it's certainly better than what most of the people we know have. Please, just back up off a brother!"

Crystal couldn't believe her husband of the last ten years was speaking to her like this. Everyone in his office must have heard what he was saying to her and probably even thought she was a nagging wife.

"Donnie, I'm really not trying to aggravate you. I was just calling to see when you were coming home. I was hoping you could go with me to the dinner fellowship at church tonight. Since you haven't been with me all year, I thought this might be a good social function to go to." Crystal continued in a single breath, "People ask about you all the time, and frankly, I'm tired of going everywhere and doing everything like I'm single. I need my husband, that's all. If I'd known asking you if you'd be able to spend some time with your wife was a crime, I wouldn't have called you." She softened her position not wanting to sound as if she were in an attack mode. "I really am thankful for you and all we have. I really am."

"Yeah, whatever." Click.

He hung up on me. What in the world? Hearing the dial tone, and having to press the talk button without saying good-bye left a sinking feeling in the pit of her stomach. Crystal sat back in her chair and looked towards the ceiling. *Where is the man I married? Lord, only you know. Maybe he's having a bad day. But recently, everyday has been a bad day.*

Immediately, the telephone rang.

"Hello?"

"Hey. I'm not trying to be nosy, but are you ok?" asked her brother-in-law, Stephen.

"So you heard?"

"Yep, and so did several other people. I was walking down the hall when he kicked his office door. I've already given little brother my two cents worth. In his defense, it has been pretty hectic around here today, but that was not called for."

"Thanks Stephen. What would I do without you?"

"I've often wondered myself!" he said chuckling slightly. Stephen's voice was comforting to Crystal.

"How long do you think you'll be there tonight?"

"I'm about to leave in a few minutes. Donnie and Amanda are working on a proposal right now. I'm not sure how much longer they'll be."

"Oh. Well, I guess I'll see him whenever."

"Do you want me to bring you something to eat?"

"No, I'm fine. I'm going to sauté some shrimp and rice in the Chinese wok we rarely use."

"Sounds good, want some company?" Stephen asked hoping she'd oblige.

"I think you'd better go home to your own wife tonight."

"Yeah, yeah, yeah. You know how that goes."

"Stephen, be good now."

"Yeah right. I think I'll go to Applebee's for a minute. I need to unwind before going home. If you need anything, you know how to reach me."

"Ok, have a good evening."

"You too."

Once again, Crystal hung up the phone. This time it was a more positive conversation. Stephen had a way of making her feel at ease, unlike his brother who'd recently turned into someone she could no longer recognize.

Chapter 1

Let Me Bend Your Ear

"What? Girl I can't believe you are actually in town... Yes I'll be there. See you soon. Bye, girl."

Crystal Moore pressed on the gas pedal from excitement and then reached over to turn the volume level to six. Track number nine on Kirk Franklin's latest CD was her favorite pump up the volume gospel song. Bobbing her head to the music, she wore the biggest smile she'd had in a long time. She was so surprised to see Melissa's name appear on her cell phone when it rang. Melissa had called to say she was in Charlotte for one day and would be staying overnight to attend a meeting for work. *My girl is in town. Thank you Lord, you always give me what I need when I need it, and right now I need some companionship—preferably from my husband, but Melissa will work too.* "You're da bomb!" she said out loud and pointing her index finger towards the ceiling of her car.

Melissa and Crystal had been much closer since reaching adulthood than when they were younger. For all intents and purposes, Melissa was Crystal's sister, although they were actually cousins. Melissa lived in Charleston, South Carolina, and for years they had spoken almost everyday. More recently, there had been some distance growing between the two of them, and Crystal didn't know why. Well, at least she didn't know details as to why. Melissa did tell her that her relationship with Charles, her boyfriend for the last eleven months, was over, but didn't elaborate about the breakup.

Crystal told Melissa that she had planned to attend Bible study. As a matter of fact, she was just a few miles away from the church when Melissa called. Melissa asked Crystal to meet her afterwards at Starbucks for some girl time. Crystal agreed and hoped she would be blessed by attending study, but at the same time hoped the blessings would come quickly, so she could leave and go see her girl.

After the Bible study was over, several people stood around the church entrance chatting about the week's events and their jobs. Crystal discreetly excused herself through a side door, not wanting to become engrossed in conversations with any of the deacons, elders, and sisters of the church. She had one thing on her mind and that was getting to Starbucks as quickly as she could.

While pulling out of the church parking lot, she called Melissa's cell phone to find out where she was. Melissa said that she was sitting at a table in the back of the Starbucks located on the corner of Broad and Church Street. When Crystal arrived, she saw a Chrysler Pacifica with South Carolina plates and assumed it was Melissa's rental car. Hurriedly, she parked and went inside. Melissa was sitting in the far corner busily using her laptop computer to take full advantage of the free wireless Internet access Starbucks offers. Melissa didn't notice her walk in. Crystal ordered her usual, a decaf white chocolate mocha, then walked over to the table where Melissa was still engrossed in whatever was on her computer screen.

"Hi there," Crystal said as she set her cup on the table.

Melissa let out a high-pitched scream and stood up. She grabbed Crystal, and they hugged and kissed each other on the cheek. "Hi, sis. How are you?"

"Don't 'hi, sis' me. Why didn't you tell me you were coming to town?" Crystal asked.

"Don't be mad," Melissa said. "I didn't know until yesterday afternoon, and since I would be out today, I worked well into the evening. I didn't even have time to get good rates for a flight, but the drive wasn't bad; gave me a chance to think about some things. Girl, I have been working hard all day long." She sat down, and Crystal joined her. Melissa continued to use the computer while talking with Crystal.

"So how are you and Donnie? I'm not taking you away from him am I? I don't want him getting mad at me like he used to when we'd have girls' weekend, Melissa said hesitantly."

"No, it's not like that anymore. I'm sure Donnie hasn't made it home from work yet." Crystal took a sip of her hot beverage. "He's been so busy and preoccupied lately, I don't know what's going on. Girlfriend, I feel like there's trouble where paradise used to be."

"What's going on?"

"I don't know. I guess it's business. I know the agency has been trying to get a big account for a while, and Donnie has been working late on that. I hardly ever see him anymore."
"I'm sure he's doing it for the both of you. Advertising can be very demanding. Sis, be glad you have a man who not only works, but also co-owns the company. Speaking of which, how is Donnie's 'fine' brother, I mean, uh, business partner? Is he still all that and a bag of chips with a super-sized drink?"

Crystal laughed. "Stephen is doing well. He's been working just as hard. They're always tied up in a meeting or entertaining clients somewhere when I call or stop by."

"Girl, take advantage of Donnie being gone. I know…I'm not married; but hey, if I were you, I'd make sure the house and you are hooked up when he does get home. I hope you aren't hounding him about being home more. He probably needs your support right now." Melissa paused, "Things come in seasons, you know that, don't you?"

"Yeah, I know. I don't hound him; I just want to spend some time with my man. I feel like I'm taking a backseat to the business. I know I have a good man," Crystal said. *That is, I hope I do.*

"Sis, I hope and pray I find a good, God-fearing man one day. If he owns his own business, that'll work too," Melissa said smiling like that wasn't such a bad idea.

"You will. I know it. There's a man that God is preparing for you right now, and you'll know he's the right one when you meet him. Hopefully, he won't take off running in the opposite direction!" Crystal said as she threw a napkin at her best friend.

Melissa turned her attention back to the computer screen as if she hadn't heard a word Crystal said. Crystal took in the crowded room. Soft jazz echoed through out from the Dolby surround sound speakers that were strategically placed along the gold colored walls. A blender ground ice to a slush while more iced coffee drinks were ordered in the distance. The strong aroma of fresh-brewed coffee made its way to the back of the building. The place was filled mostly with young couples drinking frappuccinos and other colored drinks. Crystal felt younger than she was, almost like she was in college again. "Thanks again for inviting me here," Crystal said. "I love being here this time of the evening. Girl, my life lately has been school, church, school, church, and did I say church?" Melissa laughed and shook her head. Crystal continued, "There's a different feeling in the air in the evenings. I swing by a few times a week and treat myself."

"You look like you deserve a treat," Melissa said.

"Girl, this stuff is bad for you. But sometimes a sista just has to indulge and ask for forgiveness later! I'll spend the next few days trying to work off this whipped cream," she said patting her already flat stomach.

"Girl, please. You always stay in such good shape. I know I need to back up from the table, but food just tastes too good," Melissa said looking down and patting her stomach. Melissa always admired Crystal's skin, hair and figure. Crystal was so beautiful with her light brown skin and hazel eyes. Her hair was long and flowed over her shoulders. Most days, she wore it pulled back into a ponytail. She had the ability to lose weight when she needed to and never appeared to struggle with food or anything else in her life. She had been health conscious since they were younger. Deep down, Melissa wished she had it in her to lose weight, but as long as Lane Bryant was in business and nice clothes were available for big boned women, she was content.

They talked about thirty more minutes. "Well, girlfriend I need to head home. Three stacks of un-graded papers are calling my name."

"I hear you. Some days, I don't know whether I'm coming or going. I have so much work it's not even funny. To top it all off, I had to fire my assistant and the corporate office has denied my request to fill the position. So now, I not only have to do all of my normal workload, I now have to do my own copying, faxing, filing, new hire orientation, and the list goes on. I am beginning to think human resources isn't my cup of tea. The workforce seems to be getting dumber or the people born after 1975 are just lazy. I haven't quite figured it out yet! Human resources or teaching ninth graders; hey, we have the same job, wanna switch?" Melissa stopped, laughed at herself, and continued talking. "Let me get out of here. A room at the Hilton awaits me! I'll call you tomorrow before I leave."

They hugged each other tightly and Crystal walked Melissa to her car where they said their good-byes. Melissa was the first to pull onto the busy street. She tooted her car horn, and Crystal reciprocated before going in the opposite direction. Crystal missed Melissa, especially now that she was alone more. She longed for a female friend—one with whom she could share her thoughts, hang out, and go shopping. Some days, she felt as if she would lose her sanity after dealing with teenagers at school all day, then going home and having no one to listen to her unload. The trouble was, most days, by the time Donnie got home, she was already in bed.

Crystal thought about Melissa's words over the next few weeks. She examined herself, wanting to see if there was something she could do to make things better in her relationship with her husband. Since he wasn't with her very often, it would be hard to do. She already made lunch for Donnie and stuck messages inside of his attaché. She called him at least once daily, but more often than not, she ended up instead talking to her brother-in-law, Stephen, when she called the office.

She was careful to make sure the house was clean when Donnie arrived and prepared his favorite meals, which ended up being garbage by the end of the week. With all the dinner meetings and ordering in, Donnie usually wasn't hungry when he got home. Crystal even made sure she put on some of her sexiest sleepwear, so if she was asleep when Donnie came home, he might be inclined to wake her after he pulled the covers back to get into bed. Deep down she felt that he was so busy and tired that none of those things seemed to matter. She didn't want to seem pushy or ungrateful, but she wanted her husband back—the one she had before the new clients, new commercials, and the new attitude.

Chapter 2

March

"I need more, more, more, Jesus, more of you…" Crystal sang to the top of her lungs as Joanne Rosario crooned eloquently in the background. Still on a spiritual high from Bible study, she drove faster than she should have to get home. Even with the music blasting, she could still hear the large raindrops beating down on the car's exterior. *Let me slow down before I kill myself out here.*

Rain poured from the sky as if a hurricane was bearing down on the city. The shower arose suddenly just as Bible study was over. Even with the wipers on high speed, Crystal still couldn't see more than twenty yards ahead of her. As she came to her senses and slowed on the two-lane road, she saw a person walking towards her in the downpour. *Who in their right mind would be out here in this weather without an umbrella?* As she approached the pedestrian, she noticed the person looked like Sierra, a girl from her English class. *Was that Sierra? It looked like Sierra.* She wondered if she should slow down or keep driving. Crystal was very much aware that people ran all kinds of scams on unsuspecting motorists these days. As she passed the girl, she realized it was Sierra. *Maybe she needs a ride.* She slowed the car, stopped and put it in reverse. Sierra was a thirteen year old, who always appeared to have something going on, whether it was confrontations with other students or teachers or chronic absenteeism. She stopped by Crystal's classroom between classes to chat and often wanted to tell Crystal what was going on in her personal life. On many occasions she'd told Crystal that she wished her mom was more like her and that she was her favorite teacher.

Crystal rolled down her window just enough to ask if she could help. The rain, finding the crack, started to sprinkle her left arm.

"Mrs. Moore!" she said startled.

"Sierra, what in the world are you doing out here this time of night?"

"I've got to get away; I've got to get away. I can't go back, not now. Please don't make me go back." She spoke hysterically and was looking in the direction Crystal's car was headed.

"What...? Girl, get in."

Crystal drove about a quarter of a mile, before pulling into the Blockbuster Video parking lot where she parked her BMW. Immediately, she regretted being the Good Samaritan. *What is wrong with me? Why didn't I just keep on driving* she thought to herself. *I really am not in the mood for playing Dear Abby tonight. It was so stupid of me to stop at night... but why am I complaining? No one put a gun to my head and told me to pull over to help this girl.*

Donnie had finally promised her that he would be home early. Crystal had already called to tell him that Bible study ran late and that she hung around for a few minutes to speak to the Pastor. She told him she would be home shortly. They hadn't eaten dinner together on a weeknight in quite a while. Now, she was going to be even later. *I always do this, the right thing. Then, I get mad at myself for being who I am. Miss Goody Two Shoes strikes again.* Nonetheless, the child obviously needed some help; and Crystal could tell from school that she needed a friend even more.

"Ok, what's going on? What has you so upset that you are walking out here...by yourself...in this weather? Girl, you could have gotten your behind snatched up out here, and no one would have known about it," Crystal said trying hard not to shout. What if I wasn't who I was and someone stopped and pulled you into their car?

You know, they still haven't found that fifteen year old girl that went missing last summer."

"Mrs. Moore, I ran away from home. I had to go."

"What?"

"Yeah, I can't go back there. He was beating me and she didn't do anything, she just stood there crying. She's scared of him."

"She who? Your mother is afraid of your father?"

"He ain't my daddy."

"Ok, slow down. Tell me what happened," Crystal said while thinking Sierra hadn't paid attention during the grammar lessons in class.

Right before Sierra could speak; Israel Houghton's voice silenced her. I am a friend of God...was the ring tone Crystal assigned to her cell phone. She held up her finger to let Sierra know she needed to take the call. *I knew Donnie would call the minute I parked this car.*

"Wait a minute, Sierra. Hello? No, everything is ok. Blockbuster Video. No, I'm in the parking lot with a student. She ran away from home and I saw her walking down the street near here so I picked her up. I'll explain when I get home. Not long. I'll call you when I'm on my way. I know what I said, but this is important too. I'm sorry. Bye."

The last thing she needed was for him to be mad at her. She had a long day and was looking forward to winding down at home. Her third period class seemed to have been high on something because no one wanted to pay attention and several students disrupted her lesson asking to go to the restroom. Then, at the end of the day, someone decided not to shower after his or her PE class, and the entire room reeked of funky underarms. It gave her sinuses a run for their money. To make matters worse rush hour traffic was no rush. She wondered why it took an hour to drive twenty miles. The only good thing about the whole day was Bible study. The discussion got so intense that the Pastor lost track of time. The lesson was one that would stick with her for a long time—you must meet people where they are. *Didn't Jesus first meet the needs of the people and then minister to them?* Abruptly, she decided to stop thinking of why she didn't want to be in the car with Sierra and to see if God could use her at that moment.

"I'm sorry Sierra; please continue telling me what happened."

"Mrs. Moore, I don't wanna bother you. I'm just gonna go. Forget you even saw me tonight." She opened the door to step out into the rain. The rain had lightened up a bit, but was a steady drool that had distorted the view of the Amoco gas station, which was across the street. There wasn't any Cascade sheeting action like in the commercial to make the view through the windshield better either.

"Sierra shut the door." *Before my interior gets wet, and my car ends up smelling like raw fish.* "You can't go back out there. You're already soaked."

Reluctantly, she shut the door. Crystal was glad too, because she did not want the inside of the car any wetter than it was.

"Tell me what happened, please. I'm listening. You can trust me."

"Nate started fussing at me time I got home from school. Mamma wasn't there because she worked a double shift today. She works at Shoney's waiting tables. He sits at home all day and watches talk shows while my mamma works to support his no good ass. We moved in with him last year when my mamma's other boyfriend put us out. Nate knew my mamma from Shoney's because he used to work there too. Then, he got fired because he clocked in one Saturday, took off, and got one of his boys to clock him out. The manager found out about it and fired both of them. I think he likes me and wants to get with me...that's why he's so mean to me."

"Ok, you're rambling. What happened tonight, Sierra?"

Crystal thought once again about home; she needed to get there. She knew Donnie was going to be very upset with her. *It was supposed to be our night to relax.*

Sierra went on talking, "Well, when I got home, I went into the kitchen to make me a sandwich, and he was in there drinkin' a beer. He said that I'm always eatin' up all of the lunchmeat and if it were up to him, he wouldn't even buy me nothin' to eat. I told him that since he don't have a job, then he don't have nothin' to say about what gets bought or eaten. So he told me that I was livin' under his

19

roof and I better not forget that either. When my mom got home, he
started tellin' her that he is not gonna to have me bein' disrespectful
to him in his own house. I told her that all I said was that he shouldn'
be tellin' me what to eat when he don't even buy no groceries. He got
mad all over again and pushed me into the wall. I was walkin' past
him to go to my room. I 'raised' up at him like I was gonna hit him
and he pulled off his belt and started in on me. Miss...es Moore, I had
just had enough because he's always puttin' his hands on me.

"Has he touched you sexually?"

"No, he just likes pushin' me around or into things. According
to him, he's just tryin' to get my attention. Tonight, he hit me with a
belt for bein' [she held up her fingers to indicate quotations]
'disrespectful.' He ain't done it in a long time, but he fights my
mamma all the time. On the weekends he goes out with his friends
and after he comes back, he starts with my mamma. He loud talks me,
bumps into me, and does things to scare me—like kickin' my door
when he walks down the hall. My mom don't do nothin'. Maybe, she
thinks that since he's not beatin' me it's ok. Umphh...our life sucks.
I'm for real."

Sierra couldn't hold it in any longer. Tears that had been
building up began their exodus down her face. "As long as I can
remember, we always lived with some man. She always movin' in
with one of her triflin' boyfriends." Crystal handed her a Kleenex
tissue from her purse. "We ain't never had our own place. I don't
even respect her. I know she definitely don't have me at the top of her
priority list." Sierra had all of the ghetto moves and gestures a girl her
age would have, down to the neck and eye rolling.

"Well, you know what, Sierra? I know you are pretty upset,
but you need to call one of your family members to see if you can stay
with them for the night. After that, you and your mom need to talk.
I'm sure that she's worried about you. Here, take my phone and call
her now. She needs to know that you are ok. You talk to her, and
wherever you need me to take you, I'll go. You know you don't
belong out here in the rain, it's dangerous."

Chapter 3

April

Before putting her key in the door to go inside the house, Crystal sighed. *Lord, do I have to go home to an empty house day after day?* She walked back to her car and backed out of the driveway. *I just can't do it today. The remedy to every girl's blues is to shop!*

Crystal drove to Northlake Mall to pass time. She was sure that the Coach store would have just what she needed, but after surveying their current selection, then walking around the mall for two hours without buying a thing, she decided to go home. She pulled her cell phone from her purse as she drove back towards the empty house, and pressed the number three—where Moore Brothers was stored in speed dial.

"Good afternoon, Moore Brothers, this is Amanda, how may I help you?"

"Hi Amanda, this is Crystal. How are you?"

"I'm fine, Crystal. Donnie has someone in his office. Would you like to hold?"

What else is new? "Is Stephen available?"

"He's in Donnie's office as well," she said matter-of-factly.

"Ok, well tell Donnie that I called please."

"Will do. Have a good one," she said and hung up the phone.

Something about Friday afternoons drove Crystal crazy. Sure school was out for two whole days, and she looked forward to the last period ending. But every Friday afternoon she was lonely because she had lots of rejuvenated energy and no one to share it with. Her fellow teachers usually looked forward to being with their families on the weekends, so they usually weren't available to hang out with her. Settling onto the sofa in the family room, she tried journaling to find her inner peace.

After writing for about fifteen minutes, Crystal became tired of herself and her thoughts. She tried hard to think of somewhere to go to unwind. In the heart of downtown Charlotte, there was a nice little coffee house called Java Maison. They held open mic night on Fridays. Crystal knew people went there to relax, and she always wanted to go with Donnie, but their schedules never permitted it.

Usually Crystal spent a lot of time at church functions, but this night, she didn't want to be with any of those people. Although they were like a second family to her, they were not her family. Once more she tried to reach Donnie, but he was still in a meeting. She decided to lie down and take a short nap. After she woke up, Crystal decided to go to Java Maison alone.

The drive downtown was hectic with weekend rush hour traffic. After circling the block three times to find a place to park, she finally pulled into a parking deck. The warm April air was refreshing as she made her way to the coffee house. When she walked in, the crowd seemed to be buzzing. There were a lot of college-aged people and several couples dressed as if afterwards they might be on their way someplace else. Crystal found a table near the rear of the building, and while making herself comfortable, took in the scenery. The energy in the room definitely needed to be shared with someone other than herself. After a few minutes, a tall and rather feminine acting man, wearing a soft pink oxford shirt and khaki pants, approached the mic and began to speak.

"Self-proclaimed," he began.

"I am a self-proclaimed psychologist.

I take and follow my own advice.
No one has ever been able to tell me what to do,
Therefore, I tell myself.
So far, I've been pretty good at it.
Only I know what to do to keep myself safe, to keep myself in control.
I know, you say I have control issues.
You don't have to say it, for I am a self-proclaimed control freak.
I am a self-proclaimed passionate individual.
I love, I feel, I am.
I think, I write, I love, I am."

The man had hand and facial gestures to accompany every word. He was serious about what he was sharing. Crystal imagined him to be a regular there—maybe even a real poet. He continued...

"I am a self-proclaimed lover; a lover of the black male.
I love brown skin, coffee with cream and without, sensual, chocolate, toffee.
The essence of man is seen in a black man."

Crystal's assumptions were right. He was gay. His voice became louder...

"I am a self-proclaimed champion.
I am champion over so many things.
You tried to tear me down more than once, but it didn't work.
Why you ask? Because I am a self-proclaimed defeater.
A defeater of haters!" He snapped his fingers in a circular motion.

I am a self-proclaimed artist.
I see the good in even the tiniest things.
I feel souls, life, and passion in others.
I am a self-proclaimed recluse.
I hide myself inside myself.
You won't get to know me like that because my heart has been hurt too many times.
You don't need to know me.
I am self proclaimed."

The crowd applauded. It was a good performance to say the least. A few people were heard saying, "Go Quentin," as he exited the small stage.

Several others followed with, basically, the same repertoire. She enjoyed it though; it was different and didn't involve hormone raging fourteen-year-olds. She stayed long enough to enjoy a blackened salmon sandwich and a white chocolate mocha. When Crystal arrived home, Donnie was in bed, knocked out. Sometimes Crystal asked God what was worse, having a man and being alone, or being alone and not having a man? He never answered.

Donnie had always been Crystal's perfect man— strong, supportive, and a truly "got-it-together kind of brother." Those were things she loved about him and hated all at the same time.

Crystal wondered why he got so angry with her for trying to help out her student the other night. She understood they were supposed to spend time together, however, didn't the fact that she was on her way from church and needed to help a child out count for anything? Night after night, she was home alone, waiting for Donnie to come home. The one night *she* wasn't home, everything went haywire. She was the one taking the heat for what was wrong in their relationship. *I wouldn't be me if I didn't try to help. Yes, it was stupid to stop for someone at night; but like I told him, I recognized Sierra so I didn't see any harm in stopping. He thinks I involve myself in other people's lives too much. I don't have anyone else's life to get involved in. Ours is virtually nonexistent these days. I can't help it if I'm compassionate. Isn't that what I'm supposed to do? I guess I do get overly involved at times, but that is 'who' I am. He knew 'who' he was getting when he married me.*

That night was a nightmare. Sierra called her mother, but no one answered. As Sierra sat in the car crying, Crystal called the Department of Social Services. She couldn't leave the child out there alone. Besides, she would never forgive herself if she later found out something else had happened to her. Crystal always remembered the number to DSS. She was instructed to take Sierra to the hospital, and she stayed to speak with the social worker on call. Crystal couldn't see much of anything while they were sitting in the car, but Sierra had several bruises on her wrist, arms and upper body. Sierra said she was trying to get away from Nate, but he was holding her wrist with one hand and hitting her with a belt with the other. She said it had not ever been that bad, but she had had enough that night. Crystal didn't blame her. She never experienced such drama as a child. She stayed as long as Sierra needed her, and as long as the social worker would allow.

Crystal hated to see children suffering. The poor girl needed a stable family. She'd confided in Crystal a few times when she stayed after school for tutoring earlier in the semester. Her mother sounded trifling. Crystal tried not to be judgmental, but her mother sounded like a woman who thought she couldn't survive without a man around. The men she chose were just as trifling as she was. *Why wouldn't she be home when she knew her child was just badly beaten? Maybe she was out looking for her. What mother would let her boyfriend beat her child like that? Maybe she was afraid.*

The situation was very difficult for Crystal. She was supposed to be an educator to her students and that was all. She hurt deeply for Sierra. She couldn't imagine living like that. The social worker assured her that Sierra could not go back into her home without a full investigation. In the meantime, they would place her in a safe place. Crystal gave the social worker her contact information in case she needed to reach her for anything. Sierra thanked her teacher and gave her the tightest hug Crystal had ever received. Crystal knew Sierra was scared; Crystal was scared for her.

After explaining what had happened with Sierra, Donnie seemed to calm down. Nevertheless, the spirit of the evening was gone. Crystal quietly ate the dinner Donnie kept warm for her, and they called it a night. They did not watch the movie they were planning to watch on HBO, nor did they take the bubble bath she looked forward to. Donnie was a great masseur and could always massage out the knots she had between her shoulders. He always did that when they had one of their soaking sessions. It had been such a long time since they had spent any time like that together. She used to love the way his hands felt on her wet shoulders as they relaxed and listened to soft contemporary jazz. Donnie used to light vanilla scented candles and place them, strategically, throughout the bathroom to create just the right mood and shadows.

She noticed wine glasses on the edge of the oval shaped tub and a bottle of chardonnay leaning in a pool of melted ice. Although he understood why she was out, he looked very disappointed, and she felt like she had let him down. She hated that feeling. They both felt that the evening would be the beginning of something very special for them. She thought they deserved it so much and now she felt she'd messed things up. Crystal figured she would have to do something very special to put them back on course.

The sight of Donnie used to send chills down her neck like she was a teenager. He used to look so handsome when he'd come home from work each evening with his portfolio full of drawings. Crystal always imagined marriage to be that way. She always prayed that she'd still be in love after many years.

Donnie and Crystal were married ten years earlier after dating for four years. Donnie had been an answer to her prayers. Her father used to tell her, "Find a young man who will be good enough to be a husband some day."

Crystal didn't want just any boyfriend. She wanted her boyfriend to be sent by God. They met when she was a sophomore in college. Donnie passed her one morning as she was walking down the stairs of the Student Life Center. She didn't pay him any attention, but he noticed her. He approached her as she browsed the student store while waiting for her next class.

"How are you doing today?" Donnie asked. He had his best masculine voice on.

"I'm fine." Crystal said while continuing to browse.

"Are you a transfer student?"

"Why would you think that?"

"I don't think I've ever seen you around here before," Donnie said smiling coyly.

"Well, since the school does have a student population of over 25,000, I'd imagine it is quite impossible to remember every face. Am I right?" Crystal didn't mean to sound as rude as she did and immediately regretted it.

"Ok, my bad! I'll leave you alone, sister!" he turned to walk away, then stopped. He turned back around. "I passed you on the stairs and couldn't pass up the desire to at least speak to you. Don't fault a brother for at least trying. Since you appear to be busy *browsing*, I'll leave you alone. Sorry to bother you, Miss Lady!"

Umph! He is fine. Girl, what's wrong with you? You are about to let a fine brother walk away because you're acting stank!

Crystal tried to sound apologetic. "I'm just wasting time between classes looking around. No, I am not a transfer student." She smiled playfully. "I was here last year, but spent a lot of my time at the library. My parents told me they were not sending me here to waste money. I took that as meaning I'd better keep my head in a book and make them proud of their investment. This time last year when I was between classes, you wouldn't find me anywhere near this place. Too many distractions here, but I feel like I have a handle on things now. I'm a big girl!"

"Well, big girl, do you have a name?"

"Crystal."

"Nice. Sounds exquisite." He raised his eyebrow as though intrigued. "I'm Donnie," he said flashing a toothy smile.

"Is that short for Donald?"

"Nope, just Donnie." He said it as if he had answered the question before. His smile was gorgeous and a ray of sunshine to her. His teeth were perfectly aligned and pearly white. *He's fine and has good oral hygiene...possible husband material.*

Donnie, asked her where she was headed, and she told him English Literature. He walked her to class that day. What she remembered most about him from that day was what still attracted her to him now. Besides his smile, he had the most beautiful and flawless pecan colored skin, big brown eyes, and the prettiest eyelashes for a man she had ever seen. His eyelashes were so long, they almost touched the lenses of his glasses when he wore them. There was still something about seeing him walk into their home that made her smile. He wore a suit and tie most days with perfectly shined shoes. He had nicely groomed, silky black hair. Crystal never could figure out where he got it from because his mother had the coarse, must be relaxed, hair like many black women. The pictures she'd seen of Donnie's father didn't appear to give any indication of a 'good' hair gene in the family. But not only did God send her a boyfriend who would be good husband material, he sent a husband who still had good boyfriend tendencies. Or at least he used to, before things got so crazy at work.

After that night, she knew that she needed to do something to make up for disappointing him. They used to go to Bible study together, but it had been a long time since he'd been. Donnie told her he would not work late that night, and had asked her to not go so that they would be able to spend time together.

How could he ask me to skip church? What's happened to our marriage, and when did our spiritual life together become so one-sided?

Chapter 4

Mama Knows Best

"Oh, oh, Jesus! Oh Jesus, help me, please! Help me Lord!" Her legs and arms were shaking uncontrollably as sweat poured from her forehead. Instead of screaming in agony, Crystal shouted praises to God as she tried to hold the same yoga position as the crazy woman on television held. She couldn't stand having the anorexic looking woman tell her what to do, so she put the DVD player on MUTE, pumped up Tye Tribbett, and copied what the woman did. Very determinedly, she held the position as long as she could before calling it quits.

Whatever woman! You're crazy! You need a pork chop and Jesus! She picked up the remote, and then pressed the stop button. *I'll revisit physical fitness another day!* Grabbing her room temperature bottle of Dasani spring water from the kitchen island bar, she sat on the sofa. Thoughts of her parents filtered into her consciousness. They lived in Pennsylvania, and she didn't talk to them as often as she would like to because they were always traveling. One year after she and Donnie were married, they relocated to Pittsburgh to be near her father's aging family. Since then, they'd spent a lot of time "seeing the world" as they like to put it. She always thought that was strange,

29

primarily because they had moved there to be closer to family. "We ain't got no more babies to feed," her mother always said whenever Crystal fussed about never being able to reach them.

Crystal went upstairs, took a quick shower, and stretched out on her bed. She reached for the telephone to see if she could locate her parents on their cell phone. The phone rang three times, and Crystal was about to get discouraged. Then she heard that comforting voice, the one that had cheered her up so often when she was down.

"Lila Jenkins, please." There was a pause, "Hi Mom."

"Hey baby, don't be playin' like that on the phone. I was thinking 'how did a bill collector get my cell phone number!' How you doin'?"

"I'm fine." Crystal sat up in the middle of her bed twirling her hair like she was an eight-year-old girl."

"Well, good. You'll never guess where we are.

"Uh oh, you two just can't sit still, can you? Are you in the country? Uh, I guess that was a dumb question. Uh, let me guess. Cheyenne, Wyoming?"

"Very funny. No, not quite. Your daddy and I are in Indianapolis."

"Nap Town? What in the world are you doing way over there? I 'swanny,' I can't keep up with y'all. I wish I had time like that."

"You do, don't you? Where's Donnie taking you this year? Ya'll had planned to go to the tropics, hadn't you? Did you decide between Aruba and Cancun?"

"Yeah, we'd talked about it…but we're not going anywhere. The problem is I have the time, but he doesn't seem to get a free moment anymore."

"You need to go somewhere and relax, so you can come back with a grandbaby for us," her mother interjected. "That'll slow us down for a minute!"

"Mama, don't start that. I don't think that's going to happen any time soon. You have to be intimate to have babies, and there hasn't been any of that going on around here for a lo…ng time." She sighed deeply, not really wanting to express what had been going on in her marriage, but at the same time she was desperate for someone to confide in. "That's why I'm calling. I really need someone to talk to. I can't talk to Melissa about this. One thing I remember very clearly is you telling me not to discuss my marriage with my unmarried friends and family."

"I'm glad you feel like you can talk to me. Wait a minute; we're in a hotel. I want to get near the window, so I won't lose my signal."

"You didn't drive the RV?"

"No, we flew. Chile, your daddy signed up for those E-savers in his e-mail. He saw that we could fly here for $99 and just had to do it. You know how he is. We're just hanging out. Tomorrow, we're going shopping at a mall near the football stadium." Crystal could hear her mother rustling around in the room. "I'm by the window now. Your dad is downstairs. He said he was going to go find some cranberry juice. He'd better not be sitting down there at that bar."

"Now you know Daddy's got to have him a little bit of Malibu in his cranberry juice every now and then."

"Mmm...hmm. He better not come back up here with liquor on his breath, that's all I have to say. Go ahead baby, I'm all ears."

Crystal lay flat on her back and crossed her right leg over her left knee like she did when she was a teenager. She didn't know where to begin. "Mom, I have a feeling Donnie doesn't love me anymore. He doesn't touch me...at all."

"Really?"

"I'm for real. It's like I don't exist anymore. I've asked him what's the problem, but he always says it's work, and I'm stressing him out."

"Did he have any problems performing when you were 'doin' it?"

"Mom!" She paused. "No, it's not that..." *Why am I even having this conversation with my mother?*

"Girl, don't be embarrassed, you're married. I expect you to be getting some...some of the time!"

"Momma!"

"What? You said you wanted to talk to me, remember? Now, if I had just asked you about your sex life without you talking about it first, that would be a different story."

"I know. It's just …I feel weird talking about sex with you. Anyway, it's like this; over the last few months he's been distant… almost like he's here, but he's not here. He goes in early and comes home late. I used to be able to stop by the office and hang out, but now he acts like that's a problem. I end up talking to Stephen more than I talk to Donnie. Lately, Donnie's been trying to make me feel like I'm the problem. He says I've been nagging him, but I really haven't. I'm doing the same thing I have been doing for the last ten years. Usually, I call him after school because I've been dealing with teenagers all day and want to talk to an adult. I stop by when I'm in the area; I still cook, clean, keep myself up… the whole nine yards."

"Do you think he could be involved with someone else?"

"I don't know. I don't even like the thought of not trusting my husband, but the thought has crossed my mind. Besides, how could I find out without hiring a private detective or following him?"

"I don't know. I'm sure you've been in prayer about this, right?"

"Momma, I call on the name of Jesus so much, He's probably looking at His caller ID and rolling his eyes!"

Her mother laughed out loud. "Girl, no matter how old you get, you are still silly!"

"I've even prayed that if I were doing something wrong, God would show me. Then, I'd correct it. It's Donnie, not me. He's going through something, but I don't know what it is or why he won't talk about it."

Lila looked out of the hotel window at several families playing in the swimming pool below. She sighed as she thought of memories she'd tried to leave in the past. She knew she needed to share her own story of betrayal with her daughter. "You know, families should tell their children about family curses and demons that they've had to battle against." She paused, "Your dad cheated on me when you were younger."

"Oh Mom! I didn't know. You two look so happy now."

"I'm not saying this to scare you, but don't rule it out as a possibility. I love Donnie as my own son, but sin is present all over the earth. Don't think that you have a protective barrier around you and your household. The devil goes to and fro seeking whom he can devour. Look at Job in the Bible. He wasn't messing with nobody and old Satan came in and just ran rough shod all over him and his house."

"So what should I do? What did you do? Why you ain't ever tell me that?" *Oooh, did that just come out of my mouth?*

"Honestly, I've tried to separate that time in my life as far as the east is from the west. Your father and I have moved on and that heifer is dead now anyway! She died of breast cancer about ten years ago. We both went to her funeral."

"What? You've got to be kidding me."

"No. Remember right after Melissa and Floyd moved in with us? Your dad and I would go to our "appointment" every Saturday morning and Miss Minnie from next door would come over and sit with ya'll until we got back?"

"Yeah, she was a sweet lady. He had an affair with Miss Minnie?"

"No, chile. Miss Minnie was an old lady! It was a woman at work. There were times when I would go have lunch with him at his job at Freightliner. One day I made lunch for him and took it there to surprise him. I was the one who got surprised when I saw his car windows all fogged up in the parking lot..." She stopped as the pain of that day came back fresh like it had just happened all over again.

"Oh Mom, and we never knew any of this had happened. Where were you going on Saturdays, though?"

"Marriage counseling with the Pastor. I beat the 'you-know-what' out of that woman and your dad. He got defensive...said I was paying more attention to you kids than him, and she gave him the attention he missed at home. A lot of times it's someone at work."

"Please, don't say that. I don't know who it could be. All of the women in the office are white, although that doesn't mean anything," Crystal said weakly.

"Over the years, I forgave him, but it was so, so hard. It wasn't until I was at church one Sunday, and the Pastor said to forgive someone and let it go. That's when I actually let it go. I carried around a lot of resentment toward him and her for more than two years before I let it go. It killed me inside, and I actually thought that I was getting ulcers because I let it tear me up. He's been nothing but golden since then. I love him now, and I loved him then, too. Baby, I didn't want my marriage to be over, so I tried to work things out with him. I was insistent. I told him to find another job and cut it off with that woman, or I was going to cut something off!"

Crystal couldn't believe what she was hearing about her dad.

"Baby, I'll be in prayer for you and your marriage. The devil tries to destroy us by throwing all kinds of things at us —stuff we'd never imagine. Always be prayed up because you'll need it. But don't assume he is cheating because of what I said. I just wanted to let you know what happened to your father and me. You keep right on praying. Pray that not only your marriage will be restored, but also his desire for you will be rekindled. Sometimes, you need to stop talking to people and talk to God. He doesn't mind. He might be looking at His caller ID and thinking, 'That's right, lean on me, girl'!"

Crystal listened to the wise words of her mother for a little while longer, and then ended their conversation. She continued to lie on her bed pondering what her husband might be doing or going through without her knowledge.

Chapter 5

Blood is Thicker Than Water

Her mind and body were so tired after the workout and the disturbing conversation she had with her mother. She tried to think of something else, but her thoughts wandered off to Sierra. *Lord, please protect and comfort her wherever she is.* Crystal assumed that her inclination to help Sierra came from her mother. Crystal was an only child, but when she was in fifth grade, her two cousins, Melissa and Floyd, moved in with her family. She and Melissa were the same age, and Floyd was a year younger. Crystal's aunt was the black sheep of the family. She always had something going on with her. To tell the truth, drama followed her wherever she went. If something could be smoked or drank, she found a way to smoke it or drink it. She would be missing for days at a time, and her mother would always go to the children's rescue. On the other hand, Lila had so much compassion for children. Although her sister didn't physically abuse her children, she did expose them at a very young age to drug abuse and sexual misconduct, which ultimately led to the Department of Social Services removing the kids from her care. Crystal still remembered her mother crying late one evening about what had happened and saying that she would have to do what needed to be done. Her dad agreed with her and said he would support all of her efforts to keep her family together. After about four weeks, Melissa and Floyd had to move in with them. Life as they knew it changed after that.

Crystal remembered being excited at first. Melissa and Floyd always made her laugh when they would spend the night. They slept over a lot. She never realized how much until now. The family never talked about her aunt's drug problem in front of her. Thinking back on it now made her realize what a nice life her family had before they came.

Until they arrived, her family had been the picture perfect family. Her parents had two cars, and they both worked. She had a lot of material things other children in their neighborhood didn't have. In fact, she was usually the first kid in the neighborhood to get whatever new toy or gadget came out. She loved the attention although a lot of kids resented her and called her names as they rode their bikes past her house.

They lived in a nice suburban neighborhood. Their house had three bedrooms and two bathrooms. Lila's sister always called them rich. As a child, Crystal never could figure that out, but now she understood. When her aunt looked at her parents, she probably felt as if they were blessed, and she wasn't. But, for the life of her, Crystal couldn't understand why people did that to themselves. She often wondered why people resented others for making their dreams come true. She knew that God blessed everyone differently, but she also knew that looking at other people's blessings and being envious or jealous didn't make a good case before God.

Lila and her sister had sibling rivalry issues that were deeply rooted. Lila was better looking than her sister. When they were younger, children cruelly teased her aunt because she didn't look anything like Lila. It hurt her deeply. Truthfully, Crystal was also very sensitive to such issues. She constantly prayed that one day black people would stop being jealous of each other, celebrate their differences, and accept each other as they were. She had no problem relating to her aunt's pain because she was quite different from the other kids in the neighborhood herself. She learned to deal with it as a child, or so she thought. Sometimes, she painstakingly recalled the way children used to make her feel…like she wasn't good enough because she wasn't as dark as they were. Even now, the pain still hurt her, but she pushed it to the back of her mind.

When she was younger, Crystal's family had a dog named Smokey. Smokey was a German shepherd and a true yard defender. He used to terrorize the kids in the neighborhood, and they were afraid to pass her house. Crystal figured it was payback for the way they treated her. Her dad always felt that having Smokey was a good thing because it kept unwanted kids out of his yard.

Melissa and Floyd made the transition into their household uneventfully. They had spent so much time there in the past; so it wasn't a big deal for them. Not until weeks into the move did the family start seeing problems.

Her parents began receiving calls from the school about Floyd acting out in class. He did a number of things that were uncharacteristic of his normal behavior. He talked back to his teachers and used foul language. On one occasion, he threw a chair across the room because his teacher wouldn't let him go to the restroom.

Melissa's grades slipped. She had decent grades prior to moving in, despite her circumstances. Crystal's parents figured it would be an adjustment and vowed to work with the teachers, no matter what happened.

Reflecting back on that time, Crystal realized her parents were probably heroes to Melissa and Floyd. Nevertheless, she resented them both because they took so much of her parents' time. Too often, they would get into trouble in school, and then her parents would have to spend all evening lecturing and disciplining them. She felt it took too much of their time and energy away from her— their own flesh and blood. Crystal loved and still loves Melissa and Floyd, but secretly, deep within her heart, she still wished she didn't have to share her parents with them.

Crystal's parents only had her, and she did not give them many problems. The stuff they saw in Melissa and Floyd was new to them. Things like not cleaning up after themselves or washing their hands after using the bathroom drove her parents crazy. Crystal assumed her aunt had never made an effort to teach them about cleanliness or hygiene. When they would spend the night, it was a part of the nightly routine, but a routine they were not used to. Every morning for weeks, her mother would have to redirect them to the bathroom to wash their faces and brush their teeth.

Underneath they were good kids, but given the circumstances for the first ten years of their lives, they lacked basic socialization skills. Witnessing drug abuse, sexual promiscuity, and having a mother who did not care, profoundly hurt the innocent children.

Lila remained faithful to Melissa, Floyd, and Crystal; she was always there for each of them. She consciously dedicated herself to the last eight years of their childhood to ensure they did not become statistics, but graduated high school. Crystal and Melissa went away to college. Floyd took a job working in a factory, but enrolled in evening classes at the local community college.

Chapter 6

Early June

Praise the Lord. Crystal packed up her things as the last bell rang for the day. It signaled that school was finally out for the summer and she couldn't be happier. No doubt about it, the students were getting on her everlasting nerves. By all appearances, no one wanted to read in this new millennium. They were not interested in learning new vocabulary, nor did they even attempt to speak correct English. Crystal sincerely hoped that the fall enrollment would be different. She often wondered if she were kidding herself by thinking she could make a difference, but she couldn't give up either. Teaching was her passion. She felt that she had to try to make a difference in someone's life…someone like Sierra. Wherever she was, Crystal prayed Sierra was all right. She hadn't seen her since the evening she left her with the caseworker. Crystal wished she could help her, but because of her job, she knew she couldn't. She prayed for her continually, and hoped their paths would cross again one day.

She had seen her parents stressed by bringing someone else's children into their home; it was enough for her to say, no thanks to that option. She felt conflicted because there were so many children who needed the kind of stability she and Donnie could provide.

Maybe in time, God would change her heart and open her mind; but for now, she knew it wasn't a good idea.

Crystal looked forward to her summer breaks. She had from June until the first week of August to re-group and rediscover herself. She always felt as if she got so bogged down trying to help everyone else that she didn't have "Crystal time." *I've got to get together with my girl. We need to do something together since I'm basically single these days.* She missed Melissa. They had only exchanged e-mail messages since her brief visit in the spring. Crystal also worried about her sister living in Charleston by herself and prayed for her daily. Melissa always knew she was just a call away. Crystal prayed she would find true companionship in a holy and righteous man, but she feared Melissa had something to hide from her. That was the reason she was being deliberately quiet.

Crystal used to love being a wife, especially Donnie's wife. But teaching high school aged kids, wifely duties that were going unnoticed, obligations at church, and attempts to maintain her sanity left her feeling a little drained at times.

At other times, Crystal felt very lonely. Perhaps, it stemmed from being an only child for so long. When she was younger, even with Melissa and Floyd around, she was still often very lonely. They were always getting into trouble for one reason or another. Too often they were being punished, so she still didn't have anyone to play with. That was the main reason she liked teaching so much. In some ways it gave her a chance to be a kid again. Children were always around, and she felt needed. She often wondered what it would have been like if she had other siblings, real siblings. Although Melissa and Floyd were like her siblings, it wasn't the same.

Crystal missed her husband and didn't know what to do to stay busy. She didn't want to nag him, but she needed her man. Donnie and Stephen were also entertaining the idea of opening another office in Charleston, SC. The thought of that made her feel sick to her stomach. He'd be gone even more and probably overnight. She was beginning to think there wasn't ever going to be any time for her or their marriage again. It seemed that Donnie was married to the business, and she wondered if he intentionally stayed away. At times when he did come home, he immediately went into the home office, which was next to their bedroom. "Why do I continue to feel guilty for feeling the way I do?" she often wondered. Each day, she thanked God for Donnie and their marriage because many married women had no idea where their husbands were. Others probably knew but didn't want to admit or accept it. Crystal was sure about one thing, she didn't need a warm body in the house; she needed the man she married to be the same man she married some of the time. It was so difficult trying to manage two careers and a marriage at the same time. Donnie told her on more than one occasion that she did not need to work. However, he failed to realize that although financially things were going very well, she desired something more…something to give her fulfillment. Working in a high school environment with teenaged kids gave her fulfillment and was something she was passionate about. For her, passion was something that was felt and lived—daily. She didn't just wake up and want to do it; it was something that was in her bones. Passion was something she longed for at work, in life, and in love.

Chapter 7

Meet the Family

Stephen Alexander Moore was Donnie's incredibly fine brother. Stephen looked like a model from the cover of a magazine. He was masculine and beautiful all at the same time. His skin was absolutely radiant, and he was the essence of the black man. Stephen stood tall, broad, and muscular. He was a cocoa brown brother with a square chin and looked like a black superhero. His stature commanded everyone's attention anytime he entered a room with a smile that illuminated even the darkest atmospheres.

Donnie introduced Crystal to Stephen after they had dated for about two months. She could still remember Stephen's face as he walked into Donnie's dorm room. He looked as if he'd seen a ghost while Donnie introduced them.

"What's up, Bro? This is the incredible young lady I have been telling you about. Stephen, this is Crystal, Crystal, my big bro, Stephen."

"Hello, nice to meet you. I've heard a lot about you."

Crystal extended her hand for a formal greeting, but instead of taking it, Stephen just stood there looking at her with a big smile. Actually, it was more like a grin.

Donnie cleared his throat, "Uh, Bro?"

Crystal felt a little uncomfortable because Stephen appeared to be smitten with her.

"My bad, where are my manners? Hello. Nice to meet you," said Stephen. She wondered if she met his expectations, and what had Donnie told him about her. Did she look like one of Donnie's previous girlfriends, or did she remind him of some other woman? What was the grin all about?

Finally, Stephen reached for her hand, but held it for longer than the customary few seconds. He looked into her eyes, and for a split second, it seemed as if he was flirting with her. She brushed it off and figured it was her paranoia.

Donnie admired and highly respected his brother. Stephen was five years older than Donnie and had a phenomenal mind. Stephen had been at the top of his graduating class, finished his bachelor's degree in three years, immediately went to grad school, and completed his MBA in half the time it takes most people. He lived life as if he had something to prove to the world. Donnie often wondered where he got his energy.

The night Donnie introduced them; he took them out to dinner at a quaint little Italian restaurant not far from campus. Donnie said whenever Stephen came to visit; he would always take him out too for something to eat. Apparently, Donnie had told Stephen quite a bit about his new relationship with Crystal. Over dinner, he asked her several questions about her family, home life, and her major. He also inquired about some of the honors she'd received. Without a doubt she knew he was sizing her up. After dinner, they all went to the movies. What happened after the movies blew her away. As they were walking out of the theater, Donnie and Stephen got into a long discussion about the long-term socio-economic effects of something and African Americans. They were very deep into their conversation—so deeply that she felt as if they were in a sociology class and had forgotten she was around. She felt like she should have been taking notes during such an intense exchange.

43

That night was an extremely good night for her. It gave her some insight into what life with Donnie might be like, that is, if they got that far.

Crystal found his brother to be a truly amazing man, and she was glad that Donnie had someone like Stephen in his life. They worked so well together, and the misnomer that family shouldn't work together was not true for them. They were perfect business partners, and she was very proud of them both.

Stephen had a special place in her heart. He was like a big brother as well as a special friend. They had a lot of fun together. If she called the office and Donnie was not around, they could have a 30-minute conversation about nothing. He made her smile. If there was ever a time when she felt down, Stephen knew how to make a sister feel good about herself. Whatever it was their parents taught them about how to treat a woman, stuck. Stephen was tender, loving and the most chivalrous man she had ever met in her life. There was something about southern men she really liked, but he was a cut above the rest. He opened doors, carried things, and held her hand to assist her out of a car. Whatever a woman needed, he was there to help. Donnie was a gentleman as well, but Stephen had him beat in that area.

Stephen got married a few years after his brother. Most everyone thought of him as an eternal bachelor. His wife, Pam, is not the woman Crystal or Donnie thought he would have chosen, but she was very nice. They live in the same neighborhood on the same cul-de-sac with one house separating them from Donnie and Crystal. Since Stephen and Donnie had always been very close, it was no surprise when the house on their street went up for sale, Stephen was the first to bid on it. He and Pam moved in shortly after getting married. Pam had a son who lived with his father. Crystal didn't know why, but her son's father had custody of him. Pam never saw him and, rarely spoke of him. They were all surprised when Stephen asked Pam to marry him. They'd been seeing each other for about 6 months, but it just never appeared to be that serious. She had a very dry personality and never really seemed happy or excited about anything.

misnomer
interpretation that
is known to be
untrue

Sometimes, she wondered if he was really happy with Pam because she knew it took a special kind of woman to love the Moore men.

Occasionally, Pam and Crystal would do things together, but they certainly didn't have a lot in common. Crystal couldn't imagine what had attracted Stephen to Pam, but he appeared happy when they were first married. She tried for the longest time to figure out what type of relationship they had. Honestly, neither one of them looked really happy anymore. Crystal thought Pam was clinically depressed, but she never told her that. As the years passed, Pam stayed inside all day with the blinds closed. When a car circled around in their cul-de-sac, sometimes she would move the mini blinds just to peer out and see who was circling, then she'd go back to the couch. Sometimes, Crystal called her to see if she wanted to go to Wal-Mart or the mall, just so she could get out of the house. Pam always used the excuse that she had so much to do, though their house seldom showed evidence of her doing anything. Crystal liked to just drop over, unexpectedly, after school to see what she was doing. More often than not when she did, Pam would still be in her bathrobe and have her hair tied up with a scarf.

She worked occasionally, but never held a job for long. She went to the local community college and had an associate degree in business. She usually worked during tax season at H&R Block, but not much else during the year. No one knew what went on in their house. Knowing Stephen for as long as she had, Crystal knew what she saw was not his mode of operation, not at all.

Serious med. illness that negatively affects how you feel, the way you think & how you act. Unable to function as they used to. Often they have lost interest in activities that were once enjoyable to them, & feel sad & hopeless for extended pd. of time.

Chapter 8

Same Thing, Different Month

Excruciatingly hot didn't begin to explain the way the weather had been all summer. The weather in North Carolina was like walking into the bathroom right after someone finished a very hot shower. Crystal enjoyed her summers because they gave her a chance to relax, to breathe. A teaching career was not the type of job where you could just call in because you didn't feel like working. As a teacher, she had other people's education and future to consider. At the beginning of summer break she preferred to wind down until she got into a comatose state. Then, gradually, she'd do some reading, write some poetry, and travel a little. This summer, however, had been unlike most. Usually, she and Donnie would have already planned some type of getaway, at least for a few days. But due to the business going extremely well, he told her he'd have to wait until maybe late summer or early fall until things slowed down, if they went anywhere at all. Crystal knew that things usually got busier during that time because of back to school advertising and preparation for the holidays. Again, the success of the business came before their marriage, which she felt was just as important.

He strolled in the house later and later every night, kissed her on the cheek or forehead, and then went straight to the computer to continue working. This had gone on all year long, and she was beyond being tired of the situation. *If he's going to come home only to continue working, what good is he to me?*

Months had gone by since the night she helped Sierra, and they had been going through the motions. Things had been the same way before that night, but had really been strained ever since then. *What was so pivotal about that night? That was months ago?* Yes, she loved her husband, but the luster of the marriage was gone and needed some major polish.

Chapter 9

July

Crystal woke up to the sound of something falling in the shower. Donnie had already slipped from the bed and into the shower, yet she hadn't heard a peep. She didn't even hear him come in last night. For all she knew he could've slept downstairs. She turned over and looked at his side of the bed. Her vision was blurred as she viewed the wrinkled pillowcase and covers that had been pushed back.

"Coffee, I need coffee," she mumbled as she moved her legs around under the soft white Egyptian cotton sheets. Donnie always tossed the comforter back during the night, and she missed the weight of it on her body and legs. She looked over at the large red digital numbers on the clock. It was 7:15. She sat up, took a deep breath, then placed her feet on the cold cherry step stool, which led to their beautiful matching rice bed. She inhaled the pleasant aroma penetrating the morning air in their bedroom. It was the aloe-scented Ivory body wash she'd bought last week at Wal-Mart. The scent made her want one thing, her husband. *What do I have to lose?* Instead of going downstairs to make a fresh pot, she opened the door to the master bathroom. She rubbed her eyes like a child just awakened as she opened the door. "Good morning," she said sheepishly.

"Good morning, what are you doing up?" He turned the water off.

"I heard the commotion in here. What happened?" she asked feeling that the reason she'd be up so early ought to be obvious.

"Oh, I'm sorry," he said closing the top of the body wash. Reaching for a long, thick black bath towel, he stepped out of the shower. He started to dry off his back and lower extremities. Crystal was growing more excited. In spite of everything she still was very attracted to the man she pledged to be with forever.

"Let me help you," she said as she pulled the towel from his hands. "Crystal, I have an 8:00 meeting."

"Come on honey," she paused, then continued, "we haven't played the 'race against time game' in a long time." She poked out her bottom lip like a little girl. She stood in front of him and kissed him on his chest. "Pleeease."

"I can't. I need to shave. He reached past her for his navy blue Tommy boxer shorts that were neatly folded on the sink. Stepping into his boxers, he hastily explained to her why he didn't have time to make love to her. "We've been going back and forth with a car dealership for a quite a while and he's finally approved the latest ad we've done for him. I need to get to the office so we can get this thing underway today. Stephen is all excited about it because he's the one who does all the smoozing for the agency and he landed the deal in the first place." He reached for his rechargeable electric razor and began to contort his face for an accurate shave. The buzzing sound annoyed Crystal. *Once again, I'm in second place.* As he tried to line out his mustache, he changed the topic of conversation. "I want you to take a trip for me," Donnie said. "I know you've been a little upset with me for working so much lately, and I want to make it up to you." He tilted his head back to outline his goatee. "Well, kind of."

"What do you mean 'kind of' and why do I get the feeling that there's a catch coming that I'm not going to like?"

"Well," he said placing the guard on his razor and trimming the entire mustache and goatee. "I'm not blind. I know that things between us are not where they used to be. How they got that way, who knows?" He turned off the razor and placed it back in the charger on the counter. "Well, no one is to blame. We've both been busy with our jobs, and time has…"

Before Donnie could complete his sentence, she chimed in, "No, *you've* been busy with *your* job." She made sister-girl moves with her neck and hands. *Where'd I learn that?* "I've been on vacation for over a month now." Immediately after the last word left her lips, she knew in her heart that she shouldn't have said anything.

He was about to put toothpaste on his Crest Spin Brush when he became defensive. "Here we go again. You're bitter. You know I've been working hard and when you own the business, you have to be on the lookout not only for your own pockets, but also the pockets and pocketbooks of those who work for you. We wouldn't have the lifestyle we have if I…"

"Donnie, please." She threw up her hands to signal surrender. "I don't want to argue. What is this proposition you want to make with me?"

He turned away from the mirror to talk to her face to face. "Well, you know we want to expand our business into South Carolina, right?"

"Um hmm." She looked down and surveyed the dust and hair that rested along the floor. "Don't tell me, you're taking a second residence in South Carolina, and you'll be home on the weekends, right?"

"Very funny. No. Let me finish my thought, please. I feel you need something different to do, and since we don't have anything planned as of yet, I want you to go with Stephen to the Black Businessman's Conference in Charleston."

Puzzled, she looked at him as though he were speaking a foreign language. *Are you crazy, deranged, or both?* "The Black Businessman's Conference." She repeated it slowly, as though the proposition was totally absurd. "Be real, isn't there a more politically correct title for a conference? Besides, why would you go and suggest something idiotic like that." Her voice went up an octave, "I don't wanna go nowhere with Stephen. We cool and all, but a trip, no thanks."

"You don't actually have to attend the conference, just go. You can pamper yourself and get the works—all on me. It's at a luxury hotel in the heart of downtown. We both had registered to go, so there are two rooms reserved. Things have changed, and one of us must stay here to meet with some potential clients from Chi Town. There is a plus side; you will be able to hook up with Melissa. I'm sure she'd love to see you and spend some sister time together like you used to." Yeah, you are right about that. I do need to see my girl, but not by tagging along with Stephen."

"Donnie thanks, but no thanks. Going to Charleston with Stephen is not my idea of a vacation. I want us to do something together. You promised me that we would do something exotic this year. You have thousands of flyer miles and we, yes I said we, never go anywhere anymore. You go all over the country on business, and this is the only time of year that I can really do anything other than during the Christmas break without there being a hassle at school. Do you remember, we talked about you taking a couple of weeks off, and we'd take advantage of the last minute flights this summer? There are so many travel specials going on right now. Before you know it, it'll be time for me to go back to work."

"Baby, please. Work with me."

Baby? When was the last time you called me baby?

"The conference is in Charleston." He paused and looked at her to see if her facial expression would change. "Did you hear me? I said Charleston. You love the low country area. The last time we were there you said you'd like to go back and visit some of the shops and take in some of the historic sites. You've been moping around here since you started summer vacation. There are things you could do to occupy your time too, you know. Don't make me out to be the bad guy."

"OK, so I should be the bad guy for wanting my husband to be my husband?"

"There is no way that I can take off right now. I'd go myself if I could. Like I said, we registered last year and honestly, we can't afford to send anyone else from the office. We're swamped right now. God has blessed our business beyond what we had expected. Do you remember praying with me that we would be able to have a 'booming' business one day? Well, that day is here. That's a good thing, right?"

So you remember God now? I guess that's encouraging. "Yes, Dear."

"Crystal, I don't need sarcasm. I need support, and that is something I feel like I get very little of lately."

No he didn't.

"I thought it would be a good way for you to get a little R&R, do some shopping, and get out of the house. I don't want you to disappear in here like Pam does. I'm worried about you, and I care. I *thought* this would make you happy."

"Donnie, I'm grateful that you love me enough to want to do this for me, but the truth is, I have no desire to go to Charleston or anywhere else right now, unless you are going."

"Just think about it. The conference begins next Monday. Stephen is driving down that morning."

"I've already given you my answer." Having said that, she stormed out of the bathroom—leaving her sexy husband with clean teeth and baby smooth face in his boxers, but wondering what her problem was. "Coffee, I need coffee…and a lot more," she said to herself as she stepped into her slippers beside the bed.

As much as she loved her husband, he had a way of trying to solve things in a way that she wouldn't. She started the descent down the stairs in search of the red container of Folgers coffee. *Now if he was complaining about not spending enough time with me and I suggested he go off somewhere without him, wouldn't that make him think I didn't want to be around him?*

She put three cups of water in the carafe, loaded the filter and scooped out three scoops of grounds.

I really don't understand what's going on with him or our marriage, but I have needs. I'm not just talking about sexual needs either. I need my man, my friend.

She pressed the ON button, and the water began to percolate immediately. She couldn't remember the last time they had laughed together. Now, every week there was a different story. *We don't even go to Sunday morning worship services together because he's always resting. He's getting away from all of the things that used to be important to him, especially his relationship with God. But who am I to judge? I just want to feel close to him again. So much time has passed, and so many feelings have been kept inside. It will take God himself to work things out to where we can be like we used to be once again. Right now, I'm just a trophy wife or an inconvenience.*

More and more the word roommate kept coming to mind. She felt like her husband was her roommate and that he was trying to get out of spending time with her. She didn't know when she had become such an inconvenience to him. She pulled out an oak barstool and sat at the island bar in the kitchen to wait for the coffee to finish brewing. *We share living space, and that's about it.* She prayed that God would renew her marriage and her heart for her husband.

Chapter 10

Monday: New Beginnings

Crystal and Donnie said their goodbyes over breakfast. It was a rare occasion because she was usually still in bed when he left for the office. That morning, he summoned her to the breakfast table where he had prepared grits, eggs, bacon, and toast. She was surprised at the spread. He even sliced the cantaloupe she bought last week and made a pot of her favorite "girly" coffee.

"So, what got into you this morning? Do I need to call you Emeril up in here? Why make me breakfast now, when I'm leaving?" *What's up with that? So now you celebrate, when I leave?*

"Look, don't ask questions, just sit down and enjoy. I'm going to miss you. Usually, I'm the one leaving you here alone. It feels funny knowing that you will be gone for almost a week."

"Hey buddy, this was your idea. You and your brother are to blame, so keep your sob stories to yourself." She threw her napkin at him to show him her playful mood. She was getting excited about going. Stephen stopped by the day after Donnie mentioned going to Charleston to her. He wanted to make sure that she knew he really wanted her to go. He showed her the schedule of events for the conference, and told her that there would be some down time; they could go "hang out" as he put it. Since she and Stephen were pretty close, she didn't mind hanging with him. She still wished Donnie were taking her somewhere else though.

After breakfast, Donnie dressed, kissed her on the cheek and left for the office. He told her to call him after they arrived at the hotel. That was it.

Stephen rang the doorbell at 10:00. As she opened the door, his million-dollar smile made her feel like it wasn't such a bad idea after all.

"Let a man handle that," he said as she pulled the handle out on the black leather Pullman.

"Whatever. I just want you to know I ain't no punk, Bro!"

"I know you can hold your own, Miss Lady, I was just trying to be a gentleman."

That was Stephen though. He delighted in things like that.

Stephen weaved in and out of traffic on southbound I-77. They got to the South Carolina border in record time.

"Uh, is there a reason you are driving so fast? Do you like paying speeding tickets? Are you going to miss an event if we don't get there by a certain time?"

"My bad, I'm used to driving by myself. I'm sorry if my driving is scaring you. Naw, the opening reception isn't until tonight at seven."

"Well, you can let up a little then. My life was starting to flash before me. How about getting a sister something to drink. I could go for some iced tea right about now."

Stephen got off the interstate at the next exit with a BoJangles' Famous Chicken 'N Biscuits. They serve the best iced-tea of all fast food restaurants. He ordered two large iced teas, and they were back on the interstate. As he merged onto the highway, he inserted a Gerald Veasley CD, and Crystal reclined her seat to relax as she sipped her tea.

In no time they were in Columbia, SC. She barely remembered going through Rock Hill and Chester.

"Thank God for the inventor of the seatbelt!"

"So you've got jokes, huh? I distinctly remember getting caught in your dust one night after you left the office, and you weren't even driving on the freeway. So, which is worse, driving above the speed limit on a secondary road or driving above the speed limit on the highway where everyone is driving fast? Either way, we're both breaking the law."

"Well, although this would not have been my first choice of places to be this week, I would like to get there in one piece. You are carrying precious cargo here."

"Don't I know it"?

"Excuse me?"

"Nothing."

She wondered what he meant by that, but she let it go. She and Stephen had been good friends for years. If she had to go somewhere without Donnie, he would be her first choice as an alternative. She was very comfortable with him.

Crystal must have been dozing when her cell phone began to vibrate.

"My driving must not be too bad. You felt comfortable enough to go to sleep over there." She saw Stephen's beautiful smile flash at her as she scrambled to find the talk button on her phone.

"Hello? Hey...somewhere in Columbia. Ok, I will. Bye."

"That was quick."

"It was just Donnie checking to see where we were."

"Really?" he said sarcastically.

"What does that mean?"

"Are things ok between the two of you?" he asked.

"Yeah, why are you asking?"

"I'm just a casual observer, that's all. I work the same hours he does, so I know the amount of time he spends away from you."

"Ok, and aren't you spending the same amount of time away from Pam?"

"That's different."

"How? She's still your wife. I think you Moore men are just workaholics. Time at work is time away from your family."

"Ok, I shouldn't have said anything. Let's just change the subject."

"No, come on. Why are you acting like that? You started it. What are you trying to say?"

"It's like this, you care that Donnie isn't around. I don't think Pam cares one way or the other. We can go all week without talking, and it doesn't bother her or me. She's so lost within herself that I'd rather be at work than to see her moping around the house. Little brother on the other hand has something to go home to, and he still works like a dog. I just don't get it."

"And I don't get you. I figured you'd be on his side since the two of you are in business together. Don't you need to work in order to be successful? I thought ya'll were inseparable."

"Yes, we do have clients to take care of, but we also have employees who do a lot of the leg work. We have the flexibility to come and go as we please most of the time. We both work hard because we like it, but there is no reason for him to put in as many hours as he does. I'm not trying to imply anything; I was just saying it was a short conversation, that's all."

"Don't get defensive. Donnie says you all have been pretty swamped. Are you saying that you aren't?"

"Like I said, we are very busy, but we have employees who we pay very well." He changed the subject. "Check out the lay of the land. Everything down here is so flat. I love the south."

"Ok, Stephen. We'll change the subject. Can we take a restroom break? The tea is starting to get to me. We just passed a sign that said a rest area was coming up." They drove two more miles, and then Stephen pulled into the rest area. They both went inside. As she washed her hands and checked her make up in the mirror, she reflected on the conversation they just had. She felt for Stephen because she hated to see Pam hurting him like this. She wished Pam would get some help for herself and they'd go to counseling together. It hurt her to see him hurting, even though he didn't say a word about it. She could read between the lines because she knew her friend.

They got back into the car and headed for the exit that said I-26 East Charleston.

"Do you want some nabs, or do you want to stop somewhere and get something to eat?"

"I would like to eat something light. I may treat myself to some place nice tonight while you are at the opening event."

"I don't think so, girlfriend. You are going with me."

"Oh no you don't. Donnie said for me to relax, and that is just what I am going to do. Besides, I didn't bring formal wear or any other type of wear to be hanging out with you at some conference."

"The opening ceremony is a formal event. It is about thirty minutes of introductions and light business announcements. After that, everyone let's loose and it is a par-tay! High dollar skeezers wait in the lobby for the party to begin every year! You can just hear "ching ching" going through their minds!

"So you want to use me to fend off the skeezers, huh?"

"No, I didn't say that," he said smiling.

"You didn't have to. All you have to do is wear that gold band of yours and that should be enough."

"You've been married too long. Don't you know a gold band is intriguing to a woman? In fact, it's a magnet! It means nothing these days. I left it at home anyway. I rarely wear it anymore."

"Alrighty then. And why not? Are things that bad for you?" Crystal said trying to sound optimistic.

"Yes," he said matter-of-factly

"Ok, well let's talk about that later. We came to have a good time, right?"

"Right, but you still haven't responded to my proposition. Will you accompany me to the opening ceremony? You know family sticks together, right?"

"Well, if it will keep hoochies and skeezers away from you, then yes, I'll go. I have to look out for Pam! I do need something to wear though. Let's hit Saks Fifth Avenue on the way in. There's one in the city, and it might be near the hotel. If it is, you won't be seeing much of me this week!"

Stephen took her to Saks as requested, and she found a nice selection of after-five wear. Stephen went to the men's department to look for a tie.

She tried on several dresses, and then decided to see if Stephen was nearby to offer an opinion. She found him sitting outside of the dressing area with a small bag.

"What did you buy?"

"Just some LaMale. It is supposed to drive women crazy! I didn't see a tie I liked. I was looking for something a little more conservative than what I brought with me."

"And what women are you trying to drive crazy? I thought you wanted them on their best behavior. Sounds to me like you are tempting them and I'm really starting to feel used now."

"No, don't be like that. I've wanted to try this ever since I saw it in Ebony Magazine. The bottle is shaped strangely though." He pulled the bottle from the box and showed it to her. It was in the shape of the male physique."

"Hmm, that's interesting!" She raised her left eyebrow checking out the shape of the bottle. It was a half male body with the chest muscles and male body parts accentuated. "Come here and tell me what you think of these two dresses. This one is the one I'm favoring, but give me your opinion."

She turned around for him; he nodded his head to signify not bad, then looked away. She went back into the dressing room and changed into the next one. Stephen's face lit up when she walked out. She wore a conservative, yet sexy, red tea length dress with an asymmetrical hemline. "I can tell by your expression that you like this one."

"Yep, classy," he said smiling from ear to ear. "That's you right there. All eyes will be on you."

A sales associate passing by chimed in. "Awwww, that was so nice. You two must be newlyweds, huh? My husband stopped giving me compliments years ago!"

"We're not married... well not to each other ... never mind," Stephen fumbled as he tried to explain himself.

"Honey, he sounds like a keeper," the lady said. Stephen looked at Crystal and smiled.

She paid for the dress and they left the mall in search of the conference hotel.

Once again, he got her Pullman and his bag from the car. She grabbed the cups of melted ice and the snack wrappers, then went inside. Stephen checked them in since both rooms were listed under his and the company's name. She was in 829 and he was in 808. They made small talk as they waited for the elevator. Professional looking brothers in business suits made their presence known in the lobby. A few sisters were seen hanging around the hotel lounge.

"See, I told you," said Stephen. "Look over there. Even this early in the day, sisters are on the prowl. I told you that high dollar skeezers would be here!"

"You need to stop! Hey a woman's gotta do what a woman's gotta do!"

The elevator doors opened, and they went to the eighth floor. Stephen pulled her bag down the hall and headed for 829.

"You don't have to do this; I can pull my own bag to my room."

"Woman please, you let me pull it all the way from the car to the elevator and down the hall this far. What are a few more steps?"

"I know you didn't just say 'woman' to me."

"Yeah I did, and…"

"Whatever."

They arrived at 829 and Crystal put the electronic card in the slot and then waited for the green light. When they entered, Stephen looked around as if he expected someone to be inside hiding. It left her feeling a little uneasy; almost like he was assuming the role of husband for her.

"Uh, I could use a little nap. What time is the opener?"

"You could use a nap? What? You would think that you had made the drive down here. You mean to tell me we are in the deep dirty south, and you are going to stay cooped up in this hotel room?"

"Stephen! What do you want me to do? Didn't I tell you that I came along to get some R&R? This was your brother's idea, so don't be forcing me to do something I didn't want to do in the first place."

"Why are you getting all edgy? I thought we were getting along well. I just want you to have a good time and not regret coming with me. I come every year to this event and there is a lot to see and do while it is going on. I would enjoy your company, that's all. I'll let you get your beauty rest. You know where to find me."

Having said that, he walked out and pulled the door shut rather loudly.

What the heck that was all about? Why is he acting like I let him down? All she wanted was to relax in her room with her books and vanilla candles for a few hours. *He already twisted my arm into going to something I didn't want to go to. Maybe he wishes Pam were here instead of me. She needs to get a grip and realize what she's got. He's acting better than my own husband.*

Chapter 11

Party Time

"Hold on, I'll be right there." Crystal was trying to zip her dress up the back when Stephen knocked on the door. When she opened the door, he just stood there staring at her.

"You seemed pretty ticked at me when you left here, Bro. What's up with that?"

"My bad. I'm cool, everything is everything," he said making hand gestures like a rapper. He walked into the room, but was careful to stay near the door.

"Good, because I would hate to have to *read* you up in here! Is my zipper stuck?"

She turned around so he could check for her. "It's stuck on something, right...?" she asked twisting her arms around her back and over her shoulder trying to get to it.

"Stop moving, please. Yeah, it's stuck in the fabric. Hold up." He gingerly pulled the fabric, and while lifting up on the zipper, finished zipping her up.

"Merci beaucoup."

"You are so very welcome," he said smiling and trying not to look directly at her.

"Let me grab my shoes, and I'll be ready."

Stephen walked across the room and sat down on the sofa in the lounging area near the window. She went into the bathroom to do one last makeup check and slipped into her new three-inch heels. She bought them in Charlotte a few months prior, figuring she'd wear them out on a night on the town with her husband, not someone else's.

She and Stephen walked to the elevator, pressed the down button, and waited for a set of doors to open. All four seemed to be going up. Crystal could imagine people standing on all ten floors waiting for doors to open. Soon, more people began to gather. A mid-forties looking brother walked up with a white woman who wore a silver sequined dress. Crystal wondered if she was his wife, although neither of them wore a wedding ring. While they waited, she decided to make small talk with Stephen.

"Did you call Pam?"

"Yeah, I called to let her know I was here. She was watching *As the World Turns*."

"Donnie called me before I could call him. He told me to tell you that Billy Martin stopped by the office."

Stephen rolled his eyes. "That man just won't give up. I don't like to lose money, but if he took his business elsewhere, it wouldn't be too soon. He drives me crazy. He owns a Toyota dealership in Matthews and expects us to personally guarantee his business will grow. We can't make guarantees like that."

"Oh, he's the guy? I've heard Donnie grumbling about him before."

The elevator doors opened. It was jammed packed with people of color dressed in after-five attire. At the same time another elevator opened. "Ya'll go head, here's another one," said Stephen. They walked a few steps and went inside the empty elevator. Crystal felt especially attractive since she hadn't been dressed up in a long time. Her Mary Kay foundation made her skin look flawless, and her new lipstick, Crimson Passion, complimented her new dress. Her hair was flawless and rested just below her shoulder blades. It looked silky and soft. Stephen eyed his sister-in-law from the corner of his eye and envied his brother. The descent from the eighth floor seemed to take forever.

As they got off the elevators, the sound of soft jazz filled the lobby. They were looking for the Chelsea Room. As she and Stephen approached, they saw several people standing on the outside, holding glasses of champagne and red wine.

"Would you like something to drink?" asked Stephen.

"No, not now. Go ahead and work the room, I'm sure you're dying to mingle. Most of the time at social engagements, you're the 'man'."

"Whatever. Let's find a table first. How about over there beside the palm tree?" He pointed to a table near the wall but close to the podium.

"Ok."

"I'll be right back. I see Cameron Galliard, he owns a CPA firm here."

Stephen walked off as she sat down and tried to blend in. So far, they were the only ones at a table set for eight. She felt a bit awkward being there with him. Even though she felt strangely comfortable with him, at the same time, it felt as if she were out with another man. Crystal could see Stephen across the room talking to Cameron. Cameron was an attractive caramel-colored man with a baldhead. From across the room it appeared that he was drinking brandy. Stephen fit in easily with those guys.

In no time a tall model-looking woman, wearing a very tight fitting long red dress, approached Stephen. The back was v-shaped, and the point ended right at the bottom of her back and left nothing to the imagination. She was not wearing a bra, and by the looks of it, she wasn't wearing any under garments either. *Maybe she's wearing a thong.* She was all up on Stephen and Cameron, and they were eating her up. She looked like she could be right off the set of a music video.

Cameron walked away, and Stephen and Miss Rump Shaker were left alone in front of a champagne fountain. As they talked, she flirtatiously touched his arm. For some reason Crystal felt heat rising inside her like never before. *What is wrong with me?* She felt jealous and didn't know why. *He ain't my man.* She got up and walked around the room—all the while hoping that something or someone would distract her to keep her from thinking about what was going on across the room. She walked toward the exit that led to the powder room, but surprisingly heard Stephen's voice from behind.

"Where are you going in such a hurry? You were walking up outta here like you were going to put out a fire!"

Ain't that the truth, not that I want you to know it. "I just need to go to the ladies room. Is that all right with you?" She sounded snappy, and she knew it.

"What's your problem?" He looked at her as if she were a crazy woman? "Where's the attitude coming from? I am simply checking on you to make sure you're ok. What in the world happened while I was gone?" Stephen looked around the room as if he expected to see something.

"You would have to ask." *Why did I say that?*

"What the heck does that mean?"

You over there flirting and everything.

"And why do you have an attitude?" Stephen was visibly perturbed.

"You know what, Stephen, nothing. Just nothing, I really need to go to the ladies room. I'll be back in a minute. Go ahead and finish working the room, will you?" She walked off feeling his stare in the back of her head. When she got to the restroom, she checked her makeup. *Of course I don't need a makeup check; I just left my room less than thirty minutes ago.* All the same, she hung out for a few minutes to waste time.

What the devil is wrong with me? That's probably it, the devil. Lord, help me. I don't know why I'm acting this way. As she walked out, she noticed Stephen standing with another woman. This time it was a Naomi Campbell looking sister with short hair. She tried to walk past them without him noticing, but just as she saw a clear path to the table, he called out to her.

"Crystal, over here." She walked over and couldn't help noticing that the woman gave her the once over with her eyes. She did the same and put on a fake smile.

"Shana, this is Crystal. Crystal, this is Shana Maxwell."

After they exchanged pleasantries, Stephen told Shana it was good meeting her. Then, he pulled Crystal and headed in the direction of their table.

"What was that all about?" she asked

"That woman just invited me to her room. I used you; I'm sorry, but I had to get away. You women are about as bad as the brothers these days."

"Not all of us. Some of us do have morals...*although I'm beginning to wonder about my own.* Where do you know her from?"

"I just met her, that's my point."

"Lord, have mercy."

The music stopped and a short light-skinned man approached the podium to test the sound system. He wore Malcolm X style glasses and had a large gap between his front teeth. "Testing 1-2-3. Testing 1-2-3."

"Good evening everyone, I'm Dennis Johnson." His voice didn't match his outward appearance. Instead, it was attention grabbing, and he sounded like Barry White. "It gives me great pleasure to kick off the 15th Annual Black Businessmen's Conference ball. We have a few announcements to make before the festivities begin…"

He made a few jokes, reminded conference goers of the change for the breakout sessions the next day, and introduced the conference officers. After that, a local minister, who was also a member of the conference, said a long singsong-like blessing for the food. The night was officially kicked off. Attractive men and women dressed in black and white served the catered meal. As Stephen and Crystal ate, they made small talk with other attendees who had joined their table. After a decadent chocolate kahlua cheesecake, she was satiated and ready for a little dancing to burn off the calories. A bit earlier she had finally made up her mind that since she was there, she might as well have a good time. After chatting with the others and enjoying the conversation with Stephen, she felt more relaxed. Maybe it was the kahlua, or maybe she was escaping into another reality— one where she didn't feel so lonely.

"Crystal, your emotions have been all over the place today. I'm really feeling the new you, though," Stephen said in a lowered voice as he leaned over.

"I'm sorry. I never got over the conversation we had in the car on the way here. It's been bothering me. I keep thinking you not only know something, but you're also hiding something from me. I don't know what to believe. But now's not the time. We can talk later. This is the first time I've been out like this in a long time. I decided that I'm going to enjoy myself, even if I am with you!"

"I didn't mean anything by it, Crystal. I agree, let's just enjoy ourselves while we're here."

"We be cool!"

"OK, Miss English teacher."

"Hey, you may not know it, but the Crystal outside of the classroom is a totally different woman."

"I'll bet," he murmured. He thought she didn't hear him, but she did.

Come on Stephen, don't do this to me.

After everyone appeared to have satisfied their appetites, the band took the stage and began to play soft jazzy sounds. Couples began to make their way to the dance floor in the middle of the room… They both sat and watched as men led women by the hands and vice versa. Stephen began to get the dance itch, but was unsure if he should ask Crystal to dance. Slow dancing seemed somewhat inappropriate, but simply observing others wasn't his idea of a fun night either. Stephen leaned in.

"You look like you could dance a hole in that floor."

"What gave me away?"

"The way you're gyrating in that chair is a dead giveaway. May I?"

He extended his arm.

"Let's wait for something a little more upbeat."

"I feel you."

Just then, the band began playing an upbeat song from the early 90's.

"Come on girlfriend; let's show these people what it's all about."

They danced until she felt perspiration spreading across her forehead. She noticed a few men checking her out and women looking at Stephen. He danced as if he felt the music in his bones. He always smiled when he danced; giving the impression that he was really enjoying moving his body. They had fun, and after three songs, she yelled above the music, "Let's take a break." She turned to walk away, but he gently took her by the arm and pulled her to him.

"Thanks for coming here with me," he said in her ear.

"You're welcome, friend. That band is off the chain!"

The band began playing a song by After Seven. The mood was changing in the room. Stephen already had her by the arm, so they just went with the flow. At first they started off dancing as two friends, but as the song continued, it captured their hearts. The embraces began to grow tighter. *Oooh, this feels so good.* Crystal started feeling uneasy. She wanted to fight the temptation to give into his embrace, but it felt so right, at least for the moment. She hadn't been held this tenderly in a long time and longed for the warmth and the closeness.

"You know, I haven't been this close to a woman in a very long time?"

"Alrighty, then. Maybe you should've asked Pam to come here with you."

As he put his lips close to her ear, he whispered, "Now is not the time to be talking about Pam."

Once again, she felt a bit uncomfortable, so she dropped it and just danced. Soon she began to feel as if she were flying. Euphoria filled her bones, and she began to feel alive within. She took long deep breaths. Thoughts raced through her mind about the man she was dancing with and vivid pictures fueled her imagination. Quickly, she knew that she had to ask God to forgive her for what she was thinking and feeling. She loosened her embrace.

Cameron and his date made their way over to Stephen and Crystal. She felt him and Stephen give each other "dap" behind her back. When the song was over, they went back to their table.

"Would you like something to drink?" asked Stephen.

"If there is water, I'll take a glass or bottle."

Stephen went off to find some liquid refreshment. She saw Miss Rump Shaker walk up to Stephen. They exchanged what appeared to be small talk, and then he made his way back to the table.

"Is Miss Thang trying to make her move on you again? Do I need to pull off my earrings and break out the Vaseline?"

"Whoa, hold up. It's not like that. I told you, women don't care these days. She saw me out there with you but didn't care."

"Like I said, I'll break out the Vaseline!" She playfully reached for her earrings.

"That won't be necessary," he said laughing. "Would you like to walk around outside or something? It's getting a little warm in here. You know what they say about our people and heat!"

"Yep, sounds like a good idea."

They got up and walked out into the lobby, and then walked out of the front door. The humid summer air rested on their faces. It was a pleasant, welcomed break from the Chelsea Room.

"I saw a nice garden with benches over that way from my hotel room," said Stephen.

They walked around the corner where there was a softly lit flower garden with wooden park benches. Stephen took off his suit coat and put it down for her to sit on.

"What a nice evening. Check out the moon," he said.

Stephen sat down next to her and put his arm on the back of the bench. She was thankful for the space between them because it made the sky gazing platonic.

"Sometimes, I sleep on our deck at night. I find it comforting to gaze into the sky. It gives me hope of a better tomorrow."

"Are you serious? You sleep on your deck?"

"Many nights. You know the hammock I ordered a couple of years ago from that shop down here? That thing is nice."

"If you say so."

"I say so."

Just then, sea gulls flew over.

"Where are they going this time of night?" asked Crystal. "They always amaze me. They look like they're just floating in the air when they fly."

"Who knows, maybe they're going somewhere to get their party on!"

"Ok, too much dancing for you," she said

What started out as a warm and humid breeze, soon turned brisk. Crystal's body jerked quickly as chills ran down her spine.

"You cold?"

"Yes, I got chilled all of a sudden."

"Do you want to go back inside?"

"No, not really. I'm enjoying this. I haven't been outside at night in a long time. Can I put your coat around me?" She stood so that he could lift his coat from the bench.

"Sure. I didn't want you to get a tear in your dress or a splinter from the bench."

She smiled. "I appreciate your thoughtfulness, but I could use your coat in another way right now."

Stephen moved his coat and draped it around her shoulders. For some reason, having his coat around her made her think of him having his arms around her. She felt comforted in a strange sort of way.

Chapter 12

Don't Say a Word

They sat still, not saying a word for what seemed like several minutes. With everything so peaceful, they both simply enjoyed the beautiful surroundings and the night sky. She was really content spending this time with him. It was as though she were in another world. Truthfully, she wished that were the case. She had to keep reminding herself that she was not simply married, but married to this man's brother. *What is wrong with me?* The fact that she was allowing herself to even dream about him or feel some of the things she'd been feeling all night made her wonder if she was losing it.

"Crystal, do you ever wonder if marrying Donnie was the right choice for you?"

"What?"

"I'm sorry," he said inwardly wishing that he could retract the question.

"Why would you ask me something like that?" *I've wondered a lot of things lately.*

"I apologize. I don't mean to make you uneasy. I'm sorry."

"You didn't answer my question. We were sitting here quiet, and then you ask me something like that."

"Don't take it the wrong way. I know I made the wrong decision when I married Pam, and its times like this that I know I did."

She wanted to smile deep inside, but knew in her heart that she shouldn't. He was feeling what she'd been feeling all night too. *God help me. I'm feeling so weak right now.*

"No, I've never questioned it. Our marriage isn't perfect by no stretch of the imagination, but I haven't regretted it."

"I'm not trying to get all philosophical or make you feel uncomfortable. I just thought we had some chemistry tonight and decided that I'd take the chance on exploring that with you."

"What do you mean?"

"Nothing. I'm just rambling. Must be the kahlua cheesecake!"

She sat quietly because it felt like they were going in the wrong direction; one they both knew was forbidden. Besides, she'd already had doubts about her sanity tonight.

"Why don't we go back inside?" she suggested.

"Good idea." He answered very quickly as if they both were trying to avoid what could potentially happen, should they decide to stay out there any longer.

As they walked back into the lobby, they heard the electric slide playing.

"No black function would be complete without the electric slide," said Stephen.

"You know it. The band must be taking a break."

They walked back inside the Chelsea Room and jumped right in.

Stephen yelled over the music, "It's universal. Doing the electric slide is listed in the *Black Person's Guide to Being Black.* You can't be black and not know how to do it. That would just be un-black!"

They danced and laughed for the next twenty minutes. Finally, she had to take a break. They walked back to the dinner table where she grabbed a napkin from the center of the table and dabbed her forehead.

"Dang, check out this table. These people have been getting their drink on!" There were glasses with cherries in the bottom and stir straws all over the table. They were probably feeling real good wherever they were.

"Stephen."

"Say no more, I'm wiped out too."

They got up to leave. Stephen waved to several people as they exited.

"Do you know everybody?"

"Why? Does it bother you?"

"Ex...cuse me?" she said playfully rolling her neck.

"There you go again, getting all touchy!"

She didn't say a word; just kept walking. This time, there was no waiting for the elevators. They arrived at the eighth floor in what seemed like record time. She stepped off first and turned towards 829.

"Have a good night, Crystal," Stephen said as he got off and walked down the hall in the opposite direction.

"You too."

Something felt real weird about the moment. For Crystal, it felt like a point of no return. She continued walking, and so did he. She kept expecting to hear him call out her name or something, but he didn't. She heard a door close in the distance. Apparently, he reached his room before she did. Walking into her room and removing her shoes, she turned on the television to see what was on. She was too wound up now, and sleeping was the last thing on her mind. She didn't see anything that she wanted to watch, so she pulled out a book that she'd brought, and then found the rainwater fragranced candle that was packed at the last minute. She went into the bathroom to get matches from her cosmetic bag and a clip to pin up her hair. She had planned to wash it first thing in the morning since it smelled rather sweaty, but at the moment didn't want to take on that task.

She passed by the mirror next to the door and admired her body. She looked good in the dress that Stephen had basically picked out for her. She struck the match to light the candle and inhaled the smell of the freshly struck match. For some reason she liked that smell. She switched off the overhead lights and turned on the bedside lamp—intending to read after taking off the dress. She reached around her back to pull the zipper. *The stupid thing is stuck again.* Frustrated, she stamped her foot, then squirmed and squirmed, tugging at it, but it wouldn't budge. The dress was too form fitting to get out of without moving the zipper. She thought about the old wire hanger trick, except there were no regular wire hangers in the room, and she didn't pack any clothes on hangers. The closet only contained the ones, specifically, designed for closets in hotels.

As she walked towards the bathroom trying to figure out how to get the dress off, there was a knock at the door. *Who could that be?* Stephen seemed to be in a mood when they got off the elevator, so she knew it wasn't him. She went to look out of the peephole. There was a woman she didn't recognize.

"Yes?"

"Tabitha?"

"Not in this room, sorry."

"Ok." The woman said as she walked away. Crystal could hear her murmuring something to herself about room 829.

As she started messing with the zipper again, the phone rang. It was Stephen.

"Hello?"

"Are you asleep yet?"

"No."

"I'm sorry."

"Why?"

He took a deep breath. "Crystal, can we talk face to face?"

"I don't think that would be a good idea."

"Why not?"

"Stephen, I'm not dumb, and I'm not naive. I know something is going on and I'm not sure if I want to analyze anything. We don't need to have any discussions. Whatever you need to say to me, you can say it over the phone or not tell me at all."

"Where's all of this hostility coming from?"

She sat silent, enjoying the scent of the rainwater candle.

"Crystal?"

"I'm here, Stephen."

74

"Sorry to bother you."

"OK," and she hung up the phone. *Donnie, how could you. Now, look at the situation facing me.* Crystal pictured an angel on her right shoulder and the devil on the left fighting.

She sat on the bed reflecting. She thought about what, if anything was going on between them. On the other hand, the real dilemma was how she was going to get out of the dress.

She tried the zipper once more, as if something may have changed since the knock at the door and phone call, but it still wouldn't move. She continued to sit there thinking about Stephen. *He looked so nice tonight. He is such a fine man.* She knew why all of the women were looking. *Good eye candy. I admit it! Any woman would be lucky to have him.* Just then, the phone rang again. It was Stephen.

"Crystal, please; I really need to talk to you face to face. I have to tell you something."

"Stephen!"

He wouldn't back down. "Can you meet me in the flower garden in five minutes?"

"Stephen, I..."

"Please, just hear me out."

"OK."

She had no idea what she was going to be getting herself into, but it was intriguing to say the least. Since she couldn't get her dress off, she reached over her shoulder and zipped it back up. She left the candle burning and grabbed the pass key and a light jacket.

When she got to the flower garden, he was already there, sitting in the same spot as before. The moonlight made his jet-black hair glisten, and he had the most serious look she'd ever seen on his face.

"Stephen, what are *we* doing here?"

"Please, sit down."

He looked so serious. She was getting a little nervous. *I shouldn't be here; I know it.* She wanted to be there, but didn't actually want to hear him say what she thought or secretly hoped he would say.

"Crystal, since we've been here, actually since we left your house, I've felt so at ease with you; then again, I always have. I know that this might be the end of our relationship as we know it, but I cannot go another day without telling you this. I love my brother and would not do anything intentionally to hurt him. But...I have the biggest crush on you, and I have for years. Sometimes, Donnie comments that I act like I think you are *my* wife, not *his*. The truth is, for years I have secretly wished that were true."

"Stephen, I..."

"Please, just hear me out. OK? I take advantage of every opportunity that arises to be near you." He paused as if thinking how to stress the seriousness of what he'd just confessed. "I do anything I can to be near you. I love to hear you speak. I love the way my name rolls off your tongue. I feel something very special for you. Tonight, for the first time, I know you feel it too. Why else would you be jealous when the other women were flirting with me? You don't have to admit it because I know. I wanted to put it out there because...I have to let it out, Crystal. I know this might sound lame, but it's the truth.

"Remember when I came to get you this morning? I imagined that I was picking you up so we could elope. I don't love Pam, and anyone who knows me knows that. Marrying her was a huge mistake, but I'm in it now. I don't know what to do. I'm with her, but my heart belongs to you. It has for years. Often, I've thought that maybe I was in love with what you stand for. You are any brother's dream. Not only are you beautiful, intelligent, and cultured, you also have a big heart. I simply want to be in your presence whenever I can. I'm sorry Crystal; I just had to let you know."

"Stephen, I don't know what to say. I do feel something for you too, but we both know we can't act on those feelings. This is so wrong. Why did you tell me this?" She paused and sat quietly for a moment. Stephen didn't speak either. "We could have gone on the way things were. This is not fair to Donnie or me."

"How do you think I've felt all this time? Is that all you have to say?" He asked as if his feelings were hurt by what she said.

She just sat quietly. Her heart was racing; palms were clammy.

What have I gotten myself into? How do I get out of this conversation? I shoulda kept my behind at home and told Donnie no when he suggested this. The admission had aroused her in a way she knew she should only feel for her husband. She knew it would be crazy to act on those lustful feelings, especially with her brother-in-law. *This sounds like a scenario in a soap opera.*

As they sat quietly, she imagined them dancing again. She refused to allow herself to think anything else about him.

"I need to go," she said standing. As she stood, her legs felt wobbly. Walking as fast as possible, she went inside. She bypassed the elevators and headed straight for the stairs. She hadn't realized what she'd done until she reached the fifth floor. That is when she began feeling the effects of going up stairs in heels. She got off on the sixth floor, hoping she wouldn't get to the elevator and when the doors opened, would find Stephen inside. She pushed the up arrow. It opened immediately as if it had been waiting for her. The walk down the hall seemed to get longer and longer. Her head was spinning, and she felt a serious headache coming on. She always got a headache when she was stressed. *What am I stressed about? I told him without hesitating that I was not going to entertain the thought of anything happening between us.* She questioned why she hadn't told him that she loved her husband and that he was wrong for even making such comments. Hindsight was always 20/20, but now she was left wondering if he read more into what she didn't say, than what she did say.

Chapter 13

A Sin and Reality

When she got to her room, the scent of the candle hit her in the face. *I left it burning?* She immediately kicked off her shoes and reached over her shoulder to begin unzipping the dress. "Crap!" she yelled. She'd forgotten the zipper was stuck. She sat down in front of the credenza and put her face in her hands. *How do I get myself in these situations? Sometimes I open my mouth to say too much, other times, too little.* With so many thoughts flooding her mind, she sat back in her chair, and stared at the flower print on the drapes. She was very concerned with how she would get past this with Stephen. Driving home would be impossible. There would be too much sexual tension in the car. *Sexual tension?* She questioned her sanity again. *Did I just think that? I swear, I must be going crazy. I am thinking of my brother-in-law and the word sex in the same thought. I need to lie down.*

She got up from the leather captain's chair and moved to the bed. She crawled onto the bed and pulled the comforter back revealing the crisp white sheets. Lying down, she curled up into a fetal position. Her body ached to be touched, and she wondered whether it were the power of suggestion or for real. She wondered if she were at home, would she be thinking about Stephen. *Probably not.* On occasion, she'd imagined what being in a relationship with him would be like, but that was all. *That's normal.* She figured all women did it, just like men—regardless of whom the other person was. *It's ok to fantasize, isn't it? Girl, of course not! There's a commandment about that. This man just poured his heart out to me, and I left him sitting outside, alone. What's wrong with me?*

Someone was knocking at the door again. This time, she walked to the door and opened it without looking through the peephole. There stood Stephen.

"May I come in?"

She was frozen.

"Please. Just let me explain what that was all about. Hear me out, and then I will never speak of this again. I promise."

She stepped to the side as he entered the room. They stood near the door, not near the bed. She was barefoot and went to the closet to get some slippers. Stephen walked up behind her and took her hand in his.

"Crystal... I never want to hurt you or my brother. I love you both too much. I'm sorry for causing you pain tonight. That was not my intent." His thumb caressed her index finger, and his eyes were filled with tears. Her heart started pounding, and so did her head. She wrestled with the fact that they were about to go down a forbidden path. It made her scared and excited, all at the same time. She hadn't felt like this in a very long time. She hadn't felt wanted or desired in a very long time. She pulled her hand from his, but then he touched her face as if it were familiar to him. She closed her eyes responding to the desire. His hand was so tender; he was tender. He looked deep into her eyes, which looked like spirals to her. She felt mesmerized gazing into them. When exactly, she didn't know, but they melted into a kiss. His lips touched hers and hers touched his. She melted into him; the kiss became passionate. *Hold up! I'm kissing Stephen...Stephen Moore?* She pulled away.

"This is so wrong, Stephen."

"I know, but I can't stop. I love you so much, I always have. I don't want to hurt you, but I *want* you so badly."

Tears began rolling down his face. He put his arms around her waist. She couldn't resist hugging him back, and they began kissing again. He caressed her hair and held her tighter and tighter. She wanted to melt into his arms and give into temptation to make love to him. She fought with all that was within her to pull away, but she didn't.

She knew she was going some place God didn't want her to be, but her free will told her something else. The battle between good and evil wore her down.

Stephen's breath became labored as though he could devour her right there in front of the closet. He took his cues from her, and when she did not hold back her feelings, he unzipped her dress with one smooth movement. He slid the spaghetti straps off her arms with no problem and the dress fell to the floor. She was wearing a black-laced bra, which he unhooked as though he was a master at undressing women. He guided her through the door to the bedroom where they glided onto the already unmade bed. He was gentle with his caresses and every kiss was exactly like she'd imagined. He looked at her and she at him in the candlelight. The scent of rainwater filled the room. She unbuttoned his shirt and touched his chest. It was a perfectly chiseled chest—one that most women would die for. His arms were strong and muscular. She couldn't believe she was actually doing it, but she wasn't about to stop. His hair was silky and soft as she ran her fingers through it. They lay on the bed kissing, caressing, moaning and wanting each other until finally, he pulled away. It was only long enough to step out of his trousers and boxer briefs and to remove her remaining matching undergarments. He looked deep into her eyes as they crossed the line- the point of no return. His eyes rolled back as she closed hers. He felt so good to her. After being celibate for months she was more than ready for him. They moved in motion to their own rhythm. He made love to her and her to him. They didn't want to stop. They couldn't stop. It felt wonderful to her. He called her name over and over in low whispers. She whispered back, careful to say his name. They rolled around in the covers like people do in the movies until they both experienced sinful pleasure.

Chapter 14

Post Act

They lay together. Quiet. The only audible sounds were their breathing, which was slowing down. Crystal felt elated, yet low down. For the life of her, she could not tell herself why she allowed this to happen. To tell the truth, she felt like an outsider looking at the two of them together. Then, she began to cry softly. She had another man's seed on her body, and here they were, lying in bed together like it was where they were supposed to be at that point in time.

"I love you, Crystal." He pulled her close to him as she made an effort to get out of the bed. Her beautiful dress was at the foot of the bed, and she really wanted to hang it up. She needed to do something to momentarily take her mind off what had just occurred between them. She was lying in his arms facing him, and he pulled her even closer. He caressed her face and wiped her tears with his thumb. He leaned in and kissed her on the tip of her nose. Nonetheless, she still remained very quiet. He placed his cheek on her forehead. Reaching up, she stroked the back of his head. He leaned in to kiss her and they kissed again, making love with their tongues. Soft kisses. Hard open mouth kisses. All lip. All over. Stephen kissed her down her spine, which made her quiver all over. She kissed his chest and lingered around his neck. He thoroughly enjoyed the spot near his Adam's apple. They kissed and held each other tightly as though it would be their last time together. In Crystal's mind, this *would* be their last time together. It would be their only time together.

"You haven't said a word."

"Stephen, I don't know what to say. I'm afraid to say anything. I know you've been pouring out your heart tonight, but like I said, I'm afraid. I'm afraid for me, I'm afraid for us."

His embrace grew tighter, and they lay there until they both fell asleep. The dress remained on the floor.

Crystal awakened to the commotion of ghetto-sounding women walking down the hall. They were talking very loudly, and with all that ruckus, they sounded like they had had one too many forty ounce malt liquors. *Obviously, they're not conference goers.* Stephen shifted a little under the covers, then she remembered that she had been dreaming about him.

"What time is it?" he asked sheepishly.

"2:30."

"I'm hungry," he said turning over.

"Me too. Want to go find something?"

"Not really, I was just making a comment. I want to spend the rest of the night holding you in my arms. I know this can't go on, and I want to savor every moment."

"I said, 'me too,' remember? I need food, some crackers or something."

"Crackers? Ok, I'll go find you something. I'm sure there must be a vending machine around somewhere."

Stephen arose, dressed and left, grabbing her passkey as he exited. She guessed he was under the impression that she also wanted the night with him to continue. She arose from the bed and went into the bathroom. Walking directly to the shower, she turned the lever all the way to the red H. As she turned and looked in the mirror, she saw a completely different person. *Who are you and what have you done with Crystal?* Staring back, she saw herself in all of her sinfulness with her hair all messed up from rolling around with a forbidden man.

Her face was flushed, and she felt ashamed— ashamed, yet happy. Contemplating what had happened, she thought maybe she was caught up in some kind of game. This was truly a game. How it would end remained a mystery. She stepped into the shower and burned her left leg. She jerked her leg back, and quickly moved the lever from the red-hot zone. Before attempting to step in again, she waited a moment for the temperature to adjust. Then, she let the water run all over her face and head. She stood there for what seemed like minutes before moving. She obsessed about feeling clean again. She wanted to erase the terrible mistake that she had just made. Squeezing out a little of her cucumber melon scented body wash onto the loofah pad, she began washing her neck slowly. It wasn't long before she heard the door slam closed. She closed her eyes as the warm water drizzled over her head and face again. A moment later, she felt arms around her waist and opened her eyes to see Stephen standing in front of her. He kissed her, and it reminded her of a similar scene in *How Stella Got Her Groove Back*—except, she didn't have micro braids and this was no movie. They both enjoyed allowing the water to bathe them as they embraced each other. Taking the loofah from her, Stephen turned her around, and gently lifted her wet hair, and kissed the back of her neck. He then proceeded to wash her neck and back. He reached around and washed the front of her body. She melted and felt intense feelings deep within herself. He stopped.

"I don't want you to go there without me." She glared at him because she found it hard to believe he would start something, and then stop abruptly. But mentally, she did a quick reality check because she knew she wasn't supposed to be with this man anyway.

They ended their sensual shower with her washing his back. As wrong as they were, she felt very uneasy about washing him anywhere else. They both knew the situation was crazy, but were caught up. After they both got out of the shower and dried off, she walked over to the closet. She took out her black camisole and matching black pajama bottoms with red hearts.

"You even have sexy pajamas," Stephen said.

"I like clothes, which you already know," she said smiling."

"Yes, everyone knows."

"Ha ha, very funny."

Glancing over at the bed, she noticed that Stephen had pulled the covers and neatly arranged them just as they were originally upon checking in. There was a plate of fresh fruit on the adjacent night table as well as two bottles of Deer Park water.

"Where did you get this? I thought you were looking for a vending machine?"

"Actually, I went downstairs to ask where the vending machine was because I couldn't find it on this floor. The attendant at the desk mentioned that they had fresh snack items I could buy there; so, I did. Looks good, huh?"

"Yep. Thanks."

He had blown out the candle while she was in the shower, so the ambiance was gone. Nevertheless, the sweet fragrance of rainwater still filled the room. The aroma seriously clashed with the cucumber melon, which made its way from the bathroom. She saw that Stephen was wearing the hotel bathrobe.

"Do you want me to go to your room and get some clean clothes for you?"

"Sure, that would be great. I didn't want to be too presumptuous by bringing things to your room, but I guess we've already crossed that line, huh?"

"You think? What do you want me to get?"

"My Tommy duffel bag has everything I need, thanks."

She left the room and headed down the hall looking for his room. She entered and found his bag in the closet just as he said. However, he did not tell her it was so heavy. Lifting the bag to her shoulder, she left the room and headed back. On her way down the hall, she passed Miss Shana, who didn't even look at her. *Whatever.*

Entering her room, she saw Stephen sitting on the bed with the plate of fruit in his lap. She set the bag down and joined him. He fed her a strawberry.

"Check this out." He had turned on the television and Jerry Springer was on.

"Come on, Stephen- surely, you don't watch this junk."

"Definitely not! Well, not usually, but you must admit that this stuff is borderline ridiculous and funny. Ok, ok. I'll turn it off." He turned it off, and they finished the fruit. Afterwards, he got up and changed into the pair of black Tommy Hilfiger boxers and lounge pants packed in his duffel bag. *He looks so good.* He sat back down on the bed with his back to the headboard. Then, he pulled her toward him so that she sat between his legs and her back rested on his chest. Both sat in total silence, and then he reached over and turned out the light. They slid under the covers to go to sleep. He still had his arms around her. She felt him pull her hair back again and kiss her neck. He whispered "Good night, love" in her ear. She said "good night." By the time they drifted off to sleep again, it was 3:15 am.

Chapter 15

Tuesday

The alarm clock was annoying. Crystal awakened first. Disoriented, she tried to figure out where the darn thing was. Jumping to her feet, she tripped over one of Stephen's shoes, and barely missed falling on her face.

"Ouch!" she screamed trying to prevent herself from falling.

Stephen jumped up.

"What? What? What's going on?"

He saw her jumping around. She was in pain because the way she landed on his shoe really hurt the bottom of her foot. She hobbled over to the dresser where she slid the button on the alarm clock to OFF.

"What's wrong with you?"

"I stepped on your shoe, Mister, and it hurts."

"I'm sorry, come here." She sat on his side of the bed, and very gently, he massaged her foot.

"I really came down hard on it. It feels a little better now."

"I'm so sorry. Is it really 9:00?"

She picked up her cell phone from the night table to check the time.

"Yes, it is. What time is the first session?"

"It was 8:30. I need to get going. The breakout sessions begin at 10:00 a.m. I wish we could have breakfast together. What were you planning to do today?"

"First, I was going to sleep in. Then, I thought about walking downtown to see some sights, and I need to call Melissa. I didn't call her yesterday."

"Yeah, the two of you do need to hook up. At least that way I'll know you are with someone. Please, be careful. I don't like you wandering around alone." He reached for his clothes and started to get dressed.

"I won't be wandering, and I'll be careful."

"Take your cell," he said buttoning his shirt.

"Yes, Stephen."

"I'm not trying to patronize you, I care about you. You know how much."

"I'm going to walk down to the battery. I need to clear my head."

Stephen didn't respond; he just looked at her. "Dinner?"

"Yeah, call me when you get out."

"Ok. I need to go to my room."

He left.

She went to the closet to find something to wear to breakfast. Looking for her toothpaste, she opened her cosmetic bag and found a piece of folded purple stationary. She opened it and could hardly believe her eyes. It was Donnie's handwriting.

I wanted to kiss you yesterday.

Too afraid to ask or hear what you might say.

You have no idea how you made me feel.

You kissed me softly on my ear, giving me chills.

Your touch felt so good, I want you to know.

I felt a vibe from head to toe.

Standing next to you, I felt my nature rise.

Unconsciously, you caught me by surprise.

My hands caressed your face and soft skin.

Wanted to grasp you, but couldn't give in.

Your smile is like the ocean's breeze.
Cascading waves, just enough to tease.
Kissing you gently, I rubbed your hair.
I was lost in your eyes, trying not to stare.
Your lips—luscious, full, and sweet.
So soft, I wish they were mine to keep.
An evening spent with you, I'll never forget.
Looking forward to it again—I have no regrets.

It was a poem he had written for her when they were dating. She remembered thinking it sounded lame when he gave it to her, but also thought it was sweet of him. He must have stuck it in her bag before he left for work. It certainly wasn't there when she packed. She folded it back up and sat on the bed. She remembered him telling her that although he wasn't much of a poet, he cared so much about her that he had to give it a shot. She cried and ached deeply at what she was feeling. She had betrayed the one man who had always been there for her. At least used to. *What was this all about? He hasn't said 'boo' to me in months, and now he's sticking poetry in my bag like he can't get enough of me.* She couldn't imagine how she was going to function after this trip was over. For that matter, how was she going to act for the rest of the trip or the rest of the day? Stephen had just left her there as if they were a couple. "How stupid can two people be?" she said aloud. This was some *Bold and the Beautiful, Young and the Restless* mess. Her mom used to watch the soaps and say, "Black people wouldn't do some scandalous stuff like that." *Mom would be proud of me now.*

After she showered again, and dressed, she still was in a state of shock. She put her journal in her backpack and made her way to the hotel restaurant. As she walked down the hall, she passed the Chelsea Room. *It all started in there. Not really though. It has been happening for years. I just hadn't owned up to it.*

She ordered scrambled eggs, wheat toast, and coffee. The waitress asked if that was all she wanted to eat as though she was implying that wasn't enough. She proceeded to tell Crystal about the morning special which consisted of four pancakes, two sausage links, two strips of bacon, two scrambled eggs and juice for $7.99. Crystal politely declined the offer, and told her that was all. *She must think I want to look like her. I refuse to have a forty-five inch waist and swollen ankles. I like my heart and pancreas just the way they are, disease free.*

There was a copy of the Post & Courier newspaper on the table. The headlines read something about the redevelopment project on Daniel Island coming to a halt and construction for a new bridge. A man at the next table asked her if she was going to read the sports section. She said, "No" and passed it to him.

After eating breakfast, she grabbed her backpack, left the hotel restaurant, and walked down East Bay Street. At first, she walked briskly, and then realized that the summer heat and humidity would get the best of her if she kept up that pace. She slowed down and began to recount all that had happened the night before.

Stephen was a wonderful man, but so was Donnie. Although she and Donnie hadn't connected in months, she knew the man she married. What she felt for Stephen had to be temporary. Obviously, she couldn't have a long-term affair with him. She felt so foolish for even being in such a situation. Her mind was racing and she couldn't think clearly. A warm sea air whipped her hair, and she desperately sought a diversion. She entered a shop that sold decorative flags to browse and think about something else. She would have never imagined that there could be so many different types of flags to display. An older couple on vacation from Connecticut bought four flags, one for each of the seasons. She imagined they were the type of people who decorated their yards and houses for each holiday. *They probably have an Easter egg tree and pumpkins on their lawns for Halloween.*

Soon, she left the store to continue her walk. *Incoming call, incoming call.* Her cell phone announced she had a call. It was Stephen.

"Hi, beautiful."

"Please don't say that."

"Why? You are beautiful. Do you disagree?"

"What's up? Why aren't you in a session?"

"I couldn't concentrate. I was thinking about you and wondering where you were."

"I'm on East Bay Street."

"Where?"

"Don't try to find me. You need to be at the conference."

"Aren't you full of yourself? I wasn't going to try to find you, I was just asking."

"I'm sorry. I…"

"Don't be sorry. I was just wondering where you were. Truth is, I really just wanted to hear your voice. I know I left rather abruptly this morning. I was in a hurry because I had missed the opening. Are *we* ok?"

"Let's talk about this '*we*' tonight."

"OK."

He took a deep breath, and she felt an uneasy feeling in her stomach. To say the least it was awkward.

"I'm going to finish my walk, ok?"

He said ok, and then they said good-bye.

She continued her walk. She could see sailboats and barges in the harbor across the street. A whiff of cinnamon flavor drifted from a nearby bagel shop. It reminded her of her grandmother's kitchen. Grandma always had something good and flavorful for everyone to eat when she was alive. Crystal turned and walked down a side street to get to Waterfront Park. There were wooden swings that looked like park benches on the pier. She found an empty one facing the ocean, and sat down. She removed her journal from the backpack. Next, she stretched out and propped her legs up on the swing so no one else would sit beside her. She began writing and the flow was fast. Her thoughts came so quickly, she couldn't write fast enough. There was so much emotion she needed to capture before she lost momentum. The first entry flowed flawlessly.

Last night
Monday's madness, Tuesday's sadness.
We made love last night, we shouldn't have, but we did.
My heart poured out to you, yours to mine.
We were one for a short moment in time.

I want you all to myself, but I know that is not a reality.

For it to be a reality would mean lots of lives would be shattered.

I'm not for hurting others intentionally.

My heart longs for you because all I now have are my memories.

We looked deeply into each other's eyes, you held me, and I held you.

I felt your love, your passion.

You are so intense.

My body was next to yours for a moment in time.

Your heat penetrates me as I melt in your presence.

I long to feel your hair in my hands,

To feel your masculine hands in mine,

Your back, your chest pressed next to mine,

Your breath on my neck, your lips, your presence.

I care for you, more than you can possibly imagine.

I want you to know this, so if there is ever any doubt, you have this assurance.

You make me smile so wide.

No other man has ever done that.

Bringing out the little girl in me is what I love so much about you.

When we are together, it feels like time stops, just for us.

I want to stay in this place forever.

It feels so comfortable. So familiar. So free.

The smell of your cologne ignites fire within me.

I can't control the feelings I have when you are near.

I try, I fight, but I am fighting myself.

You are my forbidden fruit and temptation mustn't get the best of us again.

I care for you, please know that.

What will you do with all this information? I don't know.

But know this; you have a piece of my heart that can't be touched by anyone else.

The writing came from deep within. She felt so passionate about what she wrote. She began to cry as she reread what she wrote. It sounded so beautiful to her because it captured exactly what she felt. She closed her journal and swung her legs around so she could use the swing for what it was intended. She swung back and forth as hard as she could until a dark chocolate brother with a broom and dustpan said, "Watch out there now, you gonna go sailing through the air in a minute!" He had a strong local accent, and she had to think about what he was saying before she really understood. She smiled and slowed down. For a brief moment she had escaped from her own reality into a place she hadn't been in a long time, free.

With all that had been going on at home, or not going on, she'd felt so bogged down. Lately, she had spent so much time wishing that her husband would set aside some time with her that she had forgotten how to have fun on her own. She got off the swing, grabbed the backpack, and began the walk towards Battery Park. For a Tuesday morning, there sure were a lot of people out. A lot of them were lovers. They strolled by, holding hands, and some stood on the sidewalk kissing as if they were the only people in the world at the moment. She started wondering if any of them were married to other people, or if they really did belong to each other. She secretly wished that Stephen were there. It bothered her that she was wishing for him instead of Donnie. She knew her relationship with Donnie had changed, but she didn't know yet to what extent. In reality, it wasn't that she wanted her relationship with him to end, but she realized something after Stephen left this morning. He was what she had been wanting in Donnie for so long. She gave herself to him because she needed to be wanted, held, and touched. Her marriage to Donnie felt more like a roommate arrangement with, merely, a possibility of intimacy. She longed for passion, conversation, and adventure. Crystal walked until she reached East Bay Street again. She turned left and headed for the Battery. On the way, she passed beautiful houses with tiny, but well manicured yards. Little dogs yapped at her through closed windows. The Battery was ahead and she eyed a park bench under a massive oak tree. It had to be at least a hundred years old. She sat down under it, and took in a long, deep breath.

Lord, why have I made this terrible mistake? I know it is a mistake because I have heard over and over again 'Thou shall not commit adultery.' Lord, why couldn't I have met Stephen first? I love Donnie, and the life we were on our way to building, but somewhere we got off the path. I feel so low right now, Lord, and I pray that you guide me through this. My heart feels torn in two. I love you, and I know it hurts you for me to deliberately do what I've done. I'm weak, and I hate my flesh right now. I now understand what Paul meant in the Bible when he wrote, the harder he tried to be good, evil was right there with him.

She leaned over to lie on her stomach. Just as she got comfortable, her cell phone rang again. It was Stephen. *Why is it that Stephen keeps calling me, but my husband who should be missing me, has only called once to see if we made it here safely?*

"Hello?"

"Hey, where are you?"

"I'm sitting on a bench at the Battery. It's a park right at the tip of Charleston."

"I know where that is, I'll be right there."

"Stephen, no. Please."

"Crystal, you can't avoid me all day. I need to see you, and we need to talk. You know this. I'll be there in a few minutes." He ended the call without waiting for her to reply.

Chapter 16

Recap and Analyze

She closed her eyes because her head felt like it was spinning and laid on the bench for a moment. She heard footsteps that sounded like a horse. She looked up to see a police officer approaching on horseback.

"Ma'am, are you ok?"

She looked up at him with puffy red eyes.

"Yes, I am. I had a disagreement with my friend, and I came here to clear my head, thanks."

"Have a nice day, ma'am." Mr. Law Enforcement rode off.

She decided to sit up before someone else thought she was sick or homeless. Across the park she saw a sailboat passing by. It seemed to barely move. She could imagine the people, without a care in the world, on board relaxing and absorbing the sun's rays. She wondered whether or not they had ever made such grave mistakes as she had. Sympathetically, she fully understood how people got into these situations. In the past she had judged so many people wrongly about their mistakes. *Now it's my turn.* As she gazed at the sailboat, Stephen's car went by, and he parked about a block away. Her heart skipped a beat as she saw him walking in the distance. He wore khaki pants with a navy blue golf shirt, and a pair of fashionable dark brown sunglasses. His masculine features were very distinct: tall, broad shoulders, rippled chest and arms. He continued to walk in her direction, and as he approached, she could see a very serious look on his face.

"Hi, Crystal."

"Stephen."

"How are you doing?"

"I've been better."

He was still standing.

"Crystal, I had to see you. We need to talk, and I couldn't concentrate in my session until we came to some type of …something."

"I understand, and you are right; I can't go on avoiding you all day. Have a seat." She motioned for him to sit beside her.

They sat quietly for a minute absorbing the sounds surrounding them. Taking her hand in his, Stephen gently stroked it with his other hand. His hands were massive compared to hers and although their appearance seemed to suggest they could tell many stories, they were remarkably soft. He turned toward her and caressed her face. She spoke before he could.

"I feel so torn, Stephen. I don't want to hurt Donnie, but being with you here like this…" Her mind wandered. "Last night was so magical. Believe me; I may be trying to deceive myself into thinking that this will not end. But deep within my spirit, I know it has to, immediately."

"Me too, sweetheart. We need to put this 'crazy love' to bed." He smiled, "No pun intended. I hope you don't think I took advantage of you in any way. Like I told you last night, I love you, I always have. I made a big mistake marrying Pam, and I have envied my brother for years. The night he introduced me to you, I was so happy for him, but secretly wished I could have met you first. I long to be near you and to hear your voice. I have always loved talking to you, and all of the time we've spent together, even when others were around. I can't believe you never picked up on that. Pam asked me one day if I had a thing for you."

"Are you serious?"

"As serious as a heart attack. She's jealous of everyone because she's very insecure within herself. I do care for her, but not in the manner in which a man should love his wife. The main reason I married her is because I settled instead of waiting for the right woman to come along. I prayed for a wife, but I wasn't very specific." He sighed, and she closed her eyes. Her head was pounding.

"Stephen, my head hurts. All of this is making me sick, physically. I feel like we've gone somewhere that we can never recover from. Last night, I was so mad because I saw other women flirting with you and I wanted the same freedom to flirt with you. That is precisely why I had an attitude at the dinner. When we were dancing, I was having so much fun. I hadn't had that much fun in a long time. In some ways we've always clicked, and that's what I like about you. You are like my best friend at times and I cherish that. I was in so much conflict last night before you came to my room. As strange as it may sound, I couldn't believe that I was having thoughts about you and that you had actually told me all of those things. It felt like a dream."

He cut in, "Crystal, I don't want to cause you any harm or pain. That is not my heart's desire for you. I'll say it again; I love you... more than you know. I know that hearing me say that upsets you, but it's true. Have I thought about my brother in the last 24 hours? No, not really. I know I'm being selfish and that what we've done has changed everything for not only us, but also, both our marriages. I don't even want to mention your relationship with Pam or mine with my brother. Truthfully, I don't even want to go there yet in *my* mind. For now, I simply want to make sure that you are ok, and that we enjoy the rest of the time we have together. At some point we are going to have to face the music. But for right now, let's enjoy the moment."

"Stephen, we have sinned against God."

"I know my rationale is unacceptable. He could strike us down right here, right now, but He is merciful and forgiving."

"Yes, He is and I don't want to go on sinning against him, because I don't want that mercy or forgiveness to run out."

She grabbed her head as the pounding became more intense- it felt like her head would explode any minute. Stephen put his arm around her and pulled her close to him, lovingly. She let out a wailing cry and her entire body shook. He pulled a crisp handkerchief from his pocket and began wiping the tears from her face. Stephen's eyes were full of tears as well, but not yet streaming down his face. They gazed at each other and like magnets, were drawn to each other. They kissed each other softly, both with their eyes open, looking deeply into the other. They both knew they were wrong, but continued to do it anyway. She put her arms around him and held him tightly. He held her. It felt like a very long time. Closing her eyes, she could hear the waves crashing against the barrier wall across the street and the footsteps of others walking near their bench. An ambulance siren sounded in the distance. Someone in a car passed by with booming bass, while Fifty Cent rapped something about a candy shop. In spite of all the activities going on around them, they both felt like they were the only two people for miles.

"Let's walk."

He took her hand and they stood. She felt somewhat lightheaded and placed her hands on her temples again.

"Are you ok?"

"No, my head has been pounding all morning."

"Did you take something? What did you eat for breakfast?"

"It's more than that, I need to de-stress. Taking something will only mask the root cause of the headache. I'll be ok. Come on."

It was hot and muggy, despite being near the water. She and Stephen walked toward his car. Opening the door for her, he dropped her backpack onto the backseat. When he started the car, the music immediately came on and revealed that tracks from Jill Scott's *Running Across my Mind* had been playing. It made her smile, even though she knew she shouldn't have. Crystal still held her head in her hands. She figured that the best choices would be to eat something or find a way out of the situation she was in. The first option would be a lot easier. *Ten Excedrin tablets wouldn't cure this monster...*

They drove around the downtown area for a while until Stephen accidentally got in the wrong lane, and onto the James Island

Connector Bridge. Shortly thereafter, they turned off at the first exit, and found a restaurant overlooking the harbor. All the while, the throbbing in her head continued, and it made her feel as if she were going to throw up. Stephen helped her out of the car, and they walked toward the restaurant. In front of the building there were at least twenty steps they had to climb before reaching the entry door. Once inside, the ambience was nice with low lighting and more importantly, low noise. They were seated right away at a table with a view that overlooked a marina. A blond haired guy, who looked like a surfer dude, came to take their drink order. He looked like he could be a college student.

"Do you have rolls or crackers? The lady here is not feeling well and needs something on her stomach."

"Would you like a plate of fresh croissants with honey butter?"

"Yeah, sounds great."

"I'll bring them as soon as they are ready. What would you like to drink?" Surfer dude took their drink order, and Stephen stroked her hand from across the table. "Crystal, this makes me think of Purple Rain. I never meant to cause you any sorrow, I never meant to cause you any pain…"

She smiled. He was being corny, yet serious.

"I enjoy your company, Stephen. I don't want this to end. All day I've been reliving last night. I was so furious at you for going there, but deliriously happy that you did."

Other than the passion they shared last night, she had never touched Stephen in a sensual way. She reached over and put her hand on his cheek. He turned his lips toward her palm and gently kissed it. It sent a tingly feeling down her spine. He moved her hand from his face and held it. He looked deep into her eyes while holding her hand with both of his.

"I wish I could be all you want in a man. You don't know how I wish that for you, for us. This trip is like a dream come true for me. I want to be with you in every spare moment. I want to be your wall of strength when you need it, your place of solace when you need an escape. I love you so much, and I've waited years to tell you."

"I know. For years I've felt that connection, but refused to allow myself to think otherwise. Now, I feel like we've been given a second chance for a few days. Crazy isn't it?" She paused, "How did we get here, and better yet, how do we get out, Stephen?"

Surfer dude brought the croissants. Stephen took one and pulled it apart. She opened her mouth as he raised it to her lips. It was a large piece, but she devoured it.

"I don't know," said Stephen, continuing as if the arrival of the food hadn't interrupted them. "I'm just happy... overjoyed actually, that we have this time together. Although I love my brother and don't want to hurt him, I hope that we can have a future... together."

"Stephen, thinking about the future is the farthest thing from my mind right now. I refuse to allow myself to think like that. Let's just make the most of our time together, because you know it must end. I am letting you and myself down by dishonoring what I hold so dear—my relationship with my family and God."

Stephen didn't say a word. Silently, he agreed because they both knew that she spoke the truth.

I wonder if he is feeling as heathenish as I am.

They ordered their food and enjoyed the scenery. The sky grew a dark shade of gray as a southern summer thunderstorm was on the way. Finishing their meal, they paid surfer dude and left. Stephen wanted to do some sightseeing. Since she felt much better after eating, they decided to do just that.

They drove in the direction of Folly Beach and passed several beautiful oak trees filled with moss hanging gracefully from their branches. As they drove closer to the beach, the sky grew darker before the heavens opened up. It rained so hard that before they reached the beach, they had to pull into a public parking lot because the wipers weren't wiping fast enough. There they sat for several minutes until the rain let up. They sat quietly listening to the sound of the water hitting the top of the car. Stephen held her hand, and she looked out of the window. It was a typical low-country shower. Finally, the rain eased up enough to form a light mist. Crystal decided to get out of the car, and Stephen got out as well.

"Uh, what about your hair, Sister?"

"What about it?"

"I figured you didn't want to get your hair wet."

"Well, you figured wrong. I'm not worried about a little rain water, that's what shampoo and conditioner are for, Bro."

"See, that's why I love you. You are so different from other women."

"Let's walk toward the beach," she said.

They strolled in the direction of the beach, and she took off her shoes to feel the wet sand under her feet. Stephen took his off, and then placing his right hand around her waist, pulled her closer to him. They were hip to hip like two lovers in the movies. Walking in cadence with one another, they passed several people out with their dogs. Their owners had probably anxiously waited for the storm to be over before bringing them out. Stephen stopped and dropped his shoes to the ground. He put both arms around her, and she returned the embrace. She felt so warm and secure in his arms; almost like she was meant to be there. They kissed right there on the beach—in public. Although that was probably a normal occurrence there, for her nothing was normal anymore. They walked a while longer, picked up a few seashells, then headed back to the car. Stephen wanted to drive around for a bit, but she asked him if they could go back to the hotel and relax. She was tired and had an emotional day. She preferred to go back to her room.

"Are you ok?" asked Stephen.

"Yep, I'm just ready to shower and relax."

"Can we spend some time together later?"

"Yes. Give me about an hour to wash my hair and unwind."

"Call me when you are done."

When they arrived at the hotel, they went to their own separate rooms. She unpacked her backpack and checked her cell phone for messages. No calls. Even though she honestly didn't want to talk to Donnie, she still was surprised that he hadn't called.

She showered, and then put on a comfortable pair of lounge pants and a tank top. She laid across the bed and watched the evening news for a while before calling Stephen. He answered after three rings. "Hello?" he said sounding very lethargic.

"Did you go to sleep?"

"Yeah, I did. Sorry. I can come down there in a minute. Let me wake up." He mumbled more verbiage, incoherently.

"Stephen, go back to sleep. Call me later." She smiled at his gibberish.

"Ok."

She figured that he must have been just as tired. Emotionally, he was living the same thing she was. Chaos.

She took advantage of the change in plans and took a nap herself.

adj.
lethargic = of, causing or characterized by lethargy.

lethargy - a lowered level of consciousness w/ drowsiness, listlessness and apathy.

Apathy - lack of interest/ concern, esp. regarding matters of general importance/ appeal, indifference.

Seacrying's she forgot people who they knew were there it convention

Chapter 17

Surprise, Suprise

Knock, knock, knock! The loud banging reverberated throughout the room. Crystal had been asleep for about an hour when the knocking began. Vaguely, she remembered rising from the bed and walking to the door. She tiptoed over to look out the peephole and almost choked on air when she saw Donnie standing on the other side of the door. She stood there gawking at him, paralyzed and unable to lift her hand to open the door. Suddenly, a sharp pain radiated through her big toe, and she realized that she was still standing on the tip of her toes. Seemingly, she had frozen in time, but then the fight or flight response arose in her quickly. *Oh no! What in the world is he doing here? Where can I hide?* She turned around and took a quick look over the room like she might actually find a place to hide, and Donnie would leave. "Get a grip!" she said out loud before she realized what she'd done.

"Crystal?" Donnie called her name from the other side of the door. She had no choice but to open the door. He knocked again, and reluctantly, she opened the door.

"Hey, Baby," he said smiling. *Baby, there he goes again.*

She forced a smile, "What in the world are you doing here?" She stood in the doorway.

"What kind of greeting is that? I came to spend some time with you. Aren't you going to let me in? What are you hiding in there, another man? And who were you telling to get a grip?"

He heard me!

"I'm sorry, put your things over there. I was asleep when you knocked. The knocking scared me. Who knows what I might've said. You know how I am when I wake up suddenly." She moved to let him in. She couldn't believe this was actually happening. *Why now, Donnie?*

"Yeah, I remember the night you woke up and punched me right in the eye. I was only trying to be romantic by whispering in your ear!"

"I know, but I'll bet you learned your lesson huh?"

"Yeah right. It was kind of hard trying to explain to others that I wasn't the victim of spousal abuse!" Donnie put his duffel bag on the bed, and walked toward her smiling. He hugged her like he used to, and kissed her on the neck. She didn't melt like she always used to when he did that.

He stepped back, and still holding her by the arms, looked at her all over. "So... tell me, what have you been up to? Do you like the hotel?"

She pulled away from him and walked over to slip on her Sketchers. "I've been relaxing, and yes, the hotel is really nice. I was planning to visit the spa and get a massage tomorrow."

"Good, I'm glad you're enjoying yourself. Have you seen much of Stephen?"

Now why would you ask that? She felt a little paranoid.

"Uh, yes. We had a late lunch together this afternoon, and did a little sight seeing afterwards. To occupy my time, I walked to the Battery earlier."

"Oh. I wonder how the conference is going. Are you glad to see me?"

So making an unannounced appearance is supposed to make me forget about everything that's happened all year long? Maybe I'm the one that's crazy after all.

She faked a smile. "I'm really surprised, Donnie. I figured I wouldn't see you until some time next week. Are you staying for the rest of the week?"

"No, I drove down to spend the night with you, and to show you that I do still have a little bit of spontaneity left in me. I need to get back before 3:00 tomorrow because I have a meeting with one of the reps and the regional sales manager of Golden Corral. They want to do a blitz campaign targeted toward busy families."

"Umm hmm, so I get a few hours of you? Lucky me." *Oops, did I say that out loud?*

"I thought I was doing a good thing, Baby."

There he goes with that baby again.

Before she could respond, there was a knock at the door. *Please don't let that be Stephen.* Her heart skipped a beat. She walked to the door quickly and opened without looking through the peephole. There stood Stephen, smiling. *Lord, take me now! Take me now!*

"Look, sorry about earlier. I crashed when I got to my room. I barely remember talking to you. I hope…"

"What up, Bro?" said Donnie walking toward the door.

Stephen's face broke into a million pieces, and every emotion he could possibly have felt at that moment appeared on his face at the same time. "What the heck are you doing here?"

"Excuse me?" Donnie looked at him crazily. "I came to see my *wife*. Is that all right with you?"

"My bad, man. I didn't mean that how it sounded. It's the business. Isn't Craig McCarter coming in the morning to discuss the new proposal for Golden Corral?"

"He moved the appointment to three, so I dropped in for an overnighter."

"Did Amanda finish all of the revisions?"

"Steve!" He threw up his hands in frustration. "Everything is copasetic, man. Chill! Don't worry. I've been running the business just as long as you have. Remember? What's your problem anyway?"

He stepped closer and looked at Stephen even more strangely. "I brought a copy along for you to see. I know how you are. It's in my bag if you must see it."

"You know how I am? What the hell does that mean?"

"Guys! Please don't do this!" Crystal had had enough.

"Naw, Man, I was just asking. I know you are more than capable of handling the business." His emotions were all over the place. Stephen looked over at Crystal. She knew he was confused and hurt by Donnie being there; even though as her husband, he had every right to be.

"Well, since you don't have a lot of time, I'll get out of your way," said Stephen. He turned around and walked toward the door.

"Wait! Did I interrupt something? Did you two have plans this evening?" asked Donnie with a raised eyebrow and looking at the two of them.

"No," they both said quickly and in unison.

"I just decided to stop by. Dinner is on your own tonight, so I stopped by to find out what Crystal was up to. Go ahead and have fun tonight. Maybe, tomorrow evening we can check out that mall we passed, Crystal."

"OK," she said feeling as if her heart were in her throat about to explode. Stephen turned around and walked out, pulling the door extremely hard to close. She felt about two inches tall.

"What's his problem? He seemed to be in some kind of mood."

"Really? I didn't notice," said Crystal lying. *Lord, forgive me.*

"Oh well, I'm not concerned about him any way. I came to see my baby," he said smiling.

What? Crystal wished she could tell Donnie to go back home because the booty call visit wasn't happening. In reality, she knew in her heart that she was wrong for what she'd been doing behind his back with his brother. Donnie told her he wanted to go out for dinner since he hadn't eaten since around 11:30. Crystal got dressed hurriedly, and they headed downtown in search of seafood.

"I love the culture and the atmosphere here," said Donnie. "It's hotter than a mug here though. Can you picture being a slave and

105

working on a plantation in this heat? And what's that smell? Smells like sewage! Must be the Atlantic. Can you imagine all of the fish droppings and dead stuff out there in that nasty water?"

Crystal didn't hear a word he said because she was thinking about Stephen. *What was he feeling or thinking? He was so upset when he left. He slammed the door. What could I do? He is my husband, technically speaking.*

"Crystal?" Donnie said stopping their rhythmic pace.

"What?" snapped Crystal not meaning it the way it came out.

"What is going on with you? You've been distant ever since I arrived. Did I mess up somehow? Or did I mess up your evening?"

"What does that mean?" asked Crystal defensively.

"Come on," said Donnie pulling her arm in the direction of the restaurants.

As they walked, Donnie continued to look at his wife. By the way she was acting, he sensed that *something* was going on with her, but he dared not guess. He chose to believe that all the late nights and out of town trips were for their future, but deep down he knew his wife had longed for him and missed his companionship. He thought about the many nights he came home and paid her very little attention because he was still wrapped up in the day's events. He'd also had a lot of things on his mind recently that didn't involve work at all. He didn't even remember the last time he'd made love to his wife. For months, he'd had romantic thoughts of someone else on his mind and although he hadn't acted on those thoughts, he knew it profoundly affected the manner in which he interacted with his wife. Moreover, it interfered with his ability to hear from God. He used to be more in touch with God, but his relationship had deteriorated to an all-new low point for him. Now, he didn't even know how to begin to get back what he'd neglected in his wife or the Lord. He wanted to go back in time. He wished that he could wipe his Palm Pilot clean, refuse to allow lustful thoughts to enter his mind, schedule fewer appointments each day, and let Stephen or someone else in the office run the show sometimes. Unfortunately, this was his present and there'd be no making up for the past. More importantly, he needed to resolve an issue in his life that only God and one other person were aware of, and he didn't know how to handle it. Donnie knew what he had in Crystal, but had grown bored with her over the last year.

Mr. Corporate America. Mr. Man with something to prove to the world. His logic was, she'd love him for what he could do for her, for them in the future. What he hadn't realized was that while he was busy planning the future, his wife needed him right now.

They walked quietly down the street until they passed South End Brewery.

"Hey, there's one of those in Charlotte," said Crystal.

"I know," said Donnie. "They have great pizzas too."

"Oh, so you've been already?" *Figures.*

"Yep. Stephen and I went there went for lunch one day."

"Well, you said you wanted some good seafood, so let's see what's further on down here."

They walked a few more blocks until they reached Magnolia's. "Oh, let's go in there. I saw a review on the hotel visitors channel that they have good food presented with a very creative flare," Crystal said, trying to mask the obvious tension between them. There were several people standing outside on the sidewalk drinking wine and other drinks with olives and cherries. They walked through the crowd and went to the hostess desk. The hostess said that they would be seated in ten to fifteen minutes.

"You're mad at me, aren't you?" said Donnie to Crystal.

"Why did you ask me that?"

"I want to know Crystal," he said as they walked toward a seat in the waiting area.

"No, I'm not mad at you." Deep in her heart, she was mad at herself. She had secretly wanted Stephen, but never in a million years dreamed she'd actually be with him. Now, here was her husband who finally decided that he wanted to spend some time with her- a major inconvenience since she didn't want to be with him. Instead, she longed to be in Stephen's presence again. Not saying a word to each other, they sat and watched other people. Donnie wondered if this time apart had made Crystal realize she didn't want to spend any more nights alone, and he thought maybe the surprise visit wasn't such a good idea after all. He remembered how Crystal would take long walks through the park, spending countless hours sitting by the lake. She would use the time to meditate and seek clarity from God. Maybe she'd given up on him and he wouldn't blame her at all. At one time, they both were on the same wavelength, spiritually. They both attended Bible study together and whether or not to attend Sunday worship wasn't even an option. He felt proud to have his beautiful wife beside him in church every Sunday. They even had their own study sessions at home so they would be truly grounded in the Word. One missed session eventually turned into missing all of them for Donnie. Each week, Crystal attended all of the church events alone. He knew she probably gave everyone a good explanation as to why he wasn't there. Right now, he wished that he'd been there for her because he didn't like the cold breeze he felt. He knew one thing for sure; it wasn't coming from the air conditioning vent they were sitting directly under. He just hoped it wasn't too late.

Crystal and Donnie had dinner in a quiet corner of Magnolia's. The place was saturated with southern charm. The menu featured a number of nouveau cuisine dishes, and Donnie had a hard time deciding on which entrée to choose.

"Ewww!" Crystal snarled her nose as she read the menu.

"What? Do they serve snails or something?"

"No, I was considering the blackened mahi mahi, but I see that it comes with fried green tomatoes and jalapeno cheddar grits. I'd have to order different sides, and I'm sure the chef wouldn't like that. I'll choose something else. The grilled yellow fin tuna fillet sounds good. Comes with a potato cake and greens with pineapple salsa. Uh oh, jalapeno vinaigrette. What's with the jalapeno stuff? I'll ask that it be left off."

Donnie was glad that she was at least talking. "The shellfish over grits sounds like a plan for me. Check this out, sautéed shrimp, sea scallops and lobster over creamy white grits with a lobster butter sauce and fried spinach. Have you ever had fried spinach?"

"Actually, I have, and it was surprisingly delicious. We had it at Café Sayess in Statesville when the English Department went out for Christmas lunch. That's a nice restaurant too."

A short, brown-skinned waiter approached their table. "My name is Antwoine and I'll be your server this evening. Can I start you out with a Low Country Splash?" He went straight into a description of what it was. "It's Midori, Ocean Spray cranberry juice, and Malibu Caribbean Rum served on the rocks."

"Uh, no thanks. Crystal what would you like to have?"

"Um, I'd like iced tea with a splash of cranberry juice."

"Yeah, that sounds good. I'll have the same."

The waiter committed their drink orders to memory and waited to see if they would order anything else before the entrees.

"When he mentioned Ocean Spray, it made me think of Boston tea. Remember when we had that at Red Lobster, Stephen? I mean Donnie?" *Oh my God! Please tell me that I didn't say that out loud.*

The waiter lingered a minute— enjoying what he thought was about to go down.

"How much time have you spent with Stephen? You've only been gone for one day, and you're calling me by another man's name already!" He smiled.

Crystal smiled back at him, relieved that he wasn't suspicious.

"That's all, Bro." Donnie dismissed Antwoine, and then he put the focus back on his wife. He admired her beauty as she continued to look over the menu. Antwoine quickly returned with their Boston tea. Then, he took the orders for their entrees, being careful to remember to tell the cooks to leave off the jalapeno vinaigrette for Crystal. Donnie made small talk with Crystal, and he noticed that she was visibly preoccupied.

"Crystal, what's bothering you?"

"Donnie, not now." Reluctantly, he took her advice. He was afraid that if he pushed the issue, he wouldn't be at all happy with what she might have to say. After about fifteen minutes, Antwoine returned with their entrees. They both were impressed with the entrees they had selected. Eagerly, they devoured it as if it had been the only meal they both had had in days. Crystal deliberately focused her attention on her plate because she didn't feel like talking to her husband. Even though Donnie did the same thing, it was for different reasons.

After they finished dinner, Donnie paid Antwoine with his American Express, and then took Crystal's hand to help her from her seat. They walked through the restaurant to the front door. Miss Rump Shaker from last night was standing there with some other women. She glared at Crystal holding Donnie's hand and rolled her eyes. She cursed out loud while pursing her lips at Donnie. She looked at him like she did Stephen, as if she could eat him whole. It made Crystal feel good although she knew she shouldn't gloat. She had been seen with two very attractive men in the last twenty-four hours, and Miss Rump Shaker couldn't have either one of them. *Sorry, heifer!*

They walked quietly down the sidewalk toward the hotel. Donnie held her hand tightly. He wanted to make every moment count with his wife.

They reached the hotel in record time for Crystal. As they walked through the lobby, Crystal saw Stephen sitting at the bar alone. He didn't see her, but appeared to be nursing a green-colored drink. Stephen, like Crystal didn't drink any alcohol other than a white or red wine with a special dinner. Dolefully, she hoped he wasn't going to drown his sorrows in liquor.

They walked toward the elevator and went to Crystal's room. She went into the restroom and Donnie turned on the television. He still wondered why his wife was so distant, but decided that he would not push the issue. Instead, he purposed to try to be there for her when she got back home. He prayed that this would be the beginning of a new chapter for them despite the other issues he struggled with.

When she came out of the restroom, she found Donnie surfing the cable guide. "Hey Baby, Coach Carter is on. Wanna watch it?" He seemed excited about it.

"Sure," said Crystal as she sat on the bed. Her husband pulled her close to him so that she could lean back. Less than twenty-four hours ago, she had done the very same thing with his brother.

Chapter 18

A Day Late and...

Samuel L. Jackson was a good actor, but he was not good enough to bridge the gap between Donnie and Crystal. They watched the movie without saying much to each other. Although she would have loved to be the wife he expected her to be, she couldn't. She knew that it would be impossible to continue an affair with Stephen, yet she didn't want it to be over with him either. Furthermore, the passion she had experienced with him over the last twenty-four hours was what she had longed for with her husband all year. The effect of it all was exhilarating, and left her feeling more alive inside and out. She knew it was lust--and it was wrong, but found the toxic passion overwhelming.

She already dreaded the ride back to North Carolina. They were going to try to act as if they weren't more than friends. Suppressing the thought for now, Crystal knew that she would have to come to the realization that she had committed adultery. The fact that she kept something like this from her husband was killing her inside. The migraine crept back. Her head began to spin just like it did earlier in the day when she was lying on the park bench at the Battery. She moaned out in pain.

"What is it?" asked Donnie.

"I'm getting a migraine." Donnie knew that she got migraines when she was under extreme pressure. He recalled dozens of similar situations that caused migraines—studying for her certification exams, dealing with some of her family members, and arguing with each other. Instead of grilling her about the cause of the migraine, he decided to massage her temples, shoulders and neck. He lifted her hair to kiss her neck. She pulled away quickly.

"Donnie, didn't I just tell you I was getting a migraine?"

"I'm sorry, I wasn't trying…" Donnie took a deep breath and went back to massaging her neck. After he finished, he moved from the bed to allow his wife to lie down. He knew the routine from past experience: dim the lights, make everything quiet, and let her rest. Since they had finished watching the movie, she stretched out her legs and covered herself with the comforter. He moved to lie beside her. She was glad that she requested to have fresh linens delivered when she left for breakfast. Donnie let her rest and lay beside his wife. He watched her as she fell asleep, and desperately wanted to know what was going on with her, with them.

It's all my fault. Thoughts flowed wildly through his mind. Lately, they'd been so distant, which left him with no idea of what she thought, felt, or had going on in her own life. He had not asked her what was going on in her world in a very long time. As far as he could recollect, she'd been complaining a lot recently about missing him, and wanting to spend more time together. Misguidedly, he had grown to resent it instead of being as one as they vowed on their wedding day. Now, they were definitely two separate individuals with two separate agendas. Donnie soon fell asleep. Not only did he have a restless night, but so did Crystal.

Settled in his room down the hall, Stephen was restless as well. He couldn't believe he'd done something so stupid and outside of God's will. He had always prided himself on his values, and tried to live according to God's plan for his life. On many occasions at work, he had hung up the phone after talking to Crystal and made a beeline to the men's room to pray. He had to ask God for forgiveness for what he was feeling. She was so easy to talk to, and he loved it when she called the office. They even chatted on instant messenger at times. Sometimes, while he was traveling, she'd send text messages to his phone to see how the trip was going. He looked forward to those messages because it made him feel like someone cared.

What got into me to make me take a big helping of my brother's wife? How could I? I'm a weak brother. I hate my flesh, what's wrong with me? Thou shalt not commit adultery… This is not what I want for my life. He knew nothing good could ever come of this; nevertheless, he still felt drawn to Crystal. The chemistry between the two of them was unexplainable. Although he didn't quite remember why he married Pam, he knew why Donnie married Crystal. She was beautiful, intelligent, loving, and fun to be with. She defined the word lady. She was graceful in everything she did. She cared about everyone and had a heart the size of a Super Wal-Mart. He knew her kindness sometimes aggravated his brother. Donnie thought people took advantage of Crystal because she was so kindhearted. Stephen loved this about her.

Donnie woke up before dawn. Once again, he admired his wife's beauty. He hadn't wanted to make love to her in months, but the urge was all over him at the moment. He wouldn't dare try anything with her now; but, he wondered where his attraction had been for her over the last year. Silently, he prayed that the tension he felt was something that would blow over. He knew without a doubt that he needed to spend more time with her and he had to dedicate much more time to their marriage than he had recently. He didn't dare proposition her for intimacy now; truthfully though, the atmosphere didn't seem quite right. Mentally, he tossed around ideas about how to make things better, and he was sure he knew what to do. Ironically, something bothered him about last night. For the first time ever, he noticed indifference in his wife's eyes. Usually whenever he looked at her, he would see love coming through her big hazel eyes. But now, when she looked at him, it was as though she was looking through him.

Chapter 19

Wednesday

The phone ringer was set to high. Once again, Crystal was startled awake. *What the devil is...?*

"Hello," she said groggily.

"This is your 8:00 a.m. wake up call, ma'am," said the front desk clerk. *Why was he sounding so chipper this morning and why was he calling?*

"Thank you," she said and hung up the phone. Donnie moved under the sheets beside her. She turned over to see who was in bed with her. As she rolled over, she saw her husband waking up. He glanced at his watch.

"I had a wake up call scheduled because I thought we would have breakfast before I left."

"What time are you leaving?" she asked.

"I don't know. I need to make sure that I give myself enough time to make it back, and you know how awful traffic gets in Columbia at times."

"Ok, I'll go jump in the shower" she said getting out of bed and slowly walking across the room.

"Mind if I join you?" Donnie asked.

"Sure," she said reluctantly while rolling her eyes when he couldn't see them. He wasn't too sure if she meant it or not. However, he deliberately took it as a first step. He sat meditatively and waited until she handled her morning business, and then to hear water running in the bathtub. Once he heard the shower curtain hooks slide over the rod, he got up and went into the bathroom, handled his own business, and then slipped in the shower behind her. She turned around and looked at him with tears in her eyes.

"What's wrong, Baby?" he asked.

She didn't answer him, but turned back around. He put his arms around her and said, "I know I have a lot of catching up to do, and I'm going to make sure that I start spending more time with you. I need to make some changes at work and to my schedule, but I promise that I'll be the husband you used to know."

Too late. I don't even know if I want to know you anymore.

She turned back around and looked at her husband. "I love you, Crystie," he said as he put his arms around her waist. He held her so tight, she felt like she was going to throw up. She couldn't bring herself to say she loved him because she doubted her true feelings for him. If she truly loved him, why did she do what she did?

Crystie? "Uh, Donnie" she gasped.

"Oh, I'm sorry, Baby. I just want to hold you and let you know how much I do love you." Throbbing pains began to fill her head again. She put her fingers on her temples and began rubbing in circular motions.

"Is your head still bothering you?" he asked.

"Yes. It's throbbing right now," she said.

Once again Donnie wondered what was causing the sudden onset of pain. He moved her fingers and put his hands on her shoulders to direct her to turn back around toward the showerhead. He massaged her temples once more and kissed the back of her neck. He knew she always liked that. She didn't respond like she used to. His hands moved from her temples to her shoulders where he continued to massage. Crystal had to admit, it was very relaxing, and she enjoyed it. However, she didn't want it to lead to anything else. She moved closer to the water and broke the massage. She began bathing herself as her head pounded harder and harder. It felt as though something was inside of her skull trying to get out. Donnie reached for a washcloth and began bathing as well. He figured this was not the time. Maybe, once they were back home, things would get better. They both bathed quickly, and then got out of the tub. They brushed their teeth, applied lotions and moisturizers, and dressed in silence. At last, they headed downstairs to the hotel restaurant.

Once inside the restaurant, they seated themselves. Once again, a large-framed waitress with an island accent came to see if they would like some fresh brewed coffee. After giving their drink orders, they both walked over to the buffet line. Several people were waiting in line, and a number of couples with small children were trying to put food on more than one plate. As Crystal waited, she looked around the dining area. Across the room and sitting at a table near the window was Stephen. He had seen her before she saw him. Their eyes locked on each other briefly. Donnie spotted him too. He and Stephen spoke the unspoken greeting of brothers all across the continent—the upward nod. Donnie looked at his watch. It was 8:49 a.m.

"Must be time for the first session to begin," he said.

"Yeah, I guess Stephen will be gone all day," she said. Just then, Miss Rump Shaker walked across the dining room and made a beeline to Stephen's table. She sat across from him and took a sip from a coffee cup that was at the place setting across from him. As Crystal surveyed the table, she realized she and Stephen had breakfast together. There were two of everything, two plates, two mugs, two juice glasses, and bread plates. Suddenly, Crystal felt as if ten devils had jumped on her. She was furious at Stephen for being with that heifer. Her imagination went wild, and she asked herself a lot of questions. *Did he get with her last night? Was this a chance meeting? Was he scheming from the very beginning with me? Did Miss Shaker just invite herself to have breakfast with him, or was this the end of their evening together?* Crystal couldn't help feeling like she had been played by a "playa."

The line moved slowly as Crystal and Donnie reached the plates and silverware.

"Do you know who the woman is with Stephen?" asked Donnie.

"No, but she looks like someone out of a rap video, doesn't she?" Crystal commented.

"Dang Baby! Retract the claws! Retract the claws! Your whiskers are showing too. Aren't we catty this morning?" he joked.

"I'm sorry, but that woman has been eyeing Stephen since we got here. She all but put it in his face the night of the ball, and she didn't know if I were his wife or not. Stephen actually used me to get her to leave him alone. Some women have all the nerve," she went on without taking a breath.

Donnie wondered why she was being so protective about him, but didn't comment. She still fumed inside.

They quietly finished their breakfast, and then went back to her room.

"Donnie, this seems so rushed. Why did you come only to be here less than twenty-four hours?"

Donnie didn't know himself why he'd made the almost three-hour trip. He just felt like he needed to be there. Little did he know it was already too late. His marriage had changed, and he didn't even know it.

"Truthfully, I felt like you needed me. I can't really explain it, but something within told me that I needed to be here. Maybe, it was God, because He really does know my heart." *Mmm hmmm, He even knows the stuff in my heart that shouldn't be there.* "He knows how much I love you, and I need you in my life. You have always been the one stable thing in my life I could depend on. I don't know, Baby," he said moving closer to her as they stood in front of the mirror. "I just wanted to see you and hold you in my arms. I told you that I'd be out of town when you got back, so I guess I just missed you. When I'm traveling, it's different. I miss you, but I keep busy doing whatever it is I do. But when you're gone, well, I guess I know how you feel now."

Donnie seemed so sincere and Crystal felt terrible.

"Yep, that shoe is a little tight when it's on the other foot, huh?"

"Yep, sure is."

Donnie wanted his wife to tell him how much she loved him and that things were going to be ok, but she didn't. He wanted her to pull him to the bed and make love like they used to, but she didn't do that either. Fear suddenly consumed his body, and he felt insecure about his marriage for the first time ever.

"Do you still love me?" he asked.

"Why do you ask me that?" she responded.

"Don't answer a question with a question, do you still love me? I need to know," he said rather sternly.

"Yes. We just have a lot to work out that is impossible to accomplish on an overnighter, that's all."

"Fair enough. Let's go for a walk. As long as I'm on the road in about two hours, I should be ok." He wanted to walk in the opposite direction of where they were last night. They wandered past exquisite jewelry stores, catalog clothing boutiques, and several novelty stores. Donnie pulled Crystal into a store that sold Charleston memorabilia. Inside, there were several pieces of fine china with Charleston scenes hand painted on them, gold charms made into palm trees, dolphins, sand dollars, and hundreds of others to choose from. They browsed through all of the glass top counters, and Donnie made his way to the back of the store to look at t-shirts. They were the typical souvenir shirts. Crystal stayed near the front of the store looking at a crystal pineapple with the word "Charleston" engraved on it. Donnie noticed she wasn't with him and walked back to the counter to see what she found so amazing.

"Look at this," she said. "It is beautiful. You know the pineapple is a symbol for hospitality."

"Really?" Donnie asked realizing this was the Crystal he knew and loved; the caring one, not the indifferent one.

"Do you want it?" he asked.

"No, I was just looking at it, that's all."

"Are you sure?" he asked.

"Yes," she said walking toward the door.

"Ok then, don't say I didn't ask."

"Yes, Dear," she said condescendingly.

He smiled because that was an inside joke between the two of them. Marvin who worked for the agency said "Yes, Dear" to his wife at the Christmas party last year, and everyone had been making fun of him since. He was truly a hen-pecked husband, but a very talented artist.

They meandered for about thirty more minutes, and then walked back to the hotel.

"Go on up and get your bag," she said handing him the access card. "I'll wait here for you. Give me your car keys."

Donnie went to the room, checked the bathroom and floor for any items he may have missed. Then, he headed back to the elevator. When the elevator doors opened, Stephen was about to step off, but paused.

"Are you getting off, or are you just riding?" said Donnie.

"Ha-ha, very funny. Actually, I was surprised to see you. I figured you were gone already. Aren't you cutting it close?"

"Yeah, Crystal and I spent the morning together window-shopping. I lost track of time. I'm about to leave right now, and I'll probably break a few laws," he said.

"A-ight man, let me know how it goes. And you fly out tomorrow, right?"

"Yep, if all goes well, I'll fly to the corporate office to meet with one of their marketing people."

"Ok, well, drive safely. We need you in one piece and not in jail so we can get this contract," Stephen said smiling.

"Yeah, whatever," Donnie said sarcastically. Stephen held out his fist to dap Donnie up.

"You drive safely too...coming back with my precious cargo. I thought it was a good idea sending her here to relax and pamper herself, but I feel like she's been using the time away from me to re-evaluate our relationship. She seems distant, Man. Pray for us."

Having said that, Donnie entered the elevator, and Stephen stepped out and removed his hand from the door where it had rested during their conversation. The doors closed immediately.

Stephen walked to his room but barely remembered getting there. His legs moved him there, but he felt numb. The severity of his actions hit him like a ton of bricks. He had been dealing with the betrayal issue all morning and the adultery. Regrettably, it wasn't until his younger brother asked him to pray for him and his wife that he realized he was the cause of the problem. Hundreds of questions began racing through his mind all at once. *How am I going to work with my brother from now on? How am I going to act toward Pam? How will I avoid being with Crystal in social settings?* He had confessed his love to his brother's wife and taken her to bed. Stephen wondered if God would forgive him for willfully sinning like this. He wondered if he was who he thought he was in Christ. He had come upstairs to get his Palm Pilot, but now he wanted to get in bed and not come out of the room for a long time.

Donnie arrived back in the lobby to find no traces of his wife. He looked around the restaurant area and the gift shop with no luck. He walked outside and saw her sitting inside his car. She had started the ignition and the A/C was doing its job on full blast.

"You're all set," she said smiling and getting out of the driver's seat.

"It's almost as if you're happy to see me go," said Donnie. "You never did tell me, what's wrong with you?'

"Donnie, don't…" she said.

"Whatever, I need to get out of here anyway. I saw Stephen upstairs, and he's sweating me about getting back on time to meet with these guys," he said to her as he put his bag on the passenger seat and slid behind the steering wheel. He reached for Crystal, signaling for her to bend down to the window, and then he kissed her on the cheek. Crystal said goodbye and walked back into the building. Donnie drove off in a huff. He was a little aggravated that the plan to seduce his wife didn't go as expected. The other thing he didn't appreciate was his brother acting as if he were his dad. He sped through the parking lot, out onto the main street, and abruptly made a quick left turn in front of a trolley car full of vacationers.

Chapter 20

Regrets of a Married Man

Crystal went straight to her room and flopped across the bed. She lay there with the banging of the internal bass drum still in her head. She wanted to rewind the clock so she could relive the moment when she realized that the conversation with Stephen was going in the wrong direction. She berated herself, wishing that she had had the guts to say something with enough conviction to make him want to stop. If that hadn't worked, she wished that God would have somehow intervened and forced them to consider the risks before all of the other things happened. Now, she knew the meaning of free will and she knew that God was very displeased with her at this moment. Moreover, she was not happy with herself. Unexpectedly, her husband had just done what she had been longing for him to do. He showed that he could still be spontaneous and that he would make her the center of his life again. *He did exactly what I wanted him to, and how did I show my appreciation? I acted as if I couldn't have cared less.* Crystal wondered if she were about to lose her mind.

Donnie made it back to the office in record time. He even passed a highway patrol officer in Columbia and just knew he'd triggered the radar. He had expected to be stopped, but the officer didn't move. Believing that God had his back, Donnie slowed down and carefully obeyed the posted speed limit the rest of the way back to Charlotte.

He walked into the office without speaking to anyone. He was in a daze; and had no idea when he would be out of it. *Something wasn't right with her, I know it.* It troubled him deep within. He couldn't figure it out. To divert his attention, he decided to concentrate on the task at hand and shifted focus. He began to pull his thoughts together for the presentation scheduled to take place very soon. He sat in his leather office chair and rested his head on the back. Then, he reclined and put his feet on top of his desk. As he did this, Amanda waltzed into his office. Amanda was a loyal employee who had worked as his administrative assistant for the last four years. She was his first Caucasian assistant and fit in well with the rest of the diverse staff. She was always cheery. Usually, Donnie liked this about her, but there were days that he didn't want her brand of sunshine in his office.

"Hi, boss," she said almost as if asking a question.

"Hey, Amanda," Donnie said matter-of-factly.

"Here are fresh copies of the proposal for Golden Corral. Also, FYI, Craig McCarter has already called twice today. He seemed to be a little upset that you were out of town."

"Well, he'll see me soon enough," he said without looking at her. Amanda turned around and walked out of the office. She knew something was going on that Donnie didn't want to share. She'd worked for him long enough to know when to leave. As far as she was concerned, she and Donnie were closer than she was with Stephen. Although she admired and respected them both, she felt that it was Donnie who really took time to get to know her on a personal level.

The hour scheduled for his appointment with Craig, finally arrived. The presentation was successful, and Craig was pleased. Solemnly, Donnie asked Amanda to confirm his travel reservations for the next day, and the meeting with Craig's marketing department. He would have given anything to be back in Charleston with his wife, instead of flying off to Chicago the next day. *All Crystal wanted was to be the center of my life, next to God. My greatest ambition was to be successful and prove to everyone else that I am the man...at all costs.* He wondered if it had cost him that which was most precious to him. He certainly didn't want to be in a loveless marriage like his brother. *It baffles me. How could I have worked so long and hard for all this time? To make matters worse, how could I entertain the thoughts and feelings I've been having for another woman all this time?*

Now, he wished that he had listened to his brother's advice about working such long hours and not spending enough time at home. He recalled the last time Stephen spoke to him about what he was doing. He had said, "Bro, if you don't take care of home, home will take care of itself. If I were you, man, I'd be out of here no later than 5:30 everyday." *Was he trying to warn me?*

"Hey boss, here's your flight, hotel, and rental car confirmation," said Amanda, bringing Donnie out of his thoughts.

"Thanks, A," said Donnie. "I'm sorry for being so short earlier. I was stressing over this meeting."

"No problem. I know you, remember?" she said cheerfully with a raised eyebrow.

"Is there anything else I can do before I leave? I need to leave a few minutes early to pick up my dog from the groomer."

"No. Thanks for everything. I guess I'll see you Monday morning."

"Ok," she said. "Travel safely."

"Thanks. Have a good one."

He watched Amanda walk out of the office and reclined once again in his chair. He shifted his attention back to thoughts about his marriage.

Chapter 21

Confession is Good for the Soul

It was late afternoon when Crystal picked up the phone to call Melissa.

"Hello?" answered Melissa.

"Hey girl."

"Well, well, well. Where the heck have you been? I thought we were going to hang out and have some fun just like old times. It's Wednesday. Weren't you supposed to get here Monday?"

"Hey, hold on. I came here to relax, remember? That's what I've been doing. When can we get together?"

"How about dinner at 5:00?"

"Yeah, can you come here?"

"Sure, what's your room number?" Crystal gave her the room number, and they hung up. She went into the bathroom and touched up her hair and makeup.

Crystal could hear her cell phone announcing an incoming call and ran to find her purse. She saw Stephen's name on the display. Inwardly, she debated about answering, but pressed TALK anyway.

"Hello?" she said.

"We need to talk."

"I know, but not now."

"Crystal, this can't wait. I'm coming to your room, now."

"No, Melissa is on her way here, and we're going out for dinner. She'll be here soon."

"Well, I'll leave when she gets there," he said and hung up.

Crystal couldn't believe that he had hung up on her. *I'm bout tired of these Moore men hanging up in my face. Must be genetic.*

She was not prepared to see him and was very uncomfortable having him in her room again. She was so torn up by the mess she found herself in. Before she could get over what he'd just done, he was there knocking at her door as if his life depended on it.

"Crystal! Crystal!" he yelled banging on the door.

She hurried to the door and yanked it open. "What the heck is wrong with you?" she asked looking at him as if he were crazy.

"I need to talk to you now," he said barging into the room. He didn't pause, but immediately launched into his well thought-out speech. "I want you to hear me out. Please, just listen, will you?"

She nodded reluctantly waiting for him to continue, but still wondering what was wrong with him. *Why is now so important?*

"We messed up. I mean we really messed up."

"You're just coming to that realization?" she interjected.

"You said you'd hear me out," he said. "My brother is no idiot, he asked me to pray for ya'll. Do you know what that did to me? Huh? Do you?" He paced back and forth as if he were going to walk a hole in the floor and fall right through—just like in the cartoons. "Don't answer that. I'm sorry; I don't mean to sound like I blame you for anything." He continued, barely taking a breath. "It's just that ever since I walked in here and saw the two of you together last night, I've been crazy. It's been eating me alive. Then, this morning I saw you in the restaurant. It really got to me. I know you are my brother's wife, and this situation is all my fault." *Thou shall not covet thy brother's wife, goat...* "I should keep my mouth shut, but I need to tell you what I've been beating myself up about all night and today." He stopped pacing and then leaned against the dresser. "When I left here last night, I ached deep down. I kicked myself for putting both of us in this situation and for opening my big mouth. I was so jealous and

125

couldn't figure out why. I've seen you with him hundreds of times over the years, but for some reason last night, I felt like a jealous lover. That's not right. What kind of man am I? Do you hate me?"

Still deciding whether or not he'd lost his mind, Crystal stared at Stephen. She thought long and hard before she spoke. He wondered if she'd ever respond to his ranting and raving. Finally, she spoke.

"Stephen, I know we need to talk, but I can't, I just don't want to do this right now. I told you that Melissa is on her way here, and we're going out tonight. I'm stressed out about this just as much as you are. Funny thing though, you didn't seem too upset this morning with Miss Thing, Miss Rump Shaker, or whatever her name is at your table. You appeared fine to me. No, I don't hate you. I hate this situation, and I hate my actions. I'm wondering what will become of us; how this will all play out. On one hand, Donnie is clueless as to what my needs are. However, on the other, he is very discerning at times. I'm sure that he senses something is up with me, Stephen. Did you use me?"

"How can you ask me that? I poured out my heart to you; I can't believe you would ask me something like that. Where did that come from?"

"Was your breakfast date beginning or ending this morning?"

"Crystal, I'm not even going to answer that question because you are being unreasonable for someone who spent the night with her husband."

"Don't you know how ridiculous that sounds? Why won't you answer? And you know that I was just as surprised by Donnie's visit as you were. Did you expect me to tell him to leave?" She rolled her eyes at Stephen.

"I don't know anything anymore." He put his hands over his face and spoke through his fingers." I don't even know myself as well as I thought I did."

Before either of them could say anything else, Melissa knocked at the door. The tension lingered in the room and it was thick enough to gag on. With her heart beating a mile a minute, Crystal walked to the door to find a smiling Melissa, dressed in a short sleeve sky blue pantsuit.

"What's up?" she yelled like Martin Lawrence.

"Hey girl, come on in," said Crystal somberly. Melissa stepped inside the room and as she was about to speak, saw Stephen leaning against the dresser. Their eyes locked as they both looked at each other as if they wondered what the other was doing there at that moment.

"Hey, Melissa. Long time no see, girl!" said Stephen as he walked toward the door to embrace her.

"I know, big brother. You are still looking good. What's up with you? We're going out for dinner, you want to come?" she asked looking at Stephen and Crystal.

"No, you go with your girl here, she needs to get out," he said. He looked at Crystal and said, "I'll talk to you later." He walked toward the door, and Crystal told him she'd call him when she got back. Stephen left.

"Girl, he gets finer with age, doesn't he?" admired Melissa still looking at the door Stephen had just exited. Crystal just smiled and raised an eyebrow.

"Yep."

"What was that look for? You got a piece of the Moore pie."

"Nothing. My brother-in-law is a trip, that's all. Where are we going?"

"Well, when you told me you'd be in town without Donnie, I figured we'd go to one of my favorite places, California Dreaming."

"Uh, Stephen and I went there for lunch yesterday. It's a nice place. I can go again if you really want to go."

"Well, since you've taken the wind out of my sail, it's your choice. Even though I already had my mouth ready for some of those fresh baked croissants with honey butter. Don't tell me you had some of those too?"

"Yes, they were delicious. I'm sorry, but how was I supposed to know you were taking me there?" said Crystal, visibly irritated.

"Hold on, sister! What's with the attitude? And secondly, what did I walk into up in here?" Melissa had her hands on her hips.

"Stephen and I were in the middle of something. He…" Crystal stopped before she said too much. Truthfully, she wanted to talk to someone other than Stephen about the predicament she was in, but she was afraid that Melissa would judge her. Even across the miles, they could read each other's moods, but right now she felt less holy than she ever had in her life. The thought of verbalizing the fact that she had committed adultery with her brother-in-law made her feel sick inside.

"What's going on between you two?" Melissa sat down on the bed as if she expected Crystal to give her a long and detailed explanation. She crossed her legs. "Don't think I didn't notice the tension in here when I arrived."

"Melissa, I'm going to tell you something, and I want you to promise you won't judge me, OK?"

"Girl, I'm not God. How can I judge you?"

"You know what I mean. I'm sorry I messed up dinner plans for you."

"No problem, I love that place and always eat way too many croissants anyway," said Melissa putting her hands on her healthy hips. "How about seafood? Hyman's Seafood is within walking distance of here, and they have a great atmosphere. They have an award-winning menu, featuring a shrimp Po Boy and a crab cake sandwich to die for."

"Sounds good."

The women left the hotel and walked down the sidewalk in search of Hyman's. Melissa couldn't wait to find out what was going on.

"Ok, don't keep me in suspense, what's going on with you and Stephen? Is he finally going to leave that crazy wife of his?"

Crystal was silent and kept her gaze towards the ground. She couldn't go on. "Melissa…"

"Girlfriend, you are leaving my mind to wonder crazy thoughts. What is going on?"

"We, we…Melissa… he… I mean we…"

"Say it Crystal, WHAT? You what?" Melissa stopped right in the middle of the sidewalk demanding Crystal to finish her sentence.

"We've done something terrible, and if Donnie finds out, he'll kill both of us."

"You didn't sleep with him, did you?"

Crystal's facial expression answered Melissa's question first. "Yes."

"WHAT?" Melissa's eyes became as big as quarters. Her chin dropped, and she could hardly believe what had just come out of Crystal's mouth.

"I did, Melissa. Let's walk, I'll tell you everything. Keeping this inside is literally making me sick."

They began walking again.

"How long has this been going on, Crystal?"

"It's nothing that has been ongoing, it just happened. I know that sounds like a cliché, but it did. It just happened. I didn't plan to come here, spend some romantic week with my husband's brother, and then go back home like nothing had happened."

They turned onto Meeting Street; both were silent. When they were within a block of the restaurant, the aroma of the sea's finest met their nostrils. Melissa walked inside while Crystal waited outside. Since Melissa told the hostess they'd take first available seating, they were seated right away.

"Crystal, come on, they can seat us now."

Crystal turned to walk inside the building. "That was fast. Did you tell them you needed to hear some juicy gossip and to seat us this very minute, or you'd leave?" she leaned in and whispered to Melissa as the hostess took them to their table.

"That's not funny," Melissa said not at all amused at Crystal's attempt at humor. The server immediately came over to introduce herself, and gave them a heaping bowl of boiled peanuts. She took their drink orders and quickly excused herself.

Sensing that Melissa was impatiently waiting for her to finish her story, Crystal continued. "We have always been real close, you know that. Monday after we arrived, he wanted me to go to the opening mixer thing with him, so I did. I didn't really want to go, but he begged me to hang out with him, so I went. We had a good time dancing. Afterwards, he told me how he felt about me, and how he'd been in love with me for years. At first, I responded as I should have. I told him that we shouldn't even be having the conversation because it was inappropriate. Unfortunately, it didn't stop there. Later, when he showed up at my room, one thing led to another, and we…we ended up in bed."

"So, why were you arguing when I arrived?"

"We weren't arguing, he was upset because Donnie showed up unannounced last night. Stephen insisted on telling me about how jealous he'd felt. The whole thing is really stupid."

"I'll say. So what's with Donnie? Does he know?"

"No, he doesn't, but I don't think I can keep this from him. I'm sure it'll mean the end of our marriage, and I don't even want to think of what it'll do to his relationship with his brother."

"Hold on, so you have this all figured out, huh?"

"No, I don't. I just want it to be over."

"Who do you love, Crystal?" Melissa asked with a very concerned look on her face.

"Honestly, things have happened too fast; I don't know anything anymore. Of course, I love my husband, but I love how Stephen makes me feel inside. I wish that I had that with Donnie." She paused. Verbalizing everything made her feel as if she were one hundred pounds lighter. "I mean, Stephen and I can talk for hours about nothing and everything. He's like the male version of you."

"I know you two have always been close, but I never imagined this."

"Donnie and I have been growing apart for a long time now, and he doesn't know the first thing about taking care of me. I can't even tell you the last time we made love."

"So, in reality things haven't gotten better or worst since the last time we talked? Is he still coming home late? Do you think he has someone else?"

"Yes, and her name is W-O-R-K. Honestly, I don't know what to think."

"Well, why did he come here to see you?"

"He said he was trying to be spontaneous. Honestly, I think he had second thoughts about sending me here with Stephen."

"Did you give him any reason prior to this point in time to not trust you?"

Crystal was very hurt by the question. However, she knew that Melissa asked because she wanted to remain objective in the midst of everything. That was the reason Crystal knew she could confide in her in the first place.

"No, I've never given Donnie a reason not to trust me. When he came, it was a total shock to me. So much so that we didn't even get intimate. I couldn't, knowing I had just been with his brother the night before. He left a little upset with me. We've been on opposite sides of the table a lot lately.

"Crystal, being on opposite sides of the table and going outside of your marriage are two totally different things. Stephen is married too, remember?" She put a handful of shelled peanuts in her mouth. "Boy, this is a mess," she said while chewing.

"Thanks a lot."

"I'm just thinking out loud while I to try to make sense of all of this. See, if you had just come straight to my house when you got here, none of this would have happened." Melissa smiled.

"I don't see anything to smile about. In a matter of days I've made a mess of my life, and my family's life. Do you realize how scandalous this is—could potentially be?"

"Yes, I do. That's precisely why you need to leave, now. You can't stay here any longer. Girl, don't you know you're vulnerable? And you certainly don't need to be here with Stephen so close by. You are in a hotel--remember? Don't you know how many scandalous things happen in hotels? You're just asking for trouble if you stay. You need to be with your husband."

"What am I supposed to do? Donnie will be suspicious if I go home now."

"I've let you talk; now listen very carefully to what you know I'm going to say. You already know you've done wrong. If you haven't confessed this to God, then you need to. God forgives us from ALL sins. Girlfriend, you know that, but first, you must be honest with God and repent. I mean truly repent. Seek God for direction; He is so faithful. Trust that He will direct you, and tell you what you should do next. You ask him to help you with everything, each and every phase of this. Ask Him to protect you, your mind, and your family. Ask Him to protect your mind because I'm sure this is killing you inside. The enemy will bombard you to make you think that you are beyond forgiveness and that God is done with you. Don't listen to him. God hates the sin, not you. Do you still want your marriage, or is this something you'd pursue if your marriage ended? Girl, you also have to consider all of the lives involved in this. It's not just about you and Donnie, but also Stephen's family. Pam depends on him. What about Donnie and Stephen's extended family? This will make holiday gatherings difficult, you know?"

"I know. I haven't asked God to forgive me yet. I've felt too ashamed to go to Him with this, even though I know better than to shy away from God. I feel so unworthy of his love and forgiveness right now."

"Girlfriend, listen to me! Do you understand the words coming out of my mouth? Didn't I just tell you about that? It is the enemy of our souls who wants you to think that way. We're all unworthy of God's love, but His grace is sufficient for us all. He loves us no matter what we do or have done. Do you think that you are the first woman to cheat on her husband? Girl, please! Let me tell you my little secret: I've been involved with a married man before. I have been in the same place you are in right now. The only difference is that I wasn't married. The fact is, I knew he was married. That in itself should have been enough to stop me, but it didn't." Melissa stopped talking and looked Crystal in the eye. "Get that dumbfounded look off your face. Yes, Charles was married. The wonderful Charles whom I dated for all those months was…" She corrected herself, "is married. I didn't know it at first, but even after he told me, it didn't matter. I still couldn't or wouldn't stop seeing him because I was in too deep. Earlier this year when I saw you at Starbucks, I was a mess. I wanted to reach out to you, but I was so afraid. I knew it was wrong and I know what Aunt Lila taught us. I didn't want you to judge ME! Isn't this ironic? I was so down when I was in Charlotte, I really wanted to take my life at one point."

"Oh Missy! I'm so sorry. I sensed that something weighed heavily on your mind. Why didn't you tell me? How did you break it off with him?" asked Crystal while feeling as if she might burst into tears at Melissa's confession.

"I got through it the hard way. His wife showed up at my front door with a gun and told me to leave her 'bleeping' husband alone or I'd find myself one dead 'bleep'! That, my friend, was all the wake up call I needed."

As soon as she finished speaking, their server arrived and set their drinks on the table. She prepared to take their requests for entrees. Crystal ordered the crab cake sandwich with fries, and Melissa ordered broiled sea scallops with smashed potatoes and a side salad with house dressing. After ordering, they sat quietly. Melissa reminisced about Charles, and Crystal contemplated her future.

"I really wish that I could turn back the hands of time. I've been getting migraines for the last two days. Everyone who knows me knows that I get a migraine when I'm seriously stressed and I don't want to send up any more red flags with Donnie. I really don't have a choice. I have to pull this together quickly. Do you think I'm kidding myself, Melissa?"

"Crystal, I just want you to be happy, and to be all right. You have a man at home who loves you. Personally, I think you need to be open and honest with him, whatever that means. On the other hand, God knows him better than you do, and He'll guide you as to whether you should tell him or not. I don't know what you should do, but God does. You may be underestimating Donnie. He may forgive both of you."

"I don't know. He's been acting really weird all year. Most of the time he's acted as if he couldn't have cared less what I did or who I've done it with; then he shows up here and acts like the man I married—the one I've been used to for most of our married life together. Mom said maybe he has his sights on someone else. But what about this little surprise visit? I don't know what to do… Thanks for listening."

"You are more than welcome, and you do know what to do!" she winked her eye at Crystal as she sipped on her drink. "I want you to do me a favor though. Look deep within your heart, and find out what it is you need to be happy. Whatever that is, I will be here regardless. You've got to find happiness inside. I've watched from a distance as you've been up and down over the years. You hold a lot of your emotions inside. Truthfully, the only way for you to be truly happy with whomever you're with, is you've got to be happy with yourself first. I love you girl, in spite of your sins! That's from one sinner to another," she said winking again.

Crystal got up from the table and hugged her cousin, sister. People stopped eating to watch as they embraced. She cried a deep sobbing cry on Melissa's shoulder. Melissa let her have her moment, and didn't mind the stares from people at the other tables.

"I'll be back," said Crystal as she headed off towards the restroom.

Crystal and Melissa ate their meal without mentioning Stephen, Donnie, or Charles. After they finished, they walked to the parking lot of Crystal's hotel. There they got into Melissa's car, and she drove them to the mall. They shopped until the mall closed. Melissa then drove Crystal back to the hotel, and they sat in the parking lot and talked. Melissa took a deep breath and looked at Crystal.

"I love you, no matter what. You know that, right?" asked Melissa. The exhilaration of shopping allowed Crystal to temporarily put her situation on the back burner.

"Yes, girl. I know. I messed up and I need to go to my room, spend some time with God and seek his direction. I don't know what else to do to fix this mess." She looked down at her hands as she nervously clicked her acrylic nails together.

"Not to sound cliché, but our help does cometh from the Lord," Melissa said smiling.

"I know girl, you are right. I do need to go back home without delay. Donnie leaves for Chicago in the morning and won't be home until Sunday. This will give me a few days before I have to see him again. I truly wished that I had followed my intuition and stayed at home. I declined the offer when he first suggested it anyway. It wasn't until after Stephen called to persuade me to go, that I actually changed my mind. I wonder if Donnie set all this up to test me."

"Crystal, I'm not giving any more advice; it's not my place. I'll pray for you and your family. I'll be in touch. Let me know what is going on, OK? Are you going to be ok?"

"I have no other choice, but to be ok. I love you girl, you are truly my sister." She reached over and squeezed Melissa's hand.

"I love you too. Bye, call me in the morning."

Crystal got out of the car and walked inside the building. When she reached her room, she saw a cream-colored piece of paper sticking out from under her door. As she opened the door, she noticed her name, written in Stephen's handwriting, on the outside of the folded paper. She took a deep sigh, and felt all of the positive energy she'd received from Melissa immediately escape her body like steam rising from a boiling teapot. She picked up the paper, which read: *I'm assuming you don't want to talk to me since you continue to avoid my calls. We need to finish our conversation. I don't want to hurt you. Five minutes of your time is all I ask. Regards, Stephen.*

Crystal crumpled the paper and threw it in the trash. She had no intention of calling him tonight. Instead, she intended to do exactly what she said, pray. She hoped that God would be merciful towards her, especially now that she needed His help to rectify this situation in which she'd gotten herself. True, she hadn't consulted Him before creating the situation, and she felt so unworthy. She undressed and put on her black silk pajama bottoms and a cotton gray camisole. Once again she lit a scented candle and turned on the light on the table next to the bed. She pulled out her Bible and began perusing the Psalms of David. She knew that there would be something there for her to meditate on since David was so real. He had struggled with the very same issues facing her. Crystal prayed and pleaded with God to forgive her sins. Although she knew in her heart that God had forgiven her as He said He would, she feared what would happen in her life as a result of her sin. Even David suffered greatly as a consequence of his sins.

Chapter 22

Thursday: Far Away From Here

      The next morning, Crystal awakened determined to do the right thing, leaving Stephen and the hotel. She decided that she did not want to talk to him, at least not yet. Nonetheless, she knew she could not avoid him forever. She pulled out her laptop computer to see if there was a flight leaving Charleston that day for Charlotte or Greensboro. She wanted to get away and fast. Unfortunately, since there was not enough time to arrange advanced booking, the cost to fly back was astronomical. Unwavering, she decided to see if she could rent a car. The fee for a one-way rental was much less; although more than it would have been had she returned it to Charleston. She reserved a car and set out to leave as soon as possible.

      After finishing her morning ritual, she packed her things and headed for the elevator. When the elevator doors opened, Miss Rump Shaker stood there with another well-to-do looking brother. Crystal entered the elevator. During the ride down to the hotel lobby level, she felt the heat from Miss Rump Shaker's stares searing the side of her head like a hot comb on greasy hair. When the doors opened, she politely exited first, being careful to not run over the woman's feet with her Pullman. Although the temptation was great, Crystal successfully exited without the slightest brush against the heifer's tacky Coach sneakers.

Crystal checked out of the hotel, and then went through a side door to wait for the rental service agent to meet her in the parking lot. She sat on the same park bench she'd been sitting on just a few nights ago when Stephen poured his heart out to her. The heat and humidity were overwhelming, even though it was only a few minutes before noon. Light beads of perspiration appeared on her forehead and nose, but she refused to go inside for fear that she may run into Stephen.

After waiting for about fifteen minutes, a green and white Enterprise Rent-A-Car van pulled into the parking lot. A nice looking white gentleman pulled up in front of the main entrance, and Crystal set her duffel bag and laptop on her Pullman, then pulled it over to the van. The forty-something gentleman named Bill asked, "Are you Ms. Moore?"

For now anyway... "Yes," said Crystal.

"I'll get that for you," he motioned as he grabbed her Pullman and duffle bag.

Crystal got in and sat down on the row behind the driver.

He listened to WWWZ, which was the local hip-hop station. She wondered if he always listened to that station or was it because he "read" her voice over the phone and was trying to impress her with his knowledge of hip-hop.

"I ain't sayin she a gold digger, but she ain't messin wit no broke, broke..." The driver sang along with Kanye West. Crystal didn't know what she'd do if he actually said the words that were edited out, and she hoped she wouldn't have to find out.

They arrived at the rental lot, where she rented a mid-sized car with a GPS navigation system inside. She was all set to go in a matter of minutes.

Chapter 23

Back to Reality

For a Thursday morning, the traffic was horrendous. Crystal wondered where everyone was headed as she flowed with the traffic going west on I-26. Several tour buses sped past her as if she were standing still. She tried to clear her mind by concentrating on her conversation with Melissa the night before. Over and over, she replayed yesterday in her mind. She thought about how she had poured her heart out to the woman who had gone through similar circumstances without her knowledge. Now, so many things made sense about the recent distance they felt from each other. Melissa suffered greatly and didn't want anyone to know. Despite the resentment she harbored toward Melissa and Floyd for ruining what she thought as a child was the perfect family; they had been just that to each other, family. Crystal asked God to forgive her for her selfishness. He had given her just what she needed in Melissa, just as Crystal's mother and father had given Melissa and Floyd just what they needed.

Crystal couldn't believe that Charles was married, and Melissa hadn't talked much about their breakup. She only knew that Melissa took it pretty hard, but had assumed Charles was the one who broke things off. Even though Crystal never had a chance to meet him, she had heard about how wonderful he was and had prayed that Melissa would be happy. She recalled being really disappointed when she spoke to Melissa on Valentine's Day and heard the news that they were through. Crystal had promised her that she wouldn't force her to tell what had happened. Melissa had told her that she would explain what had happened when the time was right. She just couldn't talk about it then.

Crystal's train of thought came to a screeching halt as she noticed brake lights on the car in front of her. Traffic was slowing down, but there was nothing in her line of sight to account for the decreasing speed. Traffic flow eventually slowed to a crawl for miles. Her cell phone rang. She looked down to see who was calling and recognized Stephen's number on the screen. She didn't answer. He immediately called again, and she still didn't answer. She was in no mood to talk to him yet. She had spent several hours last night praying and reading her Bible. Fleeing the hotel was the best advice Melissa could have given her, although she missed Stephen the moment the rental van pulled out of the hotel parking lot.

Since traffic had come to a standstill, she reached inside her purse to find the earpiece for her cell phone. She called Melissa to let her know that she had taken her advice, and left Charleston. Melissa didn't answer her office phone, so Crystal left her a voice message.

"Hey girl. This is Crystal. I just wanted to let you know I left Charleston and am somewhere between Orangeburg and Columbia. I'm stuck in traffic right now; who knows what is going on ahead. There's nothing out here but trees, so maybe there's a wreck up ahead. OK, well, I'll be in touch soon. Thanks for everything." She ended her call, but kept the earpiece in place.

Slowly, the traffic began moving with no apparent explanation for the initial delay. She continued to drive, determined to focus on nothing but reaching her destination, home. She made it to Columbia with no problem and reached the exit for I-77 north without noticing that she had driven that far. She realized that she had been so intent on getting away that she didn't even do her usual ritual, finding a good radio station to listen to. She didn't have any CD's with her since she rode down with Stephen. Hoping to find a gospel station, she pressed the scan button. She couldn't find one. She pressed the tuner button to find The Big DM 101 FM. Alicia Keys, *Secrets* was playing. *Now that's ironic.* She set the cruise control and reclined her seat a bit to enjoy the long straight highway ahead. She was unaware of the earpiece in her right ear until the phone began to ring, and then she realized that it was on auto answer whenever the earpiece was connected. The call connected before she picked up the phone to see who was calling. She answered.

"Hello?"

"Where the heck are you?" asked Stephen.

"Stephen" she said.

"Yeah, it's me. Where are you? I thought you were going to call me last night after you got in. I fell asleep, and when I woke up this morning, and realized I hadn't heard from you, I got worried. Say, where are you?"

"Will you please stop interrogating me? You're making me feel like I'm on the witness stand." She saw her frowned expression in the rear view mirror. "I'm almost in Charlotte."

"Charlotte? What the...?"

"Stephen, I needed to put some distance between us. I need to get back to my life, not the fantasy we think we have."

"I know, but we need to talk."

"Talk then. I'm not going to talk to you face to face. At least not right now. You said last night that Donnie asked you to pray for us. It was a wake up call for me too. Monday night shouldn't have happened. We both know that. I think we got caught up in the moment. I was angry with Donnie, and I needed someone. It's true; I have been attracted to you for years, perhaps in love even. But in love with what you represented, not with you *per se*. I don't want to hurt you, but I'm hurting and confused. I'm too vulnerable because of the state I'm in; I need to stay as far away from you as possible."

"So, what are you going to tell Donnie? Won't he want to know why you left?"

"I'll deal with that when the time comes. Look, you went there for a reason didn't you? In the meantime you need to concentrate on your conference. After it's over, come back and figure out how what we've done affects your life and marriage. It's going to hurt a lot, I know, but Stephen, I can't be around you anymore."

"Crystal, please don't say that. I need you in my life. Talking to you, whether frequently or infrequently, keeps me going. You give me hope. Please don't cut off all ties."

"I spent several hours praying last night, Stephen. There is no other way. I need to be at peace with God and myself. Last night you said you didn't know yourself anymore. I feel like I don't know myself either. But I know this, I can't find out who I am while being in your company. Stephen, you bring out feelings in me that I should only have for my husband. The truth is that scares me." She paused. Her mind started racing. The car was cruising, but she felt out of control once again. The last few days had been a whirlwind. Even though she didn't want to admit it, the sound of his voice stirred emotions in her once again. Stephen was quiet as well. She continued, "We talk in riddles. We say that we want to do what is right, but our actions speak something entirely different. This conversation is a perfect example. I had no intention of talking to you today."

"Why not? Why did you answer?"

"I have my earpiece in, and the phone setting is on auto answer whenever I use it."

"Crystal, I can't go back to Pam."

She didn't respond to his statement. She focused on the 'semi' truck that had its left signal on, indicating that the driver wanted to merge.

"Did you hear me?"

"Yes, I did. What do you plan to do?"

"I don't know. I know that she is not the woman I want."

"Stephen..."

"Don't worry; I don't plan to make trouble for you. I love you and my brother, as crazy as that sounds. What are you going to do? Are you going to tell Donnie?"

"I don't know yet."

141

He raised his voice, "What do you mean you don't know? You're contemplating telling him about us?" His tone sounded as if he couldn't believe she would think of doing that.

"Stephen, you're stressing me. I won't do anything without talking to you. Let's talk tomorrow when you get back."

"Ok." He paused. "Crystal, I'm sorry, and I…"

"Please don't say it. I can't bear to hear it again, Stephen."

"I'll talk to you tomorrow. I'm checking out first thing."

"Ok. I'll talk to you tomorrow then. Good-bye."

Stephen hung up and Crystal detached the cord from the phone, disabling the auto answer feature. She crossed the SC/NC border and passed Paramount's Carowinds amusement park. She no longer felt as if she were in a foreign land. *I'm up out of Egypt, back to the Promised Land!* The familiar scenes of home comforted her. Twenty-five minutes later, she pulled onto her cul-de-sac and into her garage.

Chapter 24

Home Sweet Home

Her home didn't feel familiar anymore, although everything was just as she left it. As a matter of fact, even the television remote was in the same place—on the sofa in the family room. She carried her bags upstairs to her bedroom. Donnie had changed the bed linens and put on her favorite white satin sheets. She smiled to herself at the irony of the little things he was now doing. When she went into the master bathroom, a gift basket of her favorite Bath and Body Works fragrances sat on the counter. Two vanilla-scented column candles sat beside the basket. Crystal looked at herself in the mirror. Just like a few days before, she didn't know who the person was that looked back at her. While putting her things away, she prayed again that God would be merciful toward her despite her actions. She couldn't help but to feel that this would play out much worse than she could ever imagine.

After unpacking her bags, she took her dirty clothes to the laundry room and put the items in the washer. She picked up the dress with the crazy zipper and set it in a basket of items that needed dry cleaning. After that, she picked the bag back up and pulled out the pajama set she wore after she and Stephen had showered. She put the camisole to her nose and inhaled the scent of his cologne. She knew that it would be impossible to forget about him. Against her better judgment at that very moment, she speculated about what would happen if she decided to have an ongoing affair with him. He was a wonderful person, but deep within she knew that nothing good could ever come out of a union between them. Dropping the items into the washer, she set the machine to normal, and then measured and poured in the liquid detergent.

Across the miles, Stephen was thinking about her as well as he sat in a Health, Happiness, and Wholeness Workshop geared towards educating black men on the importance of a work/life balance. He also thought of his brother and how he could benefit from what was being said. He loved his brother, but unbeknownst to Donnie, the night he introduced Crystal as his girlfriend, was the night Stephen fell in love with her. At dinner that night, she had listened so attentively to the conversation he had with Donnie. He found her to be a caring, tender and loving person in that short time they spent together. From then on, he looked forward to spending time with Donnie and always hoped she'd come along to join them for Starbuck's, dinner, or a movie. He loved hearing her voice on the phone whenever she called the office for Donnie. He often e-mailed her 'forwarded messages' in hopes she would reply with even the simplest of comments.

When he began dating Pam, Crystal simply said that she wanted him to be happy, and it would be fine with her whomever he chose. He secretly hoped that she really meant that since she couldn't have him, she'd hope he'd find someone just as suitable. He never really fell in love with Pam, not the way he should have. He made love to her because he knew he was supposed to. On many occasions, he would imagine he was with Crystal, but it wasn't the same. He had prayed many times for God to forgive him and empower him to desire his wife the way he longed for his brother's. *You ask and receive not, because you ask amiss*...The prayer was never answered.

After being with Crystal, he knew the meaning of love and now understood how a man should love his wife. He had married for all of the wrong reasons; the number one reason being, his brother was married and he hated being alone. He had pressed his brother continually telling him to wake up and smell the coffee. He had attempted on numerous occasions to give brotherly advice not only by encouraging Donnie to leave the office at a decent hour, but also to do something spontaneous. For the most part, Crystal called around the same time everyday. He knew when school was out because he could almost always count on talking to her around 3:30 most afternoons. Stephen sometimes thought Donnie left the office at 3:29 just to avoid talking to her and this infuriated him. On more than one occasion, Donnie had implied that he needed to be concerned with his own wife and not Crystal. Stephen decided, after their last discussion about the issue, to let it rest. He didn't want his brother to get suspicious, and he certainly didn't want to ruin what he and Crystal had as far as their friendship. Now, looking at what he had done, he worried if the friendship he valued so much was gone forever.

He excused himself from the session and walked outside for some fresh air. He found the tropical heat inviting; the air-conditioned room he'd been in for the last forty-five minutes had chilled him to the bone. He removed his cell phone from his hip and called Melissa. He had asked Crystal for her number just in case she decided she didn't want to accompany him to Charleston. Melissa answered immediately.

"Hey girl. You left fast, didn't you?"

"Melissa?" Stephen said.

"Hello? Who is this?"

"Stephen Moore."

"Oh, hey Stephen. I thought you were Crystal calling when I saw the 704 area code."

"So you know she left then, huh?"

"Yeah," she said sighing and hoping he wouldn't probe any further.

"Do you have plans for dinner? I'd really like to talk to you."

"What about?" she asked.

"I think you know."

"Stephen, I don't want to be in the middle of anything; please keep me out of it. I can barely stand my own drama, much less yours."

"Melissa, I wouldn't think of putting you in the middle of anything. I know that Crystal confides in you, and I need some objective advice. Please, just have dinner with me, my treat."

"On second thought, that sounds like a plan. Free food and pay day isn't until the 15th, okaaay!" she said like a girl from around the way. "Where do you want to go?"

"You choose. This is your town. I'm sure you know all of the hot spots."

"So what you tryin' to say?" she kidded. "What about South End Brewery at 6:00? It's on the same side of the street as the hotel and about four blocks away heading toward town."

"Sounds good. I'll see you there." Stephen closed his phone and went back inside. The attendees came out of the room as he walked down the hall. *Oh well, this conference was a dud for me anyway, and it was my own fault.* He walked inside the conference room and gathered his things. As he exited the room, he turned in the direction of the front door and walked out into the parking lot. Once there, he walked to his car and drove toward the Cooper River Bridge. He ended up in the town of Mt. Pleasant where he followed the signs to the Isle of Palms.

The Isle of Palms was a beautiful place with huge homes lining narrow streets. Stephen parked his car and retrieved his sneakers from the trunk. He changed his shoes and began to walk towards the beach where several teens were playing with Frisbees. They appeared to be so carefree, without a worry in the world. He wondered if they'd grow up to do stupid adult things like he did. He hoped no one had to endure being in a loveless marriage or the pain of loving someone they knew they could not have; that is, at least he couldn't have her and have peace at the same time.

He continued walking until he found a bench along the seaside that was covered in sand. He dusted off the sand, then sat and watched the waves roll in. He prayed to God that the internal turmoil he was feeling would soon end. He desperately wanted to go back to secretly being in love with Crystal; back to a time when everything and everyone was still innocent. He knew that they had chemistry. In spite of that, he had purposed not to ever allow himself to think of her as more than what she was to him, his brother's wife. He had chosen never to allow himself to imagine her in his arms. Although he danced with her at their wedding, it was not the same. A few days ago, he held her tightly against him, and he wanted her more than he'd ever wanted any woman. He had imagined telling her how he had felt about her for years and imagined her responding by telling him she had felt the same way for just as long. He didn't know what had come over him that night, but he felt like it had to come out. *I figured I'd tell her and we'd joke about it, but at least it would be out. I just wanted to share it with her. I never meant to seduce her.*

Stephen prayed as he watched a yacht slowly trace the horizon. He asked God to forgive him for lusting after and pursuing Crystal. He loved her, and he knew for sure that it was love, not just a physical attraction. He didn't know how he would go on without her in his life. The one thing he did know for sure was that he had to end it with Pam and fast. He owed her that much. He couldn't allow himself to be in a loveless marriage any longer. Although he didn't love Pam as a man should, he loved her enough to end the farce they'd lived for years. He, like his brother, hadn't touched his wife in a very long time. He would talk to her and suggest that they separate as soon as he got home.

Chapter 25

A Neutral Ear

Stephen saw Melissa the moment he entered the crowded waiting area. She was an attractive, plus size woman with a short-cropped haircut. Her hair was jet black, and she looked as if she had a weekly standing appointment with the beauty salon. She stood approximately 5'6" and wore a nice wrap around skirt that accentuated her hips.

"Hey you," she said as he approached her.

"Hey yourself," he said as he hugged her and bent down to kiss her on the cheek.

"Alright," she said in a sister-girl kind of voice. "I saw some women over by the door checking you out when you came in. Don't make me the envy of the room!"

"Well, you know, what can I say?" he said jokingly while making facial and hand gestures like Jimmie Walker from *Good Times*. "Seriously though, thanks for meeting me. I don't mean to put you in such an uncomfortable position, but whom else can I talk to but you or Crystal? God doesn't talk back to me when I talk to Him! Well, at least not immediately!"

"I understand. I don't know if I can be of much help, but I'll listen."

"That's all I…"

"Moore, party of two, your table is ready," said a young girl holding a clipboard.

"Ask," said Stephen. "You must've gotten here pretty early to get our name on the list."

"No. Actually, I called right after we talked on the phone and made a reservation. This place is always jumping; it doesn't matter what day of the week it is."

They followed the girl across the floor to their seat, a cozy booth near the front of the restaurant. "Our specials for the evening are blackened grouper with rice pilaf and fresh asparagus, the soup of day is chicken tortilla and black bean, and the featured appetizer is barbeque chicken nachos. Also, strawberry margaritas are on special for $5.95 each."

"Mmm. The nachos sound good. Will you help me out, Melissa?"

"Sure, I've had them before, they're good. I'll also have a sweet tea please."

"Make that two teas, please."

Stephen didn't quite know where to begin. He figured Crystal had told her something, he just didn't know what. Melissa spoke first.

"I'll tell you what I know, then you won't have to feel so uneasy. First of all let me say, Crystal is my sister and I love her very much. I don't want to see her hurt in any way. I also love Donnie, and although I don't know you as well as I know him, I love you too. Having said that, I'll start off by saying this, Crystal told me what happened between the two of you. I know that she is torn about what to do or shall I say how to proceed with her life. I'll give you the simplified version of what I told her. Talk to God about it. I'm in no position to give advice. I know about talking to God because I've been in the same position before. The only difference was the man I was involved with wasn't my sister's husband, he was someone else's."

"Well, that sure was a mouth full," said Stephen. "I talked to her briefly today, and she sounds mad at me. She didn't tell me she was leaving, so I was shocked to find out that she was almost in Charlotte when I called her cell phone. We've been friends for a long time, and I don't want to lose her friendship. I also don't want to lose my brother either."

"What were you thinking, telling her that you had feelings for her? Didn't you know she's extremely vulnerable right now? Or was that your intent since you know the hours Donnie keeps."

Stephen sighed deeply. "Melissa, contrary to what you may think, I didn't set out to seduce her. I care too much for her to put her in a situation like that. I know it sounds crazy, but do you understand? Do you believe me?"

"You know, I wondered why I had to bear the embarrassment of being involved with a married man and suffer through the tragic way it ended. I often ask God, why He allowed me to be so weak and not to end it immediately after I found out that the man was married. I now know why. He permits us to endure things in life sometimes so that we can learn from them and share our experiences with others. Yes, I believe you." She looked down to stretch out a linen napkin in her lap. "I know what it is like to love someone you can't have or shall I say shouldn't have. I know the pain of seeing that person and not being able to reach out to them and hold them. I've endured many nights where I cried so much my eyes were raw when I finally fell asleep. I also know what it's like to think you are losing your mind when you can't get images of that person out of your head." She picked up a packet of Splenda and started fidgeting with the corners, as if she might rip the packet open.

"One Saturday morning after he had been gone for about five minutes, the doorbell rang. I thought he had forgotten something so I didn't even look to see who was at the door. When I opened the door, a woman in purple silk pajamas and slippers stood on my porch. She held a black 9 mm and proceeded to point it directly at my chest. She basically told me that Charles was her husband, and she would kill me if I didn't leave him alone. That's the clean version! Needless to say,

I'm still keeping my appointments with my therapist, Tuesday evenings at 6:30."

"What?" said Stephen as if he couldn't believe what he had just heard.

"Yes. Stephen, please don't make the same mistake I made and pursue something that you know isn't in the will of God for your life. I know it'll be hard because you have unfathomable feelings for her, but at some point common sense kicks in. Far too often, we just choose to ignore it."

"I know. Everything you are saying is true, I'm just having a hard time that's all. How do you just stop loving someone?"

"You don't. I'm so mad at myself because I haven't talked to Charles since that day. I don't know if she caught him as he left my house, or if she'd had him followed or what. I've e-mailed him and called him against my better judgment with no luck. For all I know, she could've killed him and buried him somewhere. I used to check the obituaries online, but I never saw his name. I also used to check the missing person's reports but was never able to find his name. My guess is he's still married with his life in tact, while I'm suffering. Someone opens his mail when I e-mail him at work because I always request a return receipt on outgoing messages. My guess is he's still working the same job and just chooses to ignore me. It used to make me ill, but I finally got past the physical part of grieving the death of the relationship." Melissa accidentally opened the packet of Splenda and its contents spilled onto the table. As she swept it into a neat pile with her hand, she'd answered his question. "Well, I'm no counselor, but are you really in love with her or is it what she represents?"

"What do you mean?"

"I mean do you love the kind of woman she is? Is it a sibling rivalry thing? Or do you simply love a challenge? If it's the kind of woman she is, there are other women in the world, and what about your wife? Have you prayed for your relationship with her? God can work miracles you know. Have you always wanted things your brother had? You need to think about these things."

"When I called you, I didn't realize you were so wise. I do love the kind of woman Crystal is, and I love her. Just her- even though I know it's wrong, I can't control what's in my heart. I've tried telling my heart what to do for years, but the head and the heart don't always work together. And to answer your other question, no. I don't have issues with my brother or the desire to go on quests for things that are unattainable. I didn't ask for this; well, let me rephrase that—I didn't ask to have these feelings." Stephen put his napkin on the table and leaned back. He looked as if he were pondering the future. For once in his life, he was speechless.

"Let's get off the subject for a moment. I see the waitress coming with our nachos."

They ate nachos and made small talk. The appetizer was so filling that they decided to forgo ordering entrees. The waitress returned with the check, Stephen paid her, and they left. He walked Melissa across the street to the parking garage, and she offered to drive him back to the hotel. Stephen got into the passenger side of her Volvo sedan. When they arrived at the hotel parking lot, she pulled into a parking space instead of letting him out at the guest entrance.

"Thanks for dinner, Bro."

"Thanks for listening to me. Please pray for me, for us. This is hard," he said running his hand over his face.

"Don't I know it," she said smiling.

"Have a good evening," he said.

"You too. Be careful driving back tomorrow. Keep your mind on the road, not Crystal!" Stephen smiled a heartbroken smile and got out of the car. He waved goodbye to her and went inside the building.

Once inside, he packed his bag in anticipation of checking out first thing in the morning. The pieces of conversations and memories he had had with Crystal since Monday night ran through his mind. They had connected with each other unlike they had ever done in the past. They really connected, and he couldn't help but to think that maybe something could develop between them. He kept thinking these thoughts, and then canceling them in his mind. He thought about what Melissa said about a therapist. He never really knew anyone who admitted to going to therapy, but the idea didn't seem too far-fetched at the moment. He wasn't looking for a quick fix, but he did need someone to listen. He even felt a little better after talking to Melissa in the short time they spent together.

Chapter 26

Friday: A Blessing In Disguise

The drive home was a lot longer than when he and Crystal drove down just days before. He listened to jazz CDs and thought about Crystal the entire way, although he made every attempt not to. He couldn't help but think of how they'd made love and how good it felt to have her in his arms. He wondered what wrath he'd bring upon himself for committing such sin. He prayed for God to have mercy on him and to take away the desire to have her from his heart.

Stephen rehearsed his words before entering his house. He didn't see Pam's car in the garage, and he assumed she was out grocery shopping or something. He wouldn't immediately tell Pam, but it had to be done by the end of the day or by sundown the next day at the latest. Although he knew he and Crystal didn't really have a future, he knew he couldn't be with his wife one day longer.

He took a deep breath as he put the key in the door that lead to the kitchen from the garage. He opened the door, looked around the empty kitchen, and then went back to his car to get his bag. The house was unusually quiet. He was used to coming home and seeing Pam resting in the same spot on the couch most days. He moved quickly through the house to the bedroom. He opened the door to the large walk-in closet he shared with Pam. That's when he saw it. The left side of the closet was completely bare. All of her things had been there when he left, but now, even the shoeboxes that lined the floor were gone. He dropped his bag in disbelief and walked over to the dresser to check the drawers where she kept her things. They were empty as well. His heart raced wondering what was going on, but it was evident. She was gone. He looked around the room and wondered what had happened. Fear engrossed his body as he wondered if she had found out about him and Crystal. He walked quickly across the room to call Crystal.

"Hello?" answered Crystal.

"Hey, I'm back and all of Pam's stuff is gone. Did you see anything?" he asked hurriedly.

"What? No, I haven't' seen anything. I haven't seen or talked to Pam since I've been back," she said.

Stephen held the phone while he looked around the room. On the bed they shared was an envelope with STEPHEN written on it in all capital letters. "I'll call you back," he said to Crystal and hung up the phone. He walked over to the bed and opened the envelope. A letter written in Pam's handwriting read:

Stephen,

It is Thursday and I haven't heard from you since you called to say you had arrived on Monday. I'm tired of being second to you and everything and everyone else in your life. I know you don't love me, and I've known for years that you didn't marry me because you loved me. At least you don't love me like you should, but because you needed someone and thought I needed someone, we got married. I can't do this anymore, and I'm out. I can't sit home and wonder if you are going to leave me first. I'm not as depressed or as dumb as you think. For months, I've been looking for a job and a place to stay, so don't underestimate me.

I've been wondering how to do this and finally got up the nerve to leave your trifling ass. You call yourself a Christian. If you're an example of one, I'm better off the way I am. Your church going hasn't done you a bit of good. You leave every Sunday and come back the same way, empty. That's why I stopped going with you.

I can't sit there and watch you lift your hands and say "amen" knowing what I know about what is going on in this house. A fancy house doesn't mean a thing to me if there's no love here. Life goes on, and I know that I've just made things a lot easier for you since you weren't man enough to tell me years ago. I see how you look at me, and I know you don't love me like a man should love his wife. Thanks for not calling me this week. It was a real eye opener, or shall I say it was confirmation. (One of your church words.) I'll be in touch later, and I want to make this as painless as possible. Go ahead and get your praise dance on. One of your prayers has just been answered!
    Pam

Stephen didn't remember sitting on the bed, but was stunned at what he had just read. He had planned to do the exact same thing, but she beat him to the punch. He had no idea that Pam even had the wherewithal to do such a thing. He felt saddened that he had driven a good woman to be that way, but he was elated at the same time. He hoped it would be painless as she put it. Their marriage wasn't long, but it was too long for them to have lived in that situation. He picked up the phone and dialed Crystal again.

"Hello?"

"Hey, I'm sorry. I saw an envelope with my name on it, and I had to take a minute and read it. She's gone."

"What do you mean 'gone?'" asked Crystal.

"She left me a 'Dear Stephen' letter and said she wanted to make this as painless as possible," he explained.

"I can't believe that. Oh my goodness." Crystal was stunned. She had been standing when she answered the phone, but she flopped onto the sofa. She didn't even realize that she had walked across the room while talking to Stephen. "Did she say why? I can't believe the irony of this, Stephen."

"I know. She said she knows I don't love her. Crystal, I must say she was a lot smarter than I gave her credit for. I was dreading this anyway, so it just got a little easier."

"I'm happy for you, Stephen." Crystal had to keep taking silent deep breaths because she couldn't believe this had happened. It was so much easier to make her feelings for him go away when she could rationalize that she was married and so was he. Technically, he was still married, but knowing that his marriage would soon be over made her feel very anxious inside.

"I'm happy for us."

"Stephen, please don't. Let's not get carried away here. You have to be living separate for at least twelve months in order to get a divorce in North Carolina. This doesn't give you a free pass, you know. Besides, things could change."

"I think it's too late for that. I'm coming over. I don't want to talk on the phone."

"No. Not here.

"Where then?" Crystal didn't answer. "I'm going to the office to check on something; meet me there in about thirty minutes.

She agreed and a few minutes later found herself nervously driving to Moore Brothers, Inc. She pulled into the empty parking lot and wondered where Stephen was. Then she remembered there was a rear entrance. She pulled around to the back of the building, and his car was parked in one of two spaces labeled *owner*. As she pulled into the other space, Stephen opened the rear entrance door for her. She took another deep breath and felt an excruciating pain beginning near her left temple. *Not today.*

She was very weak as she got out of her car and walked towards the tall, gorgeous man she always called "brother," but could now call her lover. His million-dollar smile beamed as always.

"Hi beautiful," he said as he took her by the hand and locked the door behind her. The touch of his hand made her flashback to the night they shared in Charleston. After he locked the door, he put his arms around her waist before she could protest and gave her an embrace. He hugged her as though he had just lost his best friend. Although it was over for him and Pam a long time ago, having everything spelled out for him in black and white made him mourn for her. It brought the slapping reality of the end of their marriage to the forefront of his mind.

"Thank you for being here," he said still holding her tightly. She embraced him as well. She loved the moment and knew it would come to an end soon. She tried to pull away, but he wouldn't allow it.

He leaned in to kiss her, and she was helpless in his arms. They kissed like two teenagers in a parked car. He continued kissing her while moving her backwards down the hall to his office. She allowed him to lead, but she knew in her heart and mind that no matter what happened, she would not and could not allow herself to become intimate with him again. They reached his office, still embraced and still kissing as if it were their last chance to see each other. Stephen backed into his desk, and pulled her close to him. He sat on top of his desk, and she stood in front of him between his long legs. He didn't try to do anything inappropriate, that is, no more inappropriate than kissing his brother's wife. Feeling somewhat uneasy anyway, she was very appreciative of that. Crystal pulled away from him.

"I can't do this," she said. I left you in Charleston for a reason. This very reason. We are dangerous together, and one or both of us are going to get hurt badly if we don't stop. We must be stronger than this burning desire. I am so ashamed of myself, Stephen."

"Well, why did you come here?"

"I didn't come here to be intimate with you if that's what you're asking." She rolled her eyes at him in disbelief at his question.

"Sweetheart, that is not what I was getting at. I mean why did you agree to come here with me? From our conversation yesterday, I thought you never wanted to talk to me again," he said.

"No, that wasn't it at all. I just needed to get out of Charleston and more importantly, out of the same hotel as you. You know, it's like the cliché, alcoholics don't need to take jobs as bartenders because of the temptation."

"Oh, ok. So you think you would have been tempted, huh?" he said smiling.

"Don't start, Mister. You men are all alike," she said.

"So this is goodbye, huh?"

"It has to be, you know that." *And I hate it too.*

"Yeah, I know. I would like for you to have dinner with me tonight though. I'll order in, and we can have it right here. Can you do that for me, oh forbidden one?"

"That, I can do," she said smiling.

She agreed to Chinese, and Stephen placed an order to be delivered. He went to a cabinet that housed a wall-mounted CD player and put in the Best of Anita Baker CD. He skipped right to *You Bring Me Joy*.

"Dance with me," he asked as he held out his hand to Crystal. *Cherish the moment girl, cherish the moment... Lord, forgive me...again.* She figured since it would be their last night like this, she would dance with him one more time. There was no ballroom setting, no formal dress, no pretense, and no words unsaid. It was just the two of them with raw, but tamed passion for one another. It was passion that would be put in a bottle, capped off, and placed on a shelf, never to be opened again. Crystal wondered whom she was fooling by thinking it would be over when she walked out of the office. She knew she wasn't fooling anyone, especially God. Turning away from Stephen would be one of the hardest things that she would ever have to convince herself to do. She loved being with him and talking to him, even before going to Charleston. *What am I going to do now?* She knew that it would take much prayer and probably a lot of fasting to get beyond the feeling she had deep within her. They held each other close and moved to the rhythm of the music. He whispered into her ear, "I love you. You don't have to say it; I know you love me too. This is the last time I'll say it."

"I love you too, Stephen." She said the words before she knew it, but she meant them. He stopped dancing, looked deep into her hazel eyes, and kissed her unlike any other time they'd kissed. They kissed for what seemed like five minutes or longer until they heard a loud knocking at the door. "Oh, that scared the daylights out of me," she said, fearing someone knew they were inside and what they were doing.

"Relax, it's probably the food." Stephen broke away and dashed for the front door. The Chinese delivery guy had arrived.

Stephen returned with the food and pulled a small blanket from the bottom drawer of his desk and spread it on the floor.

"Hold up! You keep a blanket in your desk drawer?"

"Pay close attention, please. It's from a client." As he smoothed out the wrinkles, she noticed a staffing company logo on

159

one of the corners. "And to answer your question, no, I don't do this often!"

"I'm glad you know my thoughts so well," she said lowering herself to the floor.

"Yes, I do," he said with a raised eyebrow and smiling. The aroma of sesame chicken and fried rice filled the room as Stephen opened several small boxes. Crystal removed the plastic wrapper from the forks and the paper covering from the straws. They ate and made small talk. No words were said about their feelings for one another. A chapter had ended for Stephen and his wife, and at the same time a new chapter had begun for him and Crystal. Unsaid words let them both know that they must continue on the right path; the righteous path. They both knew it would be hard and wished it didn't have to be. He knew that he couldn't go on much longer betraying his brother the way he had been. He also knew that God gave him a second chance to make some things right in his life, and he was not honoring God by being in the situation he had created for himself. He looked at Crystal as she ate, and they spoke silent words to each other through their eyes. They both knew Donnie would be home soon, and things would have to go back to the way they had been before they left for Charleston.

They finished their meal. Next, they dismantled the makeshift picnic setting. Stephen cleaned his office, and then disposed of the take out boxes. He looked at her as she reached for her car keys on the corner of his mahogany desk. He knew that their imaginary world had come to an end. He reached for his office keys, and they both walked out of his office. Stephen took as long as he could to lock his door and make sure that the building was secure. He knew that his real intent was obvious and juvenile, but he didn't care. At the rear entrance of the office, Stephen and Crystal hugged a long goodbye, and she caressed his masculine face. He kissed her on the eyelids and cheeks very tenderly, and she turned to leave. He followed behind her, and they both got into their separate cars and drove off. At that moment, Stephen regretted buying a home in the same neighborhood as his brother because he knew it would be very difficult for him to not think of her in the house alone, all night.

Chapter 27

Sunday

Crystal spent Saturday relaxing and thinking about Stephen. She hadn't seen or talked to him since Friday. It was Sunday morning, and she knew that she should have been at Sunday morning worship service before anyone else, but opted to sleep in. She was saddened by her "break up" with Stephen on Friday, but again she reassured herself that she had no other choice. She had to pull it together in order to re-ignite her marriage to Donnie if that was what he wanted.

She hadn't spoken to him since he had left Charleston on Wednesday morning. *What kind of marriage do we have left, and when did it go south? Did I do something to contribute to the distance between us?* She couldn't figure it out. *If I didn't know any better, I'd swear Donnie had something to hide.* She couldn't think of anyone at the office he'd be involved with unless it were a client. *What was up with him... just showing up in Charleston like he had something to prove or was he checking up on me? Maybe, it's my guilty conscience. I can't go on like this.*

Donnie called on his way from the airport. "Hey Crystal. I'm back in town." His voice sounded distant.

"Ok, where are you now?" She suddenly felt nervous.

161

"Leaving Charlotte Douglas. I'm about to get on the Billy Graham Parkway."

"Ok, I'll see you soon."

He arrived home in record time, or at least that was the way it seemed. Crystal's mind was restless as she thought about the events of the last week. She had to get Stephen out of her head and concentrate on her marriage. She heard Donnie's key in the door and went to the kitchen to greet him. He was struggling to get his garment bag through the door when she walked around the corner. "Hi," she said. Donnie looked as though he was surprised to see her standing there.

"Hi, how are you?" he asked. "Can you get this?" he handed her the garment bag he was about to drop. He was also carrying a large bag from Land's End. "Here, this is for you." She set his garment bag on the island bar and quickly peered inside the bag to see what he had bought for her. Inside were a soft quarter length white cardigan and a pair of light blue Capri pants.

"Thanks. I didn't know I was still eligible for souvenirs when you traveled," she said jokingly and holding the ensemble up to her body.

"Oh, it's just a little something I picked up. It looked like something you'd wear."

"Thank you," she said walking towards the island bar to set the bag down. "How was your trip? Everything all set for Golden Corral?"

"Yep, everything is a go. As soon as we can get everything together, we'll begin the blitz campaign for them. This is great for business and hopefully we'll be able to pull more national accounts because of this. My prayers are being answered."

She hadn't heard him say anything spiritual in a long time. "That's great, I'm happy for you and Stephen," she said. Just saying his name made her feel uncomfortable.

"Yeah. I take it ya'll got back safely, Friday? Did you enjoy your time away?" he asked.

You don't want to know the answer to that question. "Yeah, Stephen pulled in around noon Friday. It was an insightful trip," she said getting lost in her words.

"How so?" he asked. "Oh, did you find out who the mystery woman was?"

"Huh?"

"The woman he was eating breakfast with Wednesday morning. She looked like she could eat him alive!" Donnie smiled as if the woman intrigued him.

"He said that she invited herself to have breakfast with him. Stephen has news…"

"What kind of news?"

"Pam moved her things out while he was gone."

"Whaaat? Well, well, well. She finally came to her senses, huh? I have no sympathy for a woman like that."

Donnie's comments surprised Crystal. "Why do you say that? I thought you liked Pam."

"Don't get me wrong, I have nothing against her; I just think she settled, just like my brother did. He didn't spend any time with her, and I personally thought she latched on to him for financial security."

"I'm surprised you feel that way. Stephen was pretty shocked by the whole thing." *Although he was planning to drop the bomb on her anyway.*

"At least he didn't have to be the one to call it quits, then have to deal with all of the drama that goes along with leaving your wife. I don't know how he's made it this long."

"Donnie."

"Come on now, you know what I mean. I've just verbalized what everyone has thought for the last few years. I hope he finds a good woman soon. One he can be proud of showing off; someone like you."

Just like I thought, I'm your trophy wife. "Ok, let's talk about something else. Are you hungry?" she asked, not wanting to talk about Stephen or his woman possibilities any longer.

"Actually, I need to run to the office. Can you wait until I go over there and come back?"

"Sure," she said.

"I'll be right back. I need to go get some files. I'm not going in until later tomorrow morning. I thought we could spend the evening together. Would you like for me to pick up a movie on the way back?"

"Yeah, that's fine. Whatever you want to do. I'll whip up something to eat," she said.

"Ok, give me about an hour, and I'll be back." He walked out the door. *'One he can be proud of showing off, someone like you.'* She couldn't believe he said something so belittling like that to her. "So am I a trophy for him?" she said aloud. *He didn't hug or kiss me when he got home. An outfit from Land's End is supposed to make up for the months of distance? But then again, I didn't initiate any intimacy with him either. The more she thought about him, the angrier she became at the man who was supposed to be her husband.*

As promised, Donnie returned in about an hour. He picked up *Crash* from Blockbuster Video as well as a pack of the movie theater butter popcorn Crystal loved. After dinner, Donnie asked Crystal to relax on the couch. Before starting the movie he pulled her to him and kissed her gently on the lips. "I know I haven't been there for you a lot this year, especially this summer. I want us to start over right here, right now. I love you."

"Donnie, we don't have to rehash everything. We've both made mistakes and not been what we promised to each other. I would like it very much if we tried to make this work."

"You have my word." They watched the movie, and Donnie kept his arm around his wife until the movie ended. Afterwards, they went upstairs to their bedroom, and he gave her one of his signature massages. The feel of her husband's hands on her body felt clinical as if she was in a spa and a professional masseur was performing the task. She could not relax and enjoy what his hands did to her tense tissues. Usually a massage meant they would be intimate. Crystal didn't know what to expect since they hadn't made love in months. She felt tense anticipating being a wife in every way to her husband,

164

but Donnie didn't pursue anything further with her. She thought he would have wanted to be with her since they hadn't been intimate in such a long time, and they hadn't make love when he was in Charleston.

Crystal didn't mind the lack of intimacy that particular night given that she had a heavy heart anyway. Donnie snuggled her in his arms, whispered he loved her, and went to sleep. Crystal lay there wondering where and when things began to take a different path. For the life of her, she couldn't figure it out. She stared at the moonlight peeping in between the blinds in their room. "Donnie?"

"Hmm?" he said groggily.

"Wake up, I need to talk to you," she said, not really wanting to get into anything too deep at the moment, but feeling she needed to say something.

"What is it? What did you wake me up for?"

"What's going on with you, with us? Why don't you want to be intimate with me anymore?"

"Crystal, please, I've had a very long week, and I'm tired. Please don't stress me right now," he said sounding aggravated.

She sat straight up in the bed. Fury poured through her veins, and she knew her face and nose were immediately red with the sudden increase in blood flow.

"Stress you? I am your wife!" She knew her voice got loud. "I hardly ever see you. You don't call me. When I call you, you are too busy or quickly rush me off the phone. I've been here all summer, basically alone. You sent me away for a week, then you left while I was gone. Then, when you come back, all you want to do is go to the office, eat, and watch a movie. I'm just wondering what is going on? Do you even know when the last time we made love was? Do you?"

"So, you wake me up for this?" He sat up in the bed and turned the light on. "Don't tell me what I *don't* do. What about what I do everyday for you? I work my butt off for you. I am a provider, so if that makes me a bad person, then I guess I'm just a bad person. I'm tired of this. All you've done this summer is complain about what I haven't done. I came to Charleston to surprise you, hoping you would be happy. All I got from you was a cold shoulder and complaints about a migraine. What was stressing you so badly? Huh? You rarely get those anymore, so what was causing the tension? Was it me? I got the feeling that you didn't care one way or the other if I were there or not. You said I don't call you—you don't call me either." Donnie was obviously irritated, and it was obvious that he had given some prior thought to what he had said. "For someone who had felt like they'd been neglected, you sure didn't seem to appreciate the fact that I would drive all the way there to see you."

"Donnie, I don't want to argue with you. I just need to know where I stand. We're not the same couple we used to be. I've said it before, I feel like I've been your roommate these last few months, not your wife."

"I don't need this right now. I have enough things to deal with." He reached over and turned off the bedside light. Shaking the bed more than necessary and tugging at the covers, he turned his back to Crystal. *Maybe I need to pull a Pam up in here! He said he was going to try to make this work, and he gave me his word. It didn't even last twenty-four hours. Lord, lead me in the path of righteousness. I don't want to live in a loveless marriage, and I have no children to keep me here. His mouth says one thing, but it's clearer now more than ever that he doesn't want me, even if he doesn't know it in his heart yet.*

Chapter 28

Me Time

Donnie didn't keep his word at all. Days went by, and things were back to normal, as they had known it. The long nights continued, and Crystal saw less and less of her husband. She hadn't even talked to Stephen, which was odd because even before the trip, they would talk often. They were honoring their promise to each other and as hard as it was, it was the right thing to do.

School would start back in two weeks. At least then, she would have something to do with her time; at least for a large portion of the day anyway. She decided to take care of herself for the remainder of summer vacation. She made an appointment at Julie's Hair Works for later in the morning, and it was just what she needed. *I need to get my hair and nails spruced up for me.* She also scheduled an appointment at the spa to get a massage right before the teachers had to report back to school.

She arrived at Julie's about fifteen minutes before her appointment. There were two women already seated in the reception area, and she hoped they were waiting for another stylist. *I know she didn't tell me to come, and she's got two people ahead of me. I should have done my own hair.* Julie stepped into the reception area and spoke to Crystal. She said it would be about ten minutes before she could get Crystal in a chair. Crystal nodded acknowledging Julie's status check. The two women continued their conversation. One woman looked familiar to Crystal, and she realized that it was Pastor Fleming from a nearby church. She was telling the other lady that marriage has seven-year cycles. "See, Baby," she said, "the first seven years are the new, 'settlin-in' years. During that time, you git to know each other. You git passion and excitement. Every thang is new. After dat, the years dat follow dat are the commitment years. You ain't committin' to a person, you're committin' to a union, the marriage."

"But Pastor Fleming, I feel like all of the energy I have is going into our children. Plus, he doesn't help with anything. I'm just tired," the young woman went on.

"Don't throw away a good thang because you're bored or tired though. God neva'say this marriage bidness was gonna be easy. He ordained it, but He neva' say it would be easy."

Crystal listened attentively, while pretending to read a magazine. Another stylist called for Pastor Fleming, and she went to take her seat in that stylist's chair. The other woman and Crystal were left in the reception area. Crystal assumed she must have been going through something similar. The Pastor's words stuck in her mind as she waited for Julie.

To her surprise, it wasn't too long before Crystal left Julie's. She had a new style and a new French manicure. As she drove, she eyed herself in the mirror. *That girl know she can do some hair!* When she did require a cut or trim to her usually long mane, she always called Julie. Julie knew Crystal didn't like the ghetto styles, up do's, or outlandish colors. She kept it simple, but classy and conservative.

Crystal approached the freeway ramp but decided to take a different route home; one that would take her directly past Moore Brothers. She hoped that stopping by the office unannounced wouldn't upset Donnie, but at least then she'd get to speak to Stephen as well, in a public setting. Fifteen minutes later, she arrived at the office. Donnie and Stephen's cars were parked in front of the building. She opened the door and walked in. Amanda was coming out of Donnie's office when she walked in. "Hi," Amanda said curtly, passing Crystal in the hall.

"Hi," said Crystal in response while turning to see what her problem was. Amanda blew past so fast; all Crystal felt was the breeze of a tailwind as she passed. Crystal walked to Donnie's door and saw him sitting at his desk. He had his elbows on the desk, and his face rested in his palms. His eyes were closed.

"Hellooo?" said Crystal in a singsong voice.

He jumped. "Hey. What are you doing here?" he asked looking stressed. Before she could answer, Stephen walked in behind her.

"Well, check you out! I like it, I like it. Turn around, let me see the other side," he said looking at her hair. Crystal turned around so Stephen as well as her husband could see her new do. "You work it girl!" Stephen was smiling from ear to ear.

"Thank you," she said looking from Stephen to Donnie who only wanted to know why she was there.

"And check out the nails. You really go, girl! Getting yourself ready for school, huh?"

"Yeah, I needed a change," she looked directly at her husband.

"Well, change is good."

"Ok, you two. Are we going to discuss fashion, or did you come in here for a reason, Steve?"

"He can be rude and blunt, can't he? I don't know how you've managed to put up with it all this time," said Stephen. He turned to look at Donnie, "I came in here to see if you were having problems accessing the network. I can't view the network folders, only the local drive. I re-started my computer, but I might have to reboot the server."

"Yeah, Amanda and I were trying to figure out what the problem was when I came in early this morning," said Donnie.

"I'll let everyone know that I'll be taking the server down in about ten minutes. Good to see you, Crystal."

"Bye Stephen," she said smiling. She turned to Donnie. "Speaking of Amanda, what is her problem today? I passed her in the hall, and she was moving like a bat out of you know where! She's been rather short with me on the phone recently too. What's the deal? Is she gaining a little weight?"

"Was she rude to you?"

"She spoke, but she wasn't her usual friendly self. Is she feeling ok? Her face looked flushed."

"I don't know. She gets moody. So, you got your hair done?"

"Uh, yeah," she said sounding like that was a stupid question. I was just stopping by to say hi. Julie got me in and out in record time today," she said turning her head from side to side.

"I didn't know you were going this morning." He didn't comment on how her hair looked.

"There are a lot of things you don't know, Donnie," she said getting rather frustrated with him.

"Crystal."

"I'm not starting anything; don't even say that because I didn't come here for that. I was just stopping by. When do you think you'll be home?"

"I don't know. I don't have any late meetings tonight, so maybe around six or even earlier."

I'll give this one more try, Lord. "That would be nice. So, can I count on having dinner with you?" she asked trying to change the direction of the conversation and trying not to get frustrated with him.

"Yes."

"Great," she said getting excited for the first time in quite a while about being with her husband. *I hope I don't live to regret this."* Donnie stood from his seat and walked around the desk to kiss his wife on the lips.

"I'll see you this evening," he said.

"Ok." She turned to walk out of the office smiling. Amanda was walking back toward Donnie's office. She didn't say a word to Crystal as they passed each other. *Whatever! She better recognize who she dealin wit. I ain't at work, and I don't have to be no English teacher up in here today!*

Crystal stopped by the grocery store before going home. She wanted to broil some salmon, one of Donnie's favorite meals. She bought red-skinned potatoes and fresh green beans. She also bought a fresh loaf of French bread. It was a good feeling knowing she'd be having dinner with her husband. She hurried home, although dinner wouldn't be for several more hours. She had to know in her heart that despite the fact that she had made a mistake with Stephen, she had done everything else she could to try to make her marriage work. She wanted God to be happy with her, even if she had disappointed Him.

Chapter 29

Eminent Danger

Fine, just straight up fine! Stephen couldn't help thinking about how beautiful Crystal looked as he tried to figure out what was going on with the company file server. He restarted his computer. While he waited for the Windows screen to reappear, he prayed. *My flesh is weak; so weak. Lord, you know I don't want to have envy in my heart...I know it's wrong. You know I'm struggling right now. I've been praying about this for a long time...I know I took matters into my own hands with Crystal... Lord, you said to come to you boldly before the throne with anything, right? This brother needs some help. You know all about it, I know. Please help me.* He leaned forward with his chin in his palms, and put his elbows on the desk. He breathed in deeply. *I'm not sure if I should say this because I've always heard 'be careful what you pray for because you just might get it.' But if you have to, open a door for me to get out of here. Put me somewhere else or give Moore Brothers the opportunity to expand somewhere else. I don't think I'm even strong enough to move on my own. My mess, I know. I feel like I might just lose my mind. Maybe I should move out of the neighborhood. That might be a good start. Hear my prayer, Lord. Amen.*

Finally, the computer was working, and he couldn't be happier. When the computer came back up, AOL instant messenger automatically popped up asking him if he wanted to log on as ARTISTIC1. Usually, he'd close the window, but today, he logged on and noticed CRYSTALYTE was online. It was Crystal's user ID. It had been a few weeks since he'd talked to her online, and he couldn't pass up the opportunity to chat with her for at least a minute. He typed "Hi." There was an immediate reply that she was away from her computer. *Well, I don't need to be talking to her anyway.* He sent out an e-mail message to his staff and Donnie, which advised them to reboot all computers before trying to access the server again. About five minutes later, his instant messenger icon began flashing. Crystal had responded.

CRYSTALYTE: Hi yourself. What's up?

ARTISTIC1: Not much here, just trying to make up for lost time. I've spent most of the day trying to fix the darn server. Tech support was basically useless. I don't even know why we have a contract with them. I fixed it myself using good old trial and error.

Stephen noticed the message at the bottom of the screen that said CRYSTALYTE is typing a response.

CRYSTALYTE: I'm cooking dinner. Donnie is supposed to come home early tonight. It will be a first in a long time.

Stephen was deliberately quiet for a moment. The thought of her having dinner with Donnie made him jealous, and he allowed the enemy to take control of his thoughts and fingers.

ARTISTIC1: IMY.

CRYSTALYTE: What's IMY?

ARTISTIC1: I miss you.

There was a pause. The last time, Stephen noticed that the message at the bottom of the screen said CRYSTALYTE is typing a response. This time, the status bar said nothing. He hoped she wasn't upset with him, although he was upset with himself. After about three minutes, he saw the message that she was responding.

CRYSTALYTE: I thought we weren't going to do this?

ARTISTIC1: I'm sorry. I couldn't help it. It's like I have an angel on one shoulder and the devil on the other. I do miss you, and you did look lovely today.

CRYSTALYTE: I can't do this. I told you about dinner this evening, and I'm actually excited about it. I have to give this a chance.

ARTISTIC1: I understand that.

CRYSTALYTE: Good. I'm glad you do.

ARTISTI1: I am seriously considering leaving town. I can't keep up this charade.

CRYSTALYTE: Leave town??? Why? You can't leave. Where would you go? You're just doing this to get back at me, aren't you?

ARTISTIC1: No! It's too hard being this close and pretending. You know how I feel about you. And to answer your question, no I'm not trying to get back at you. Why do you even ask me something like that? You said you were committed to your marriage, didn't you? I honor your decision... plus I know we're in dangerous territory anyway. I need to get away and thanks to Pam, I'll be a free man soon.

CRYSTALYTE: Whatever. It's a free country; you can go wherever you want to go.

ARTISTIC1: Why the sarcasm? I don't get it.

CRYSTALYTE: Please don't leave. It would really hurt me if you did.

ARTISTIC1: You can't have your cake and eat it too. I don't know what I'm going to do. It was real hard seeing you today. I'm just keeping my options open. That's all. I just hope little brother realizes what he has. I am so thankful for our memories together, but I don't think my heart can take much more of this.

Outside, there was a loud noise that sounded like two cars crashing. Stephen heard employees running past his office to the rear office door. He minimized the messenger window and got up as well to see what was going on.

Down the hall, Donnie decided not to move because he knew someone would come in shortly to give a report of what happened. He clicked on one of the desktop icons but nothing happened. *I thought Steve said he fixed this thing.* Frustrated, he threw the pen he was holding down on the desktop. *Did the whole staff go outside?* He walked over to Stephen's office, but Stephen was still outside with everyone else. Donnie decided to check his brother's computer to see if he had a network connection. Stephen's screen saver was on and Donnie moved the mouse to make it stop. He double-clicked the Adobe icon, and it immediately opened up. Then, he remembered that Stephen had just sent him an e-mail message that he hadn't opened. *It probably said to reboot.* He stood to walk back to his office, but something caught his eye. He noticed the messenger window flashing at the bottom of the screen, and sat back down. *I know I'm being nosy.* He clicked the flashing icon to see who was IM'ing Stephen. When he saw Crystal's user ID, he leaned back in the seat.

CRYSTALYTE: It was hard seeing you too. You always have a way of making me smile. Underneath my smile is pain; pain of being pulled between two men; pain from choosing commitment over passion.

CRYSTALYTE: I can't lead a double life.

CRYSTALYTE: Stephen! Hello?

CRYSTALYTE: Are you there?

Donnie's stomach began to churn as he scrolled back up to see what else had been said. He read all that had transpired between his wife and his brother. He began to wonder what had been left out that he couldn't read. His head started to throb like it was caught between two cymbals, and he couldn't think clearly. Seemingly, time had stopped, and his feet felt super glued to the floor. At the same time his head and his hands felt very heavy.

In the distance, he heard people chattering as they re-entered the building. He listened as Stephen told the staff to wrap up whatever they had been working on and call it a day. "Calvin, lock the front door on your way out. I'm beat, and I'm going to slip out the back door and go home as soon as I shut my computer down." Stephen was getting closer to his office door, and Donnie felt even more weighed down. He turned slowly away from the computer as Stephen walked in.

"Man, you should see what happened in the par…" Stephen stopped in the middle of his sentence when saw a look on Donnie's face that resembled the expression of someone who was demon-possessed. For a moment, Stephen thought those glassy eyes looked like those of a raging monster in a scary movie. Then, it hit him like a ton of bricks. Stephen looked at his younger brother sitting in front of his monitor. Maximized on the screen behind Donnie was the AOL Instant Messenger window. He didn't' know what to say, but Donnie spoke first. His voice was deeper than usual, and his words came out slow and articulate. "I came in here to see if you could pull up Adobe before I remembered your earlier message."

"Yeah, I sent the message out right after I got it up and running," said Stephen slowly.

In what seemed like an instant to Stephen, but an eternity to Donnie, Donnie was face to face with his brother. He watched Stephen double over with his eyes bulging. Stephen never saw it coming. Donnie had punched him in the stomach so hard that his own hand hurt. Stephen, still helpless from the force of the blow, never had a chance when Donnie kicked him in the face with his knee. Pain beyond belief shot all through his face and he knew he had to get control of his senses, his body, and his brother. Otherwise, he'd risk being seriously injured or worse. He tried to stand up, but his legs were weak. Donnie wrestled him to the floor, and repeatedly punched him in the head, face and stomach. Reaching out for Donnie's arm, he tried to stop him, but he couldn't. Filled with pain and rage, Stephen tasted his own blood and realized there was a broken tooth in his bloody saliva.

"Stand up, punk! Be a man, STAND UP! I said, get up!" Donnie said, spitting as he yelled. "You think you the man messing around with *my* wife?"

"STOP MAN! Listen to me…please." Stephen reeled on his knees and tried to stand up, but the entire room was spinning.

"Don't tell me to do anything!" He punched him again in the face and Stephen teetered backwards, but regained his balance. Thoughts raced through Stephen's mind like a comet streaking through the sky. *I gotta stop this*. Stephen found something deep within him and fought back. Enraged, he wasn't going to take the beat down Donnie was putting on him any longer. Stephen grabbed his younger brother and shoved him. Donnie glared at him with widely stretched eyes.

"I've always known," he said staggering backwards. He had tears in his eyes and breathed deeply. His hand pulsated from punching the older brother whom he had always looked up to. Stephen imagined the agony gripping his brother.

Donnie's breaths were long and labored. "I've always known that you were in love with my wife. I ought to kill you right now. Don't you know I could kill you? Huh? Answer me!" Stephen said nothing. Donnie looked at him as if he could kill him with his bare hands, then walked out of the office. Inwardly, Stephen ached with excruciating pain—pain unlike any he had ever felt before. Fearful that he had internal injuries, he gingerly, walked toward the restroom to assess the damage to his face and body. Holding a small piece of chipped tooth in his hand, he entered the men's room. As he gazed at himself in the mirror, he didn't recognize the image looking back. The vision in his left eye was blurry, and it throbbed almost as badly as his left cheek, which was now red and turning a shade of blue. His lips had swollen to three times their normal size.

Suddenly, Donnie walked in making the door slam against the wall, and stood behind him. He still looked like a mad man possessed by demons. Turning around to face him, Stephen noticed Donnie's tightly balled fists. "Look, don't do something you'll regret."

"Do you think I'd regret killing you with my bare hands? Ever since I introduced you to Crystal, you've wanted her for yourself. I even saw it in your eyes at our wedding. You're the biggest hypocrite I know. You couldn't even love your own wife because you've been in love with mine for so long. Did you sleep with my wife?" He asked the question with disgust in his voice. Shifting from one foot to the other as he stood there, Donnie acted like a drunk who had forgotten where he was going.

"I asked you a question! DID YOU SLEEP WITH MY WIFE?" He put his hand in his right pocket. Horror-struck, Stephen feared he was about to pull out the weapon Donnie had always joked

177

about having, but no one had ever seen. "ANSWER ME! Have you?" Donnie lunged across the floor and grabbed Stephen by the head. Stephen was in a headlock, and he couldn't answer. Barely able to breathe, he struggled violently and fought to free himself from his brother's grip. The pain was unbearable, and he seriously considered giving up. At least then, he'd finally be out of his misery— his current predicament and the anguish of loving his brother's wife.

"ANSWER ME!" Donnie cursed his brother's name.

Exhausted from the pounding, Stephen finally let out a weak "Yes."

Infuriated, Donnie pushed him with all of his might, and Stephen's back and head hit the wall behind him. "Why?" Donnie yelled. His voice echoed throughout the restroom, and Stephen thought about all the attention the commotion probably attracted. He wondered how big the audience was outside the door. Donnie started up again. "You know what? You don't even deserve to live. I'm your brotha, your brotha. Man, we family! You make me sick!" He backed up and rested his back on the stall behind him. "And to think I encouraged her to go to Charleston with you. Did you take advantage of her?"

"Naw, man! It wasn't like that," Stephen managed to get out.

"You know what?" Donnie walked in small circles as if he were in deep thought with his right hand still in his pocket. I'm not even going to throw my life away on a piece of junk like you. There isn't any reason I can think of to ever talk to you or see you again. This is some real brotherly love here! Both of you make me sick." Taking his right hand out of his pocket, he walked over to Stephen and punched him in the gut one last time. Then, he stormed out of the men's room. He cursed Stephen's name as the door slammed. Stephen heard him exit the building and drive off, tires screeching.

I knew nothing good could ever come of this. I've just thrown everything away in my life that was important to me. Stephen cleaned himself up as best he could and edged his way along the wall until he reached the rear door. He walked out of the building while still tasting his own blood. Once inside his car, he drove in the direction of the hospital. It hurt him to breathe, and he knew that he needed medical attention. *Where's my cell?* Carefully searching around with his right hand, he found it on the passenger seat. He pressed the number three, Crystal and Donnie's speed dial number.

"Hello?"

Stephen spoke with a breathy voice. "Crystal, he knows. He knows. Donnie read our messages."

"What? Oh my God! No, please tell me you're lying," she screamed.

"I'm sorry…I'm not lying. He's probably on his way home. I'm driving myself to the hospital. I think I have a broken rib among other things."

Crystal started shaking as several natural body functions seemed to be occurring at once. She cried uncontrollably. "The two of you fought? Oh my God! What happened? How bad are you hurt? What hospital are you going to?"

"Baby, it hurts me to talk. I'm in a lot of pain. I'll give you details later. Please be careful. I've never seen that look in his eyes. I'm going to Regional Medical. Bye."

Crystal looked frantically out the window for any sign that her husband was near. She only knew of a few instances in which Donnie became enraged. He was seldom upset about anything, and usually pretty laid back. That is until recently. Lately, everything about him had changed.

Remain calm! Take the salmon out; turn the stove off. Blow out the candles; get your keys. Where's my purse? I need to get out of here. Feeling like a scatterbrain, she ran around the kitchen. Adrenaline pumped so fast through her body that she felt as though she might faint. *I need to check on Stephen before Donnie gets here and tries to take out his wrath on me.* She opened the entrance door to the garage, and the garage door began to go up. Donnie was pulling into the driveway. *No! Please God, spare my life!* He slammed his foot on the brake. His car suddenly skidded to a stop, which made the tires screech on the concrete driveway. He jumped out of the car and quickly stormed toward the door where she stood. Her heart was racing. *I'm gonna black out!*

"We need to talk. NOW!" he screamed as he grabbed her by the arm and roughly pulled her inside the house. He slammed the door so hard that the plates in the kitchen cabinet rattled.

"What? What have you done?" she cried as she jerked away from his tight grip.

"What have I done, what have you done?" he yelled. His eyes were wide with fury. She saw pain in his eyes, but she also detected something else she hadn't seen in a long time. It was a look of guilt, and it made her feel very uncomfortable. She felt like she knew her husband very well but that look of guilt scared her. *What did he have to be guilty about? Was it what he'd done to Stephen or was it something else?*

"Donnie..."

"Don't say a word to me right now. I can't believe you have been carrying on behind my back with my brother." He made hand gestures like a gangster rapper. "Naw, naw, my bad! You've been carrying on right in front of my face with my brother. What kind of woman are you? Both of you disgust me! You make me sick, and you call yourself a Christian? You are the biggest hypocrite I've ever met in my life! I just told Stephen that he was a hypocrite, but I think you've got him beat!" He laughed nervously while he shook his head. "So this is why you didn't want me in Charleston. So this explains why my own brother flipped out and acted so upset when I came to see my own wife. Aaand this is obviously why you were so jealous of the woman he sat with at breakfast that morning. You two played me like a fool. Stupidly, I thought that I was the one who wanted you to go. 'Go on, I said. Ride with Stephen. You'll have fun'. Well, I'll bet you did have fun, huh? The two of you must have thought you'd died and gone to heaven when I made that suggestion, didn't you?"

"Donnie, it's not like that. Stephen and I never crossed the line before then."

"Well, well, well. And that is supposed to make me feel better? I suggest you ride with him to Charleston to see Melissa, and the two of you interpret that as jump in bed together? You are despicable. How long has this been going on?"

"Donnie, I know we were wrong, but I am not going to stand here and let you call me names and try to degrade me. I am still your wife and no matter what I do, we are both still man and wife and children of God."

"There you go! There you go with the religion. Religion solves everything for you, doesn't it? If it itches, rub a little Bible on it, and everything will be alright, huh?"

Crystal felt so weak with guilt and frustration. She knew that no matter what she said, at that moment, Donnie was in the wrong frame of mind to accept it. She prayed silently to herself, and thought about what she should do.

"Does Pam know?" he asked as he paced the floor with his hands on his hips, and shaking his head in disbelief. "That's why she left him, isn't it? He told her, but you didn't have the good sense to tell me?

"No, Pam doesn't know. She was gone when he got home Friday."

"Well, isn't that special," he said sarcastically.

"What did you do to Stephen? Is he ok?"

"I can't believe you. I just found out you and my *brother* have been having an affair right under my nose, and all you can think about is how he's doing? The nerve! You don't even have the decency to try and defend yourself, do you? You're too concerned about your lover. He's my brother! My brother, Crystal!" He picked up a candle from the dinner table. He held it in his hand, tightly forming his fingers around the glass. He tilted it back and forth, watching the hot candle wax move slowly from side to side. Looking at Crystal with tears in his eyes, he threw it against the wall. Pieces of glass crashed to the floor, and the red wax slowly ran down the wall, stopping before reaching the carpet. "You are something else."

Crystal screamed not knowing what was going to happen next. She had had enough. She lashed out. "ENOUGH ALREADY! Yes, Stephen and I made a big mistake, an enormous one. We both know that. It shouldn't have happened. Not that I'm grasping for straws to justify myself, but you haven't touched me in months. No matter what I do, you don't respond. For the most part I spend all of my evenings

181

here alone. When I come by the office, you glare at me. It's as if I am not supposed to be there. Your facial expression shouts, what are *you* doing here? You stopped going to church with me- you don't do anything with me anymore. When was the last time we made love? You don't even know, do you? It was February 2nd. February! It is now almost time for school to start again. You haven't been sick, and neither have I. We have no health problems to my knowledge. So what's the problem? When I try to talk to you, you don't have time for me. I began thinking maybe you had someone else. I have prayed and prayed for things to be all right with us. I know that being with Stephen and lying to you was not in the will of God for my life, but I can't change what I've already done."

"I can't take anymore of this 'God talk' with devilish actions." He turned and headed for their bedroom upstairs. She followed. He snatched open the closet door and took out a suitcase. He went from drawer to drawer grabbing clothes and toiletries.

"Where are you going?" Crystal asked as she stayed on his heels like a yapping puppy.

"Don't worry about it," he said not answering her. Crystal sobbed and felt very unsure of her immediate future. Dealing with what was going on at home was one thing, but worrying about Stephen reaching the ER safely was another. Donnie finished gathering his things, walked over to her with his arms full of his belongings, and vengefully spit right in her face. She slapped him so hard that his head spun in the direction of her hand. He moved as if he were going to strike her, and for a brief moment she thought he was going to jump on her, but something came over him right before her eyes. Abruptly, he turned and walked out of the bedroom, out of the house, and out of her life for all she knew.

Thank you, Jesus.

Chapter 30

Mad Dash

Crystal stood in the kitchen to collect herself and her thoughts before getting behind the wheel of the car. *It could've been worse. It could have been a lot worse. That man spit in my face! Who have I been living with this year, Lord? What happened to the man I married? What happened to the woman I used to be? Lord, please let Stephen be ok. I know I have no right to ask you to make this situation all right, but please have mercy on Stephen; and comfort Donnie.* Crystal had never seen a violent side of Donnie, not ever. She couldn't believe he'd beaten Stephen mercilessly. She hardly believed he had acted like he was going to put a hurting on her as well. *But what else would he do? I'd do the same thing. Lord, protect me from harm and danger.* She thought Donnie might come back to confront her again later. *Everyone has their limits.* Grabbing her purse and keys, she headed out the doorway to the garage for the second time.

Oh my God! Donnie still sat in his car in the driveway. She decided to leave anyway, and ran to her car. She quickly locked the door, and nervously put the key in the ignition. Feeling like she couldn't get the car in reverse fast enough, she floored the gas pedal and maneuvered just enough to back the car out without any incident.

As she zoomed past him, he mouthed a word that rhymed with itch and narrowed his eyes with contempt.

Once on the street, she was glad that she had made her escape without any more drama. Donnie had never called her that name, nor had he ever insinuated that she was such a thing. She didn't know what was going to happen in the future, but she knew that she had to go see about the man she had grown to love and deeply care for over the years. Crystal sped through the streets of Charlotte trying to get to Regional Medical Center.

"Darn!" She ran a red light that had a camera at the intersection. A guy in an SUV laid on his horn. She barely missed sideswiping him when the lane ran out because of road construction. There were several roadblocks, and she had to circle around several times because of one-way streets. *Who designed these streets? Better yet, were they smoking funny cigarettes when they did it?*

Although, she found the entrance to the emergency room, the parking lot was full. She zipped into the parking garage across the street. Clip clop, clip clop, clip clop. She didn't realize she'd put on her noisiest pair of casual shoes as she hurriedly walked from the parking deck to the hospital. She passed Stephen's car in the parking lot near the ER entrance. His car was parked crooked as if he had only enough energy to pull in and crawl out of the car to the hospital. While looking for directions to the triage area, she practically ran into the building. She saw signs on the wall adjacent to a corridor just ahead and followed them until she reached the triage area. She didn't see Stephen anywhere, but a woman dressed in green scrubs walked toward her. She waived her hand to get her attention. "Excuse me, but where can I find someone who came into the ER for treatment?"

"What's the name?"

"Stephen Moore."

"Was he in a fight?"

Uh, oh. "Yes," said Crystal, "you've seen him?"

"Yes. I'm headed his way right now. Follow me." They walked down a long hall and made several turns. Crystal saw several people with the surrounding curtains barely pulled together to protect their privacy. She could hear people coughing and yelling out in pain.

This place is always busy. Did the city go mad tonight or what? They reached the bed with #19 hanging from the ceiling. The nurse walked in first. "Mr. Moore, someone is here to see you." She spoke to Stephen as if he were hard of hearing. Looking past the nurse, Crystal saw Stephen slightly reclined in the bed. "Oh my God!" Crystal screamed and dropped her purse and keys to the floor. She quickly moved around the nurse and reached for his hand. He looked like he'd lost a fight with Mike Tyson. Stephen had a swollen and badly bruised face. The only difference was that he still had both ears intact.

"He did this to you?" Crystal asked looking as if Stephen was on his deathbed. "Are you OK?" Stephen's eyes looked glazed over, and dried blood formed a crust on his puffy lower lip. She bent down to hug him, but the nurse grabbed her by the arm.

"Ma'am, please don't touch him at this time. We are about to take him down for x-rays. He may have some internal injuries. If you know who did this to him, you need to encourage him to press charges."

"I'm ok," Stephen muttered. "I think I probably look worse than I really am," he said.

"Well, let's let the doctors tell us that, Sugar Ray," said the nurse.

He tried to smile. "Oh, you got jokes. Aghhhh! That hurts."

"See. I told you Evander!" She motioned for Crystal to step to the side as she took the brakes off the bed. She rolled him to radiology for x-rays. Crystal followed.

After Stephen underwent a series of x-rays, the nurse transported him back to #19. "The radiologist will take a look at the x-rays, and the emergency room doctor will be in after that. Is there anything else I can get to help you be a little more comfortable in the meantime?"

"Thanks, but no, Misses Funny Man. I have all I need right here. This is my best friend," he said forcing a smile. "Oh, it hurts to smile," he said grimacing.

"Careful now," said the nurse as she left. She pulled the curtain almost closed, leaving the usual gap.

"What's the point in pulling that curtain? It's not like we have any privacy up in here!" Crystal said moving closer to Stephen. She gently touched his puffy, battered face. Tears rolled down her face. "I'm so sorry," she said beginning to sob.

"Don't be sorry. I deserved it. I'm sorry I messed your life up," he said slowly. He was visibly in a lot of pain, but did everything he could to hide it from her. It pained him more to see her upset.

"Don't talk, just rest. I'll be here as long as you need me." Crystal reached over and kissed him on the forehead. She sat down in a chair next to his bed. He reached for her hand and held it as tightly as he could. Against Crystal's wishes he began to speak.

"He saw your last instant message flashing on my computer screen and decided to read everything we'd been talking about. I didn't tell you, but I left my office for a minute. Someone had a wreck outside of our building and several of us rushed outside to see what was going on. I minimized the IM window when I went outside, and when you responded, the IM icon flashed at the bottom of the screen. Donnie went to my computer to see if the network was back up. He saw the IM flashing, and he just got nosy. When I walked back in my office, it was too late. He'd seen enough to know we weren't just chitchatting. I'm sorry, baby." He squeezed her hand gently.

"It's ok. We don't have any more secrets, Stephen." Just then the emergency room doctor walked in. "Mr. Moore, I have good news and bad news. The good news is that you don't have any serious internal injuries. The bad news, you have three cracked ribs, and there isn't a whole lot we can do about those."

"I know," Stephen barely got his words out. "I cracked a rib in high school when I played football. About eight weeks to heal, right?"

"You're right on the money. What I can do, though, is prescribe something for the pain. If you can tolerate it, you may want to try a little ice for very short periods of time. Make sure that you don't go any longer than fifteen minutes though. Your bruising will look a whole lot worse before it gets better. I will stitch up your lip, but you'll need to see your dentist as soon as possible about that tooth. Next time, tell your opponent to wear gloves, and you...please, wear a helmet!" The doctor patted Stephen on the leg and left, only to return shortly with items to stitch his lip and a prescription for pain.

He discharged Stephen and gave him instructions about what to do for the next seven days. He was to take it easy for the next few days and to resume normal activity slowly, when it was tolerable, over the next week. Crystal helped him walk to the parking lot. She offered to drive him home, but he didn't want either of them to leave their car at the hospital. "I can make it home, Crystal. I was in worse shape three hours ago when I drove here. Why don't you follow me so you'll have peace of mind," Stephen told her as she protested his decision to drive himself.

Stephen eased into the driver's seat, and waited for Crystal to exit the parking garage. She flashed her lights to let him know that she was the one approaching, and he pulled out in front of her. He drove the speed limit without any difficulty all the way home and even took the freeway to get there faster. When they pulled into their neighborhood, Crystal's house was dark. The reality of what had happened immediately sank in, and her stomach became queasy again. She continued driving over to Stephen's house to make sure he got in the house and settled comfortably.

"Come on, Bro." She helped him from his car to the house and opened the front door for him. "I don't want you taking care of me. Why don't you go home?"

"Why are you being so mean? I'm just trying to help, Stephen. It's because of us that this happened. I want to help." Her voice quivered.

"I know, but I don't want to cause more trouble for you."

"And you think that if I go over there, I'll be ok? Didn't you hear me say Donnie left tonight? Besides, the way he's acting tonight, I'm almost afraid to be there alone anyway."

"I don't think he'd harm you."

"And I didn't think he'd harm you either. He moved toward me like he was going to beat me down before he left. Then, he spit in my face, Stephen."

"What?"

"I slapped him so hard, my hand is still vibrating. It's over, but I don't want to talk about that right now." She opened the door. The house had a strange feeling about it now that Pam was gone. It looked almost the same, but there were a few items missing that she'd seen during previous visits. Blank spaces on the wall revealed that some of Pam's prints were missing, and an afghan that once draped over the living room sofa was gone. "Please get some pillows from that closet," Stephen instructed. Crystal took three pillows out of the closet and a blanket. She arranged them on the sofa and helped him settle in a comfortable position. She handed him the remote control and went to the kitchen. She rummaged around in the pantry in search of something for him to eat. While she warmed some condensed soup, she made him an ice pack for his ribs. She went upstairs to find the linen closet, and then wet a washcloth to clean his face. When she went back downstairs, he was watching CNN. He smiled when she walked in and reached out his hand for hers. She took his hand, and he gently pulled her to him.

"Awww. That hurts. Thank you. You don't know how much it means to me—your being here." She didn't say anything in response; she just smiled and nursed his wounds. His gratitude showed in his eyes. He caressed her face as she cared for him. All of a sudden she began laughing uncontrollably. "What's so funny?" he asked wondering what could possibly be so funny at a time like that.

"I know it's not funny, but this reminds me of an episode on Martin. Martin fought Tommy 'the hit man' Hearns, and his head and face were all swollen at the end!"

"Oh no you didn't!" he said trying to sit up. He playfully took a swing at her. "Ouch!" he yelled out in pain. "Ok, so you've got jokes too, huh?"

"I'm sorry, I couldn't help it," she said. I intended to kiss you on the forehead, but when I thought about this situation, that image of Martin popped in my head." Stephen moved his head as she tried to clean his face. "Stop moving around so much."

She went to the kitchen and came back with the ice pack and a bowl of hot chicken and dumplings soup.

Stephen felt like he had died and gone to an earthly heaven. Crystal was in his home doing all of the things a wife would do. Unlike the times he'd imagined in the past, she was there for real. On the other hand, he hated himself for the reason she was there.

Chapter 31

Aftermath

Three days had passed since all hell broke loose between the Moore brothers. Crystal hadn't heard a word from Donnie since she left him in the driveway. She'd tried calling his cell phone at least three times each day, but his calls were forwarded to voicemail. She called the office to see if he had shown up for work, but he hadn't. She worried that instead of trying to harm her or Stephen, he may have done something to himself. It would be highly uncharacteristic for him to do something so drastic; however, she was aware that people have been known to snap under pressure, especially when it involved marriages and family.

Stephen called the office daily to maintain damage control. He figured the rumor mill would be running rampant since he met Amanda on her way back into the building the night Donnie came after him. While lying on the couch, he worked from home using his laptop computer. Crystal stopped by several times a day to check on him and to do odd tasks like loading the dishwasher and making sure he had fresh linens downstairs.

Stephen still hurt all over. It was as if his injuries were still brand new. The pain was most unbearable whenever he took deep breaths. He often wondered where his brother was, and how things would be between them in the future. He prayed to God that Donnie would find a way to forgive him and Crystal, but he knew that his brother would need lots of time. Besides, only God had the power to ease the pain of someone who had been betrayed by his wife and his brother. Unquestionably, Stephen truly did love his brother. However, he still wished that he had met Crystal first. Even in the midst of his pain and suffering, he couldn't help thinking about her all day, everyday. He lit up when she came to check on him. He knew she was trying to be tough and not show her real feelings. On the other hand, he knew deep down inside that she loved him and his brother. He also knew that she was scared to death of what Donnie might do.

Chapter 32

Stay Busy

The day finally arrived for Crystal to report back to work. Teachers always returned to school one week before the students. It allowed them to set up their classrooms, attend meetings, organize incoming students' data, and prepare lesson plans.

Filled with excitement, Crystal now had something to focus her energies on other than her situation at home. She had grown weary worrying about where Donnie was, what his intentions were, and what the state of her marriage was. As she pulled into the parking lot at Queen's Parish High School, memories of the activities she used to love to do flashed around in her head. Excitement filled her body about the upcoming school year. She anxiously walked into the front office to make sure all room assignments were still the same. She'd had the same room for five years. Although she'd like to have a room on the western side of the building, she'd become accustomed to the quirks of her room. Smiling to herself, she recalled the way the air conditioning system made a knocking sound right before it started and the way the door made a creaking noise before it was shut completely. She greeted several of her colleagues who were also in the office. They chatted about their summers, temporary and part time jobs they had worked, and vacations they took. They spoke about children, grandchildren, and husbands. Crystal quickly excused herself from the conversations when they began talking about their spouses and what they did over the break. As a cover, she said that she was anxious to see the new paint job in Building A.

As she entered her classroom, she had flashbacks of students from the previous years. Looking over to the seat where Sierra used to sit, she silently prayed that everything was all right, wherever she was. Excited about what the new school year held, she threw herself into designing bulletin boards and rearranging desks. Soon, several other teachers dropped by and they chatted about the seemingly short vacation.

Around lunchtime, Crystal decided to try to call Donnie at the office. He'd been out of the office since their confrontation, and she thought surely he'd resurfaced by now. She dialed the number, and Amanda answered.

"Hi Amanda, may I speak with Donnie please?" Crystal tried to sound confident, as if nothing was wrong.

"He's on another line," she said in a very dry, almost irritated tone.

"I'll hold," Crystal responded.

"I really need to free up the lines. We've been very busy this morning. I'll tell him you called... Crystal," she said, pronouncing her name as if her name was a nasty taste in her mouth.

"No. I told you that I would hold, didn't I? Is there a problem with me holding? There's never been a problem with me holding before." She couldn't let it go. "So are you telling me that the owner's wife can't hold the line until he gets off the phone?" Crystal said with indignation, certain that by this point, Amanda was probably ready to hang up on her. However, she wasn't about to let this opportunity pass. "You listen to me... Most likely Donnie confides in you about stuff, BUT I am still his wife. You'd best tell him I am holding, or I'ma be over there so fast, your head will spin, heifer!" Crystal didn't know where the boldness to talk to her like that came from, but it felt good.

Without a warning, Amanda put Crystal on hold, and the next sound she heard was music in the background. Amanda had been on the scene for several years. Although she was almost like an extended family member, Crystal felt that she shouldn't take what was going on with the Moore family so personally. *Family business is just that, family business. I don't know who she thinks she is. She needs to be put in her place.* Donnie and Stephen relied on her heavily to manage the administrative side of things in their absence. Crystal figured she'd been 'feeling' herself since both of them had been out of the office recently. In reality, Crystal didn't care what she thought of her. The issues going on between her and her husband were their business. Amanda picked up the phone, "He just got off. I'll transfer you."

"Thank you very much," Crystal said sarcastically. *That's more like it, heifer.*

"Hello?" When he answered, Crystal felt nervous inside.

"Hi Donnie. Can we talk?"

"About?"

"Where have you been for the last few days? I've been worried about you."

"So you're telling me that you've been worrying about me? Me? Hmmm, let me see if I remember correctly, the last time I saw you, you were going to see about your lover. I thought *he* was your priority now." Angry didn't come close to describing the sound in his voice.

"Please, let's not do this. I want to see you. We need to talk."

"I can't see you right now, and trust me; you don't want me to see you right now either. Don't even think about coming here. I need some time." There was a long pause. "Can you do that? Just give me some time, Crystal. You are something else you know that? You have no right to be calling any shots right now. I just can't do this. Today is my first day back in the office, and I don't need drama from you. Please just leave me alone. When I'm ready to talk to you, you'll know. Oh yeah, tell your boyfriend we still have a business to run."

"Donnie," she said in a whiny voice. "You can't avoid me forever."

"Goodbye, Crystal." Donnie hung up. He left Crystal holding the phone, puzzled about how this was all going to end. As she stood there listening to the dial tone and dumbfounded that Donnie hung up on her, the principal, Ann Gray, walked into her classroom. She set the receiver down and talked with Ms. Gray for a short time, all the while trying to forget the emotions churning deep within.

The week continued, and Crystal went about preparing for her teaching duties, making worksheet copies, and attending departmental planning meetings. She kept herself as busy as possible to keep her mind occupied. She fixated on being in the right frame of mind when the students returned the following week.

The week of teacher workdays quickly came to an end. On Friday, the faculty only worked for half a day, which concluded at noon. The English Department went to Red Lobster for a lunch social. Crystal enjoyed the company of her coworkers as they laughed and sampled appetizers. Several of them made plans to play miniature golf afterwards, but she opted to go shopping alone. She spent the rest of the afternoon at the mall browsing the newest fall fashions. She shopped in Bath and Body Works and purchased a new pair of earrings in Macy's Department Store. As the day approached the early evening, the mall crowd started to change. Teenagers seemed to appear from nowhere. Perhaps, they intended to enjoy their last free weekend for a while.

Crystal left the mall and went to Harris Teeter to pick up grocery items for herself, and to get a few items for Stephen. She had planned to cook another meal for him. She hoped that he hadn't grown tired of eating the leftovers she packaged up for him. She wished there was some way that she could contact Pam. Pondering a moment, she realized that she wasn't quite sure what she'd say to her if she did have her number. *Uh, Pam, hi. It's me, Crystal. Donnie beat the crap out of your husband because he found out that your husband and I have been 'carrying' on behind y'alls back...* Crystal smiled at the thought even though she knew that it was no laughing matter. She quickly purchased rice, chicken breasts, bread, broccoli and some bathroom items.

When she arrived home, she pulled her car into the garage, put her bags in the kitchen, and then walked across the street to Stephen's. She looked through the window and saw him sitting at his desk. When she tapped on the window, it startled him so badly that he banged his knee on the corner of the desk. He whipped the chair around suddenly. "What the?" He grabbed his side, and then his knee. Regaining his composure, he hobbled over to the front door; and still clutching his side, let her in.

"Girl, don't be trying to give me no heart attack up in here," he said sounding genuinely ghetto fabulous.

"My bad," she returned. "Why you sittin' up in here wit da curtains open anyway? You want 'peeps' all up in your bidness?"

"Ok, Crystal. The Ebonics is not working for you, so King's English please!"

"Whatever," she said holding her hand up to his face to block his words—"Talk to the hand, talk to the hand!" They laughed.

"Will you have dinner with me?" asked Stephen.

"I thought you'd never ask," she said. "I'm so tired of sitting over there alone every night. I just wish Donnie would talk to me. Not knowing anything is killing me."

"I know. I'm sitting over here alone too, you know. It doesn't have to be that way," said Stephen winking his eye.

"You can't be serious? You're married. I'm married. We're in a mess already; I'm a mess. And you want to talk about us spending time together?"

"No, it's not like that. I'm just suggesting that since things are already messy, it's ludicrous to spend this time apart. Grieving separately doesn't really accomplish anything. We ought to lean on each other. We're still friends, aren't we?" he asked seriously.

"Yes, but I don't want things to *look* worse than they are. If Donnie wants a divorce, he might try to sue me for alimony or something, or he might try to make me look like a loose woman in court. Who knows? It could get real nasty. You know how you men can be when you feel like you've been crossed."

"That was a sexist thing to say," said Stephen, "but true." He smiled. "You're right. I just miss your company, that's all. Speaking of company, I'm going to work on Monday. Don's right; we do have a business to run despite the fact that it is his fault I was out in the first place. By the time Monday gets here, I shouldn't have these bruises on my face. I don't care what the employees think; I just don't want to entertain clients looking like this."

Crystal's face showed her concern. "Are you sure you will be up to it?"

"Yeah. I've been out long enough now, and I need to get out of this house. The walls are starting to close in on me in here. Besides, you're starting school, so I'll really be lonely. There's only so much I can do here anyway. I need stuff that's in my office."

"Well, take it easy. Maybe your being back in the office will force Donnie to deal with this. Then we can all come together to talk and work through this."

"Don't hold your breath. I've known him a lot longer than you have, and we both have seen how stubborn he can be."

Crystal and Stephen finished preparing dinner, and shared their meal together on the couch. In spite of all that had occurred, they decided to rely upon each other to cope with it. Enjoying each other's company, they watched the ABC Nightly News, Inside Edition and Entertainment Tonight.

"Who cares about Tom Cruise's engagement or his baby? And who is this Angelina Jolie? Why are we looking at this anyway? And this is supposed to be entertaining?"

"Stephen, look at the name of the show. It's uh *En-ter-tain-ment* Tonight. Get it?"

"Very funny. I'm just saying, people actually look at this stuff like it's their life though."

"I know, and don't let them say something that is the least bit profound or controversial. The media jumps all over it. It makes me wonder if they'd jump all over Jesus if He were here."

"Probably not. Probably wouldn't even recognize him."

Crystal gathered the dishes and walked to the kitchen; Stephen joined her. "You're on your own now, Buddy. My housekeeping duties are over!"

"Well, I appreciate everything you've done. Thank you." For the first time since he was injured, Stephen walked Crystal across the street and made sure she was safe inside her house. He felt good supporting her for a change. More than ever, he longed to hug her and profess his love, but he didn't. He was certain that God would be with them through everything they were about to endure. He wanted to be happy for once in his life, and she made him very happy.

From the outside, it seemed as though Crystal's life had crashed and burned around her with nothing left but smoldering wreckage. Nonetheless, she decided to take care of her own needs for the rest of the evening. First, she went into the bathroom to run a hot bath. Next, she poured Bath and Body Works Mango Mandarin bubbles into the water and lit candles on the counter top, and around the oval tub. When she turned on the Bose stereo Donnie had installed a few years ago, sweet sounds from Boney James' last CD filled the room. She undressed and stepped into the jetted tub. Her senses received a sweet treat, and she reclined while she did breathing exercises to relax.

She had started to drift off into light sleep when she heard the telephone ringing in the bedroom. She let it ring. Today, she didn't' want to get out, drip water all over the floor, and answer the phone, only to find she hadn't made it in time. After soaking for a while longer, she got out the tub and smoothed mango mandarin body cream all over her body. She polished her nails too, and then she remembered the phone.

Looking at the caller ID, she noticed that Donnie had called from his cell phone. When she called his number back, the call went straight into his voice mail. She wondered if he was playing games with her. The phone rang again as soon as she set the phone down. It was Melissa calling; she wanted to see how things were going. Crystal summed up the previous week's events, and Melissa was floored. She didn't know what to say except that she'd been there and done that.

"Unfortunately, it doesn't get easier," she said. "I'm going to say something and I don't want you to take this the wrong way, ok?"

"OK."

"Yes, it is a messy situation. You willingly brought this trouble on yourself. Eyes wide open. However, God will bring you through, but the choice is yours. HE is the way when there is no way. Often, sin exacts a price that we don't want to pay. Thankfully, by the grace of God, you don't have to pay for it with your life, Jesus already did that."

Crystal was amazed. Once again she was thankful for having Melissa in her life. Temporarily forgetting about her own problems, she started thinking about Melissa. She wondered how and when she became so wise. Crystal invited her to come for an extended visit to the Queen City whenever she needed to get away from her desk. Melissa promised that she would soon; perhaps during Crystal's fall break. They exchanged I love you's before hanging up.

She tried Donnie's cell once more. She was determined to talk to him one way or another. There was still no answer.

The next day, she planned to go to Moore Brothers to try to talk to her husband. She hoped she would not have to talk to Amanda. *I might just have to get straight "ghetto" if I do; the nerve of that woman.*

She had become accustomed to being home alone, but now things were different. In the past she knew that Donnie would come home eventually. Lately, her sleep was fitful. She didn't rest for fear that at anytime now; he might come home seeking revenge because of her betrayal. She prayed for her protection as well as Donnie's and Stephen's. In addition, she prayed that Donnie would be able to forgive his brother and her. Tormenting thoughts crept into her mind as she agonized over what could happen in the middle of the night or early in the morning while she was home alone. She felt very vulnerable, especially since he had been away from the house, and she had not heard from him. She just wanted him to call. At least then she might have a clue as to where his head was.

Slipping into bed, she turned on the television to peruse the Direct TV lineup. *The Village* started in ten minutes, and she had wanted to see it when it was playing in theaters. The phone rang again, and she quickly answered, not looking at the caller ID.

"Hello?"

"Hi beautiful." It was Stephen.

"Hi," she said disappointedly.

"Well, by the sound of your voice, I guess you weren't expecting to talk to me. You *could* pretend to be happy to hear my voice, you know."

"I was expecting Donnie; he called while I was in the bathtub. Now when I call him back, it goes straight into voice mail. Do you have any idea where he might be? What about where he's staying?"

"Crystal, I wish I did know. He was at the office today. Actually, I found out that he was in yesterday as well. Undoubtedly, everyone knows what's going on, and I hate being the center of gossip."

He said that today was his first day back when I called him from school. "Yeah, me too," said Crystal. The sound in her voice echoed the sadness in her heart. "I never thought about any of this when we were in Charleston."

"I'm sorry, Crystal."

"For the last time, Stephen, don't apologize again. We're in this together," she said.

"So what were you doing?"

"I was about to watch *The Village*."

"I wanted to see that movie. What channel?" asked Stephen.

"HBO."

"Can you come back over here and watch it?" asked Stephen, hoping she would say yes.

"Stephen." She paused. "I don't know…I don't think we should push it…When I left your house and you walked me back over here…" she paused.

"Don't say anything else. I know. I feel it too."

"I really want to talk to Donnie."

"Would you feel better if I came over there?" asked Stephen.

"No I wouldn't. What if Donnie comes home? I don't want another scene. No more drama. By the way, how do your ribs feel?"

"They feel pretty good considering how they did a few days ago. I can breathe much deeper today. Hold on, I got a beep. Uh oh, it's Donnie, let me call you back."

"Donnie?"

"Yeah. I'll call you right back. Bye."

Crystal twisted and turned. She just couldn't lie or sit still while waiting for Stephen to call her back. She hopped out of bed, and looked through the window. There was a light in the family room at Stephen's. She figured that he was probably sitting at the desk again. *At least he closed the curtains.* She did want his company, but had her apprehensions. *Donnie could have the place under surveillance for all I know.* She was dying to know why Donnie had called her. She was surprised that he'd be calling Stephen. She figured he would be the last person Donnie would want to talk to.

"Hello?" Stephen said, after pressing the flash button on his phone.

"How long are you going to be out?" asked Donnie rudely.

"Excuse me?"

"You heard me. How...long...are...you...going...to...be... out? Why try to hide? Everyone knows what happened. Quit playing coward and come back to the office. We have clients; they have needs that we're supposed to attend to, remember? Life goes on, you know."

Stephen's blood pumped through his veins as if it were going to boil. "I can't believe you. You better be glad I didn't press charges on your --. You jumped me, then left me; dead for all you know. And you expect me to waltz back in there like nothing happened? I have three cracked ribs, a black eye, and bruises all over my face. I have no intention of seeing employees or clients as long as I look like this."

"Oh snap! Did I do that?" he asked sarcastically while sounding like Steve Urkle from the *Family Matters* television show. Stephen could hear him muffling his laughter.

"Well, if you'd kept your hands off another man's wife, you might not have your pretty boy face messed up!"

"What else did you call me for? Your wife is looking for you."

"I tried calling her, but I'm sure you already knew that."

"Look, Bro, nothing is going on between Crystal and me. I don't care whether you believe me or not. She's a good woman; don't break her down like this. If you want to be mad, be mad at me. She's always been there for you, man, and you know freaking well that you haven't been treating her right for a very long time. Yeah, this is between the two of you, but now, it's between you and me too."

"Like I told her, you have no right to be calling any shots right now. Y'all started it, but I'm going to finish it. That's for sure."

"Why don't you just call her? All she wants right now is to talk to you."

"I'll bet she does." Donnie was silent for a moment, a deafening silence to Stephen. He spoke softly. "Why? Just tell me why? I don't get it."

"Donnie, do we have to get into this right now?"

"Yes, we do. You expect to wreak havoc in my life, split up my home, and then call the shots? Uh un. That's not going to happen."

Stephen asked, "Where are you staying?"

"Don't worry about it. I'm not homeless or destitute! You didn't answer my question…why?"

"Man, I can't control my heart."

"What are you saying? Do you love her?" asked Donnie.

This time Stephen was the one who was silent. "Yes. I do. I'm sorry, but I do."

"Well isn't that just lovely? My brother loves *my* wife. My wife! So what now?" he asked as if he really expected Stephen to give him a logical answer.

"Don, I don't know. The only thing I can say is that I am truly sorry, and I never meant to hurt you or Crystal. I never set out to destroy the life the two of you had together…I'm actually considering leaving town for a while."

"…And you think skipping town will solve our problems? It won't change the fact that you had sex with my wife and both of you betrayed me. Back to my original question, how long are you going to be out?"

"I'll probably be in on Monday or Tuesday."

"Good, McCarter will be here Tuesday, and he wants to meet with both of us."

"Ok."

"Later," said Donnie and hung up. Stephen sat at his desk, still dumbfounded. *What the?* He loved his brother, and knew what he'd done to him would never be forgotten. The damage was done.

He called Crystal to give her an update on the latest. Although disappointed that Donnie hadn't called her back, she figured he still needed more time before he wanted to see her. She knew it was for her own good anyway. She didn't want to be the evening news, a statistic or another victim of spousal abuse because he went off the deep end. She knew that she'd have to answer a lot of questions that she really wasn't ready to answer anyway. Yet, the waiting was killing her slowly every minute, every hour, everyday.

Chapter 33

Blind-sided

"Good morning… welcome back!" Crystal stood outside her door and greeted students as they arrived Monday morning. The halls were filled with students returning from summer break and reuniting with their friends. Several of her former students stopped by to hug her and share their summer activities.

"Hey, Miss Moore," said Tyron, a junior varsity football player.

"Well, hi, Tyron! Look at you! How could you leave here just a couple of months ago the same height I am, and come back so tall? Now, you're looking down at me. Did you take some height enhancing vitamins over the summer?" she asked while hugging the young man. He beamed a metallic smile. "And you got braces too? Check you out!"

"Yeah, I'ma pull all the shorties this year!"

"All right boy! You better keep your focus on school if you want football in your future. The time will come for that other stuff. Enjoy this time while you can."

"You sound like my mom!" he said with a smile that revealed that he wasn't used to having braces. "You right though. Good to see you, Miss Moore. I have Mr. King for homeroom, so I better go."

"Ok, take care and keep those grades up this year," she said as he continued down the hall.

Crystal didn't report to school in her usual fashion as she had so many years prior. The summer's events made this year different. In previous years, on the first day of school, Donnie prepared breakfast for her send off. He'd tell her to go shape the minds of tomorrow. Then he'd kiss her and say how proud he was of her. Today, she wondered if he could ever be proud of her again.

Stephen returned to work as planned. He called Crystal after the school day ended to report that the atmosphere in the office was business as usual.

"So, how did it go today?"

"Not bad. I came back to a lot of stuff piled up on my desk, but Donnie acted as if nothing had happened. No one said anything to me either, but then again, why would they?"

"He probably didn't want to stir the pot of office gossip, any more than it had been while you were out."

"I guess. We had a few meetings and met with a client. Everything was cool, but you know Donnie. He won't let anyone know anything; especially, when he knows they're suspicious. He's been pretty chummy with Amanda though. She's been giving me strange vibes, and I'm not going to tolerate it."

"Yeah, I had to 'read' her the other day. She didn't want me to hold when I called the office."

"Don has given her a little too much freedom. That won't be a problem much longer. She may not think so, but I'll nip that in the bud. I didn't want to make any more waves than necessary today."

"Ok, but be careful. Did you get a sense of where Donnie might be staying?"

"No, I didn't ask, and I left before he did. He and Amanda were in his office going over some invoices when I left."

"So it's not just me then? He still works late?"

"I guess."

Interesting.

Every evening that week, Stephen called her to report that everything had gone smoothly at work that day.

Two more weeks passed, and she still hadn't heard a word from Donnie. On several occasions she was tempted to stop by Moore Brothers after school. Instead, however, she respected his wishes and went home. Warily, she decided to drive by one afternoon just to see if his car was there. She parked across the street for a few minutes, but she didn't see anything except a few employees exiting the building, and Donnie and Stephen's cars parked in their usual reserved spaces.

Crystal was glad that Stephen was there to keep an eye on him. That was her only link to him. She didn't know how much longer she could hold on like this. *I wish he would tell me he's filing for a legal separation, divorce, or something. Not knowing what he's thinking is driving me crazy.*

So far, he made sure that the mortgage and utilities were paid. For years, they had arranged an automatic draft for those bills. Nevertheless, she worried about how long that would continue. She wondered about the concessions she would have to make in the near future regarding her living arrangements. Although she feared that he would stop taking care of the household expenses, she knew that Donnie was a good provider, financially. She was certain of one thing, though. It wouldn't or couldn't last too much longer. Fortunately, she had some money of her own that she always kept separate from their joint accounts. She was relieved that she had listened to her dad. He always told her to have her own stuff in case a man ever started tripping.

Crystal entered the house carrying a large stack of papers, and her briefcase as she had every other day over the last few weeks. When she put her things down on the island bar, she noticed that all of the things Donnie had purchased for their home were gone.

He's been here? He came in here and wiped the place out. She walked from room to room. *He had to have been here most of the day loading stuff. He must've had a moving truck.*

The CD cabinet was empty, and the sixty–inch, high definition, wide–screen TV that they had spent weeks trying to find, wasn't in the family room. The leather vibrating recliner chair that he had ordered from Ebay was gone, and so was the cherry dining room ensemble she died for. She went to the room he called the game room, and the pool table he never used was gone. His mother's antique wardrobe was no longer in the downstairs guest room.

She ran upstairs to their bedroom, and all of his closet space and drawers were empty. He had taken an entire shelf of towels from the linen closet. She slowly walked back downstairs to check the kitchen. *He took the Chinese wok from the kitchen cabinet? Come on, Donnie. Is all of this necessary?* The three Jonathan Green prints he bought for her five years ago from Gallery Chuma in Charleston were missing—the wall in the living room was bare.

Crystal felt sick to her stomach. She walked to the couch and fell face down, sobbing. It was the end for her. Things appeared so final, yet she hadn't heard a word from the man who still held the title of her husband. He hadn't spoken a word, not one, since he'd told her to stay away from him for a while. She guessed the "while" was over.

Sliding off the couch and onto the floor as if there wasn't a bone in her body, she dry heaved until her stomach and chest ached. She knew that the bathroom was probably the best place for her at the time, but she didn't care. Life as she knew it was over. *The end* she thought to herself, even though she'd known for months it had been over for quite some time.

Grieving the loss of her marriage, she lay prostrate on the floor and prayed to God. Her stinging eyes were red and raw once again. She begged God for mercy. "Lord, you are an awesome God, please have mercy on me," her voice quivered. "Lord, I am at the lowest point I have ever been in my life. I asked you for a mate years ago, and you answered my prayers. I always thought I would be married to Donnie for the rest of my life. Lord, you know the circumstances. I messed up. I was weak, and I'm truly sorry. I let my flesh take over because I was lonely, and I needed my husband. Lord, I realize this mess is my fault. I can't blame him for something I did." She paused, "Forgive me, please. Looking back, maybe I rushed into marriage with Donnie. Maybe he wasn't the one you were preparing for me." Tears poured from her eyes. "Could it have been Stephen all along? I have nowhere to go, but to you. I hate asking you to fix my mess. From the way things look here, my marriage is over. Help me Lord! Please, please. You are my helper and my redeemer!" She yelled out to God, pleading for mercy.

She apologized to God for not being a good wife, breaking His commandments, and not being committed. She slowly got up from the floor and thought about her past, and the future. She remembered the days of premarital counseling with the pastor of her church. He told them, "Romance draws you in. She look good to you, and he look good to you. The real question is what happens when you don't have *that* to keep your interest anymore? For the most part, marriage is about commitment. There will be bumps in the road, but that is when you'll need commitment to fall back on." *We failed miserably at that one.*

The Holy Spirit began to comfort Crystal. She felt Him telling her that He did love her unconditionally, and to lean on Him. She kept hearing *look ahead* in her spirit. She was sure it was God speaking to the depths of her soul. She knew things would probably get worse before they seemed better, but she needed to lean on Him. *Lean on Me. Lean on Me.* She didn't want to imagine the worse. How she could endure more? Yet, she knew the source of her strength.

Crystal went to her bedroom where she tried to rest in the peace that God was in control of everything, no matter how it looked. She took a long hot bath, and afterwards wrote in her journal for a while. Her last entry was when she was on the swing at Waterfront Park in Charleston. The pen glided across the pages.

Hurting
I've always guarded my heart.
I never wanted to be hurt or to hurt.
If I guard my heart, then I won't have to worry about either.
It was different with you.
When it came to you, I didn't guard my heart;
I let my guard down.
It was down for you to come in, to come in and steal.

That you did, and in an enormous way.
Now, I'm left to deal with why I have this empty space.
I wanted you to know my heart, but now that you know, my heart is broken.
It's broken because for once in my life, I didn't guard it.

Crystal didn't know whom she was writing about, Donnie or Stephen, but she couldn't stop. Another one flowed from her pen:

Warm Tears
Warm tears caress my face,
The harder I try to keep them from falling, the faster they fall.
I wish that the hurt, the pain of losing would wash away in those tears,
But it doesn't.
How can I make it all go away?
I have memories of good times, happy times.
Where did they go, or were they ever really there?
The tears are so warm, trickling down my cheek.
I wish I had someone to wipe my tears,
Someone to gently caress my face and make things better.
I know that I'm alone with my tears, no one to share them with,
No one to lean on, no one to turn to.
Most would judge my reason for crying,
Therefore, I keep it to myself.
Do you feel as I do?
Do you ever cry when you are alone, when no one is looking?
What does your heart tell you?
Do you ever cry as I do as you visit days gone by?
Deep inside, I long for so many forbidden things,
Warm tears caress my face, even as I write.

When the telephone rang, it diverted Crystal's attention from her writing. It was Sierra.

"Hey Miss Moore. This Sierra."

"Well hello, Sierra! I'm so glad to hear from you. How are you doing?" asked Crystal. She was so glad to hear from Sierra.

"I was just calling to thank you for what you did for me dat night. I'm glad somebody cared, even if my own family didn't…and… you'll never know how what you did for me dat night affected me. I'm so thankful," she said sounding as if she were tearing up.

"Sierra, it wasn't a problem," said Crystal while thinking things did go downhill for her after that night though. "It was so dangerous for you to be stopping for me out there that night," Crystal said.

"I know. I'm in foster care now, and I'll be going to school in Gaston County. I'm excited about it. My foster family is real nice, and I'm not going to do anything to mess it up either. I'd like to stay here at least until I graduate if they let me. I get to make a fresh start here." Crystal could hear happiness in her voice for the first time ever.

"That's wonderful, Sierra! I'd like if we could get together sometime soon. Maybe we could have lunch or dinner one Saturday or Sunday. I could pick you up, and we could spend the day shopping in Gastonia."

"That sounds like fun. I'll have to ask my foster mom, but I'm sure she'll say it's ok. She knows who you are because I've talked about you ever since I've been here," said Sierra. She sounded excited at the possibility. "Well, like I said," she made a smacking sound between words, "I basically called to thank you for caring about me. I've been thinking about you all summer. I also think about how the night you saved me, changed my life. I'll never forget it, Miss Moore. If I had a job, I'd buy you a present," she said.

"I'm glad I was there to help, and I'm glad that it was you when I stopped. Stay in touch, and let me know how you're doing in school this year, OK?"

"Ok, I will. You're my angel. Have a good night," said Sierra.

"Thanks for calling. You have a good night too," said Crystal hanging up the phone. "At least someone is happy with a decision I made this year," she said sarcastically out loud.

The telephone rang almost immediately after she hung up with Sierra.

"Hey baby. You always complain that we're out and you can't reach us, but we've been in town for weeks, and haven't heard a peep from you. What's going on?"

"Hi, Mom. I'm glad you called because I need to tell you something, and I don't want you to get upset, OK?"

"I can't promise that, Crystal. What's going on? You and Donnie still having problems?"

"He moved out... he left me, Mom." Crystal began crying again.

"WHAT? When did this happen? Why didn't you call me?"

"Mom, I'm going to tell you something and I don't want you to judge me because I've beat myself up enough about it."

"Go on," said Lila, almost knowing what was about to come from her daughter's mouth.

"I was with another man... Donnie found out about it." Lila was silent and Crystal began to get uncomfortable. Finally, she could hear her mother crying and praying. "Mom?"

"I'm here! Crystal, how could you? I raised you better than that." Her voice was loud and demeaning. Crystal detected hurt in her voice. "Didn't I tell you the devil is going to and fro seeking whom he can devour? Didn't I tell you that? Why did you do it, Crystal? How could you? I taught you better than that. I can't believe this. When I poured out my heart to you about what your father did all those years ago, didn't that have an impact on you? We have to beat these demons! They come to destroy, Crystal!"

Crystal slammed the phone down, not intending to be disrespectful to her mother, but she needed a break from the drama the day had provided her. She had been through enough as a result of her actions with Stephen, and she didn't feel like listening to any more negativity at the moment. She knew she'd have to call her mother back and apologize, but at the moment, she needed to cool off.

The phone rang, and she saw that it was Lila calling her back. She picked it up on the third ring. "Mom, I'm sorry. I didn't mean to be disrespectful, please forgive me."

"That had better been the first thing out of your mouth young lady, or you'd be seeing me in person real soon. I'm sorry for the way I reacted, but I was not prepared for you to tell me that you had succumbed to the demons that have tormented this family for years. Crystal, I've been praying that we'd be delivered from this. Me, my sister, our father, and only God knows who else, have been affected by this demon. Maybe the family is under a curse. It just won't give up, but we have to know when the tempter comes, and not be moved. Honey, we have to be like the tree planted by the water. I'm not going to preach because I know you, and I'm sure you've talked, talked and then some, to God. Please tell me that this was a one time thing… are you involved with someone?"

"It's Stephen."

"Jesus." She could hear the disappointment in her mother's voice. Crystal anticipated that Lila would hang up on her this time, but she didn't.

"Crystal, I'm going to pray for you and your family, just as I've been doing. Is there anything in particular you want me to cover?"

Whew, thank you, Lord. She didn't lecture me.

"I just want peace in my life, and if it's meant for Donnie and I to be together, then I ask that He fix it. Donnie is still distant, and prior to him finding out about Stephen and me, he still hadn't touched me, or said two words to me. Mom, pray for my strength and that I come out of this with my mind in tact. It's eating me alive. I know I shouldn't have done what I did, but I was weak. We both were."

"Does his wife know?"

"No, she walked out on him while we were in Charleston."

"Lord, have mercy on YOUR children."

"Mom, I'm scared. When I got home today, all of his things were gone."

"Baby, talk to God. He knows everything anyway. Talk to him, and in the meantime, if you need a shoulder to cry on or an ear to listen, just let me know. I love you, no matter what. Always remember that."

"Thanks, Mom. I knew you'd have comforting words to say. I want so much to be a woman like you."

"Chile, don't try to be like me, but be the best Crystal you can be. Do it for God because He gives nothing but the best to us. I can be there in a flash if you need me.

"No, there's no need for you to come be a part of my mess. I'll be all right. Just knowing that you are there and praying, means more than you could possibly know."

"I love you, baby."

"I love you too, Mom. I'll talk to you later."

"Bye baby."

"Bye."

Chapter 34

Forgiveness

The sound of rain splashing against the gutters outside of her bedroom window awakened Crystal. She lay in bed for a while longer before getting up, and then dressed for church. It had been several Sunday's since she'd been, and she knew that she needed to be in service. *Fail not to assemble yourselves together.*

She went downstairs to make a pot of coffee and to call Stephen to see if he wanted to go as well. She felt rather uneasy about asking him to go with her, but they had agreed to lean on each other, and to be friends through this until something happened to resolve it either way. Before she could call him, there was a knock at her front door. Crystal tied her robe, and looked through the peephole to see Stephen standing there smiling. Forgetting that the alarm system hadn't been deactivated, she opened the door. The alarm sounded loudly as she hurried to the keypad to disarm it.

"Wow, I don't think I've ever seen you move that fast," Stephen joked. He carried a bag in his hand from Bo Jangles. "I brought you some breakfast. Smells like you beat me to it though."

"No, I just started some coffee, that's all. I'm going to church; do you want to go with me?"

"Yes, I'll go, but I'll drive myself. We need to be careful. Even though we know how things stand between us right now, we don't want to arouse or add to any suspicion, if there is any."

"You're right. Did you bring me my favorite?"

"Yep, here's your artery clogging steak, egg and cheese biscuit."

"Like you eat healthy all of the time. What did you get?"

Stephen smiled and said, "The same thing."

They relocated to the kitchen and went over to the breakfast table. As Crystal pulled mugs from the cabinets, the phone rang. She saw Donnie's name on the caller ID.

"Hello?"

"Hey. Is everything ok over there?"

"Yeah, why?" she asked.

"The security company just called my cell, and said there was an alarm there. Is everything all right?"

"Oh yeah, I opened the front door before I disarmed it. Everything is fine."

"Oh, ok. Do you have a minute to talk?" asked Donnie.

"Yes." Crystal mouthed to Stephen that she was talking to Donnie, and she walked into the living room to take a seat on the couch. "I'm glad you called."

"Yeah, well I had planned to call you today anyway. It's not that I haven't wanted to talk to you, but I've been hurting, Crystal. You've hurt me deeper than I could have ever imagined. I never thought we'd go through something like this. "

"I know, and I'm truly sorry. I know that's of little consolation right now, but I am. I shouldn't have 'gone there' but I've been so lonely for months, Donnie. Actually, longer than that."

"I understand lonely, but I don't understand why him? I could even understand another man—but my brother? I'm still trying to figure that out. He and I have been close all of our lives; that's why I suggested you ride down to Charleston with him. You ruined my relationship with my brother, not to mention ours. I trusted him. I trusted you."

Crystal was silent. She didn't know what to say. She already knew all of the things Donnie was saying to her.

He continued, "I'm finally at a place where I can say all this. Can you imagine the pain I felt when I saw your reply in that instant message to Stephen? Y'all couldn't have been any crueler to me. It felt like my heart had been ripped out of my chest, Crystal."

Silence fell on the line. Crystal didn't know what to say to that either. She sat there quietly, feeling his pain. "Yeah, we had our problems, but I never imagined this. I don't think we can ever get over this."

She took a deep breath, "So what are you saying?" asked Crystal somberly. "Just tell me."

"Let's talk face to face. Are you going to be home this evening?"

"Yeah, I'll be here. Donnie, I'm so sorry."

"I'll see you at six."

Crystal hung up the phone and went back into the kitchen where Stephen was still sitting at the table drinking coffee.

"Cream and sugar right? I put some of that hazelnut stuff in yours." He noticed Crystal's demeanor had changed since talking to his brother. "Are you ok?" he asked.

"Yeah." Crystal was visibly upset. "Donnie is coming over this evening. I think he's going to ask me for a divorce."

"I'm so sorry, Crystal. I blame myself."

"Let's not talk about blame. What we did destroyed a man. I'm having a hard time with that. I've never heard him so down. But I can't change the past, so I'll just have to endure whatever the future brings. I know it's over."

"Let's eat so we can go to church."

"Thanks for breakfast."

They finished eating breakfast, and then Stephen went home to get ready for service. They drove separately, and did not sit near each other. Ironically, the Pastor's sermon was about recovering from mistakes, and living a glorious life in spite of past sins.

"I wanna make a special altar appeal for those of you who know you've sinned against God. The entire congregation should be making their way down here right now." He walked back and forth in front of the pulpit while talking on a wireless microphone. "For some, you done prayed and asked for forgiveness, but you haven't forgiven yourself. There's somebody under the sound of my voice who's been trying to recover from the past, but friends and family constantly remind you all the time of what you did or who you used to be. Come on down here right now. I'm here to tell you that Jesus is a forgiver, and a lover of your soul. He died on the cross on that dreadful day for your sins. You don't have to carry around the burden of sin. The good news is that Jesus arose on the third day for you and me. If you've asked him to forgive you, don't you believe that He did? I do. Won't you come? Meet Him here with me. Ask Him to lift the load, and cast your cares on Him. Come forward and release yourself from the grip of sin."

Several people poured into the aisles; so did Crystal and Stephen. The Pastor asked everyone to join hands for prayer. Stephen was unaware that Crystal stood behind him as he extended his hand to touch her. His eyes were closed, and all he knew was that he was holding a woman's hand. He wept openly, and the Pastor placed his hands on Stephen's head as he prayed.

"...Father, in the name of Jesus, we want to lift up this brother, and these people who have come boldly to the throne of mercy. Lord, we know not what he stands in the need of, but he needs you. Lord, ease his pain and let him know the burden is yours and yours alone. Lord, forgive him of his sins, and forgive the sins of everyone else at this altar. Let them know in their hearts that they are forgiven. Lord, please let these believers know that the enemy wants them to be bound, but there is victory in you..."

Stephen squeezed Crystal's hand so hard, it hurt. Tears ran down her face as she prayed along with the Pastor. After the Pastor had finished praying, everyone hugged Stephen and gave him encouraging words. Stephen noticed Crystal walking back to her seat and wondered if she was the woman holding his hand.

After service, Crystal saw Stephen getting in his car, and walked over to see if he was ok.

"Hey. You all right?" she asked bending down to speak to him through the window.

"Yeah, all is forgiven. He was speaking to me today, you know. Were we holding hands?"

"Yep, that was me. I walked down right after you did." He got out of the car and hugged her, thanking her for being the woman she was.

"I love you so much, and I don't mean that to be taken in a romantic way." He let go of the embrace. "I need to go. Take care, and I hope things go ok for you this evening. Call me later."

"I will. Pray for me. Better yet, pray for all of us."

"You don't even have to ask." He got back into the car, and Crystal turned in the opposite direction to find hers. Stephen passed her and tapped his car horn as he passed.

Crystal drove home and tried to prepare herself mentally for the meeting with the man who probably wouldn't be her husband much longer. She wondered where he'd been since leaving that night. There were so many questions she wanted answered. She prayed that God would protect them both, bridle their tongues, and help them to not hurt each other any further.

Chapter 35

Finally Over

Promptly at 5:59 p.m., Crystal heard his car pulling into the garage. Donnie still had his keys to the house and used the automatic garage door opener to let the garage door up. Crystal had a nervous stomach, and she hoped that she and Donnie would have a civilized conversation. She walked to the door, and opened it before he had a chance to.

"Hi," she said trying to sound calm.

"Hello," he said wiping his feet on the mat. He looked around the kitchen as if it were his first time ever being there. Then, he put his keys on the island bar as he always had in the past and walked towards the sofa in the living room. He sat down, still observing every detail of the house.

"Would you like something to drink?" she asked.

"Do you have any of that wonderful lemonade you used to make?" he asked smiling.

"No, but I do have some tea."

"Oh yeah, you make that ghetto–style sweet tea," he said with a visible smirk on his lips.

219

"Oh no you didn't!" she said smiling. "I do not! I don't have anyone needing a shot of insulin after drinking my tea."

She poured him a glass of iced tea and joined him in the living room. She sat in a wing back chair across from the sofa. He took a hearty sip of the iced tea, then his face turned serious.

"Crystal, I don't want to rehash anything here. I prefer that we talk like two rational people. More importantly, I want to leave here with a clear picture of what the future holds for us. Can we please talk like two mature adults and be completely honest?"

"Yes. I have no problem with that." She leaned forward to set her glass on the coffee table in front of the couch. "I need resolution or closure too," she said.

Donnie began. "Can you please tell me how we ended up here? I just don't understand."

Crystal took a deep breath. She didn't want Donnie to think she was blaming him for her actions. "I love you and I always will. Being apart from you is not something I wanted or ever imagined would happen when we got married. The day you proposed to me, we had dreams, big dreams. We've accomplished a lot of those dreams. Sadly, there was a huge price paid to reach those dreams.

Donnie, I have been a wife, a daughter, a graduate student, a teacher, a sister and a friend to a lot of people. I have been those things to you, and for others. Right now, I need to do something for me. I think our needs changed. Over the years, I've found things to occupy my mind, and my time in your absence. I'm so happy that you and Stephen have a successful business. That business has afforded me a lot of luxuries that I may not have had otherwise, but I needed a husband, not a benefactor. I didn't run to another man, Donnie. I didn't. I never had an inappropriate conversation with Stephen, or any other man prior to that one trip. I didn't leave here wanting to have a rendezvous with him, and there was no hidden agenda. I'd been trying to close the gap in our relationship for months, and you know it. As a matter of fact, even before April when I was out most of the night with that student, you knew there was a huge disconnect in our marriage as wide as the Grand Canyon. You do realize that this isn't a recent thing, don't you?

"Yes, I do—but not being on the same page and having an affair are two different things, Crystal. I've told you before; I work my butt off to have the things we have. You know how hard it is out there for a small business. It's hard competing with giant agencies. Not only do we do it, we're also very good at it. You knew going into this marriage that there would be times like these…" Before he could continue, Crystal interrupted.

"Uh, how can you say what I knew going into this marriage? Yes, I knew you and Stephen were going to be business partners, AND I knew that there would be no guarantees. BUT, I did not know that your going into business meant that five out of seven days a week, you'd be too busy to call home simply to see if I made it home safely. Neither did I know that calling you at the office would be a major problem, or stopping by to see my husband wasn't a good thing. I didn't know that I'd go for weeks, even months without making love to my husband who didn't just claim to love me, but also couldn't get enough of me at one time. I did not know that you wouldn't even take a second glance at me when I wore the sexy lingerie that you bought for me. I didn't know that my own husband would slowly fall out of love with me. Is there someone else, Donnie?"

He chuckled and shook his head in disbelief at her diatribe. It made Crystal furious. "So you're trying to pin this all on me?" His nostrils flared when he spoke. The same way they always did when he attempted to control his anger.

"No, I'm not. I…" He cut her off this time.

"So, Miss High and Mighty Christian commits the ultimate marital sin and has the nerve to try and blame me? Ain't this some bull?"

"Donnie, please. Don't be condescending to me! Aren't you supposed to be a Christian too? At least that's what you've told me all these years. Have you forgotten that you were to love me just as Christ loves the church, or did that slip your mind? For the life of me, I can't figure out what I did to you that caused you to disregard me totally." Her voice softened, then she said, "Prior to Charleston."

"Crystal, I don't know what to tell you. You always knew where you could reach me. No we hadn't made love in a while, but you know how many hours I've been working during the summer. By the time I got home every night, I was beat." He looked at her as if her suggestion that he should make love to her after work was absurd.

"Ok, look, we are not going to get anywhere by doing this to each other. Remember we said we were going to be civil. Why did you come over? What was the point of you coming by? You've already moved your stuff out of here, and you've been gone for weeks. Just say it, whatever it is, just say it. You want a divorce?"

"Yes." Donnie answered very quickly.

"Wow, that didn't take long," she said.

"I've had a lot of time to think about it. I just can't see myself married to a woman who claims to love God so much but then has no problem with going to bed with my brother. I deserve better."

Before Crystal realized it bubbling from deep within her, she began to sob, uncontrollably. Donnie didn't move. He was cold and unmoved by the sudden display of her emotions.

He continued, "I haven't talked to an attorney yet or anything like that. I know what I want; I just want this to be over. Abandonment, incurable insanity, and adultery are all grounds for divorce in N.C., and I think there is a one-year separation period required. If there is, then we're already well on our way!"

Crystal wiped her tears with the heel of her hand. "If that's what you want, I won't fight you."

"Did you think I wouldn't want that? What kind of man do you think I am? You really do take me to be a fool don't you? What brother in his right mind would stand for some mess like this? Do I look like I need to be on the Jerry Springer Show?"

His voice was loud and his temper rose. Crystal had never seen him that frustrated before. He stood up, walked across the room towards her and stood over her. Menacingly, he looked down at her, "I should have killed that sorry brother of mine, and you sit there talking about 'if that's what I want.' Humph! I, never mind… It's not worth it." He turned and walked towards the kitchen as if to leave, then stopped. "Hold up, what I'm getting upset for? You both did me a favor. Happiness is right around the corner for me. What's the scripture?" He snapped his fingers a few times trying to remember. "Uh, weeping may endure for a night, but joy comes in the morning? Well, *Joy* is going to come. That's for sure!"

Crystal wondered what had happened to the man who had been so full of the spirit years ago. He was so empty now and had been for a very long time. She wondered if his faith in God was gone, and what had happened to make him this way all along. She blamed herself for pushing him over the edge, whatever edge that was.

"Donnie, what's going on with you? Please, if this is truly over, please just tell me where and when things went so wrong for you."

He walked towards the door and opened it. He turned before walking out.

"I'll be making an appointment with an attorney this week if I can get a referral. Also, since my name is on the mortgage loan and I've been the one making payments, I'm moving back into my house. You are the one who crossed the line and took matters into your own hands. Since *you* are the one who went outside of our marriage, why don't you find a place to stay? A real man doesn't leave his home. I'll give you until the end of the month to get something arranged." He turned and walked through the door, then yelled back from the garage, "Maybe Stephen will help you out!"

Crystal sat in the chair in disbelief. She had never seen Donnie so distant or so mean. She heard the garage door and his car start. He backed out quickly, and then the garage door went down again. Immediately, she felt the need to pray for his safety in reaching his destination. She wondered where he had been staying, but was afraid to really know the truth. She thought of several possibilities, but tried to put them out of her mind. The thought of him being with another woman made her feel sick. Donnie probably felt the same way.

Chapter 36

Another Mad Dash

An hour later, she was still sitting in the same chair. She thought about the possibilities; *a new home and a new life*. That didn't help much because the pain of the impending divorce was unbearable. It hit her hard, and she could only blame herself this time. Anticipating the worse, she'd previously made a few notes on a note pad about various places to live. She knew that there were several condominiums that she could afford. She found them in a realty magazine that she picked up at Harris Teeter. She'd begin her search Monday after school. She didn't want to get into a big drawn out mess with Donnie over property. Sure, she loved her home and remembered the day that they first looked at it. She told Donnie, that it was the one, and they made an offer on it the same day. Donnie knew what was technically hers in the house, that's why he took things out that he knew were not hers. She hoped the transition would be a smooth one—that is, at least as smooth as possible.

The phone rang, jolting her back to the present. She darted up from her chair to answer.

"Thank God. Crystal?" It was Stephen.

"Hi. How are you?" she asked in a very quiet voice.

"I'm ok. How'd it go with Donnie? I saw him pull out a while ago. I've been waiting for you to call. I got worried when I didn't hear from you. Is everything ok?"

"Stephen, he wants a divorce, and he wants me out of the house by the end of the month. He's very bitter and violently angry."

"Did he threaten or touch you?" She could hear anger rising in his voice.

"No, but he got very angry and crossed the room to where I was sitting. I got worried for a minute." She told him what had happened between them and how condescending he was to her.

"I'm so sorry. Want some company?"

Ding Dong. Crystal's doorbell rang.

"You expecting somebody?"

"No," she said.

"Hold up, let me look out to see who it is." He walked across the room to his window. "Crystal, there's a police car in your driveway. I'm walking out the door right now." They both hung up, and Crystal walked to the front door, peeked out, and saw a uniformed officer. She opened the door just as Stephen reached the front yard. The officer wore a tag that said "Chaplain."

"Good evening, Ma'am. Is this the home of Donnie Moore?"

"Yes, why?" Stephen reached the front door. "Come on in, Stephen. This is my husband's brother."

"Misses Moore is it?"

"Yes." *At least for the time being she thought.*

"Ma'am, I'm here to inform you that your husband has been involved in a single car accident. He's been airlifted to Carolina's Medical Center downtown. It's pretty serious."

"Oh my God!" Crystal felt like she had been hit by a ton of bricks.

"I can take her to the hospital, officer. Thank you," said Stephen. "Crystal, get your things. I need to run back home and lock up. Meet me right here, OK?"

"OK," she said. She felt like she was in a daze. She was living a very bad dream and couldn't seem to wake up from it.

Stephen followed the officer back to his patrol car. Panic filled his body. "Officer, is he?"

"No. He was unconscious when the medics left with him though. He lost control of his car on a rural part of Hwy 51. Apparently, he ran off the road and overcorrected. Witnesses say the car skidded off the road, hit a bale of hay, a mobile home, and finally a tree, over a hundred yards away from the main road. Officer Carlowe was the first one on the scene. He is completing his report right now, and should be at the hospital by the time you get there. Go to the emergency room, and they'll get you to the trauma unit. I'm sorry, sir."

Trauma? "Thank you," said Stephen as he broke out into a sprint toward his house, despite his soreness. He ran inside, grabbed his keys, a light jacket and turned the television off. He jumped in his car and backed out the driveway faster than he ever had before. *OK, big brother, slow down.*

Crystal scurried around looking for her keys and purse. She put on her shoes and quickly opened the door just as Stephen pulled into the driveway. She ran to the car. Once again she was on a mad dash to a hospital to see a Moore brother. This time it was the one whom she had proclaimed to have and hold until death they did part. She wondered if that time had come sooner rather than later. *How much did the Chaplain really know?*

They both were quiet as Stephen drove. His mind raced, and guilt filled his body as he thought of the terrible wrong he had bestowed on his brother. He couldn't imagine anything that ever would have prepared him for the last few months of his life. Tears ran down his face as he took Crystal's hand in his. She burst into tears for the second time in an hour.

"This must be what God meant when he told me to lean on him," she said.

"We must be strong, no matter what. We must be strong." His grip was tight around her hand. "We must be strong…" Stephen's words drifted off as he cried, shaking his head. "The police officer said he ran off the road and the car flipped several times before hitting a tree off Hwy 51."

"Oh Donnie!" cried Crystal. "He was so angry when he left. This is all my fault. I shouldn't have let him leave like that."

Still weeping, Stephen managed to laugh a little. "Now you know you can't keep a grown man from doing what he wants to do—especially when he wants to leave. You and I both know that wouldn'a been a pretty sight!"

She forced herself to smile at the thought. "Yeah, you right," she said wiping her nose.

They pulled into the emergency parking lot at Carolina's Medical Center and followed the signs to trauma.

"Stephen, I don't feel like doing this again. I feel like I've done it before."

He pulled into a parking space and ran around the car to open the door for her. "Remember what I said, we must be strong. We have no choice. Whatever is going to happen...well, we don't have the power to change destiny if something was already going to happen. We can't control it, but God is still in control. Come on, he needs us." *Thanks, Lord; I needed those words for myself.*

Inside, a triage nurse escorted them to the trauma unit. A doctor pulled the curtain as they approached.

"This is Dr. Pearson. He's a trauma specialist. Doctor, this is Mr. Moore's wife and brother."

"Good evening. Mr. Moore is resting right now. We have him heavily medicated to help relieve the pain. I am waiting for a report from the radiologist to see just where and how severe the injuries are. We have an idea, but don't want to speculate."

Stephen asked, "Has he been conscious at all?"

"Yes, he's been in and out of consciousness; mostly incoherent mutterings though. You can go in for a few minutes, but right now I'll need for you to stay in the waiting area until I get the radiology reports and review them. At that time, I should have a clear prognosis."

"Can you give us your opinion right now based on what you can see?" asked Crystal.

"I really can't say. The accident was pretty serious. Sometimes what looks pretty bad to man isn't that way at all to God. If you know the power of prayer, get busy until I speak to you again." He turned and walked in the opposite direction, his white lab coat flapping behind him.

"This doesn't sound good at all," Crystal said. Stephen put his arm around her shoulder to comfort her. They walked to the waiting area, and took a seat near a small television. Headline News channel was on, and several people were gathered around watching a Texas town prepare for a hurricane that was due to hit the next day.

"Do you want something to eat or drink?" asked Stephen.

"No."

"I need something. I'll be right back. Will you be ok?" he asked reluctant to leave her, but hard pressed to make a phone call.

"I'll be fine. Go ahead."

An elderly lady sitting across from Crystal commented on the disaster that would be tomorrow's news in Texas. Crystal shook her head acknowledging the woman's comment, but thinking of her own devastation at the moment. *Lord, let your will be done. Let your will be done in Jesus' name. I know you are in control of this and every situation. Amen.*

"Stephen walked in the opposite direction of the vending machines and went outside to call Melissa on his cell phone. He brought her up to speed as to what had happened that day, and she promised that she'd be there as soon as she could get a few items packed. He also asked her to call Crystal's parents in Pittsburgh. Melissa said she would.

Stephen went back inside, purchased a cup of coffee, and joined Crystal in the waiting area.

"Did you get lost?" she asked.

"No. I made a phone call," he said. "I called Melissa for you, and I told her to call your parents. She said she would, and she's on her way."

"Thank you," she said, and he put his arm around her shoulder again. Visibly looking for someone specific, a Mecklenburg County police officer entered the waiting room. He walked toward Stephen and Crystal. "Good evening ma'am, sir. Are you the family of an auto accident victim?"

"Yes, I'm Stephen Moore, and this is my sister-in-law, Crystal. She's Donnie's wife."

"I'm sorry you're having to go through this tonight, but I wanted to let you know what happened." He flipped through several papers attached to the clipboard he held in his left hand. He read word for word from the police report.

"An eyewitness says he observed vehicle #1 traveling at a high rate of speed, outbound state highway 51 in Pineville. An eyewitness advised he observed vehicle #1 lose control and skid off the road. The vehicle had 120 feet of yaw marks before it hit the shoulder of the road. The vehicle went fifty feet before it struck a bale of hay. The vehicle continued another sixty feet before running completely through an abandoned mobile home. The vehicle went another forty-five feet before finally striking a large tree. The driver was transported to Carolina's Medical Center for treatment." He looked up from his report. "Ma'am, the car was literally wrapped around the tree. If eyewitnesses hadn't called, I don't know if we'd be standing in this part of the hospital right now."

"Thank you," said Crystal wiping away tears with the back of her hand.

"Here's my business card in case you need anything. You can also call the number at the bottom to see the car, and retrieve any personal belongings that may still be inside. If you need anything, just call that number. If I'm not available, someone at the station can help you. My thoughts and prayers are with you.

"Hey, thanks again officer," said Stephen as he reached out to shake officer Carlowe's hand. The officer exited the waiting area just as Dr. Pearson walked in. He looked around the room, and Stephen waved his hand to get his attention. They both walked in the direction of the man who would tell them the fate of Donnie's future.

"Let's step into the room over there where we can talk privately," he instructed. They walked across the room and into a small, family conference room. Stephen and Crystal took their seats, and Dr. Pearson put x-ray pictures on a light board. "Here's what's going on," he began. He pointed at black and white blobs while he spoke. "Your husband has a ruptured spleen, a bruised kidney, and a liver laceration." He turned around and faced them. "He could have a cardiac contusion...a bruised heart. These injuries have caused severe internal bleeding, and he's lost a lot so far. Medical management and transfusion is needed. We are transfusing blood now, and he is stabilizing, somewhat."

"Are you going to have to operate tonight? What does all of this mean?" asked Crystal.

"At this point all we can do is try to keep him as comfortable as possible and see what happens. The risk of surgery outweighs the benefit at this point. He shouldn't be in any pain right now with the amount of medication he's been given. Right now, we have to keep a close eye on him for fear of cardiac arrest. When the heart is bruised like it is… Well, let's just say we need to keep on praying for him. There are many scenarios that could happen. We need to get him stabilized first, then go from there. These situations can be touch and go. I'm very sorry. He's in the right place here. We'll do all we can for him."

"Is he brain dead?" asked Crystal.

"No, in fact, his head is fine. It's all of the other things going on at the same time that place this young man in danger. The body is a self-healing machine. However, when something as traumatic as this happens, our 'circuits' so to speak, get overloaded, and sometimes shuts us down."

"So what are you saying? Just be straight with us, is he going to die, or do we have hope?" she asked.

"Ma'am, I'm sorry. You probably should go ahead and call your family. But, God is a doctor too," he said. "I can't give you false hope, but I have seen my share of miracles around here too."

"No! No! No! This can't be happening, this can't be happening," she shouted shaking her head back and forth. Stephen wrapped his arms around her, and held her tightly in his arms. Dr. Pearson left the room to give them a moment of privacy. They cried together deeply. Crystal could feel her legs getting wobbly, and she fell to the floor. Stephen tried his best to help her stand up, but he was just as unsteady as she was. Finally, he just gave up trying to make his body do something it didn't want to do, and joined her. They sat on the floor of the family conference room holding each other for the next few minutes.

Dr. Pearson returned to let them know Donnie had opened his eyes, but his condition was still critical. They struggled to get up from the floor, and supported each other as they stood. They tried to gain their composure before walking out and back through the waiting area. He escorted them to a room in the intensive care unit. Donnie's eyes were open and looked very hazy as if life were slowly leaving its present home. They had him connected to a myriad of machines. He couldn't sit up or move if he wanted to, certainly not without pulling out or setting something off. There were wires and cords draped everywhere. The beeping EKG machine announced his heart rhythms and an automatic blood pressure cuff took his pressure. Stephen and Crystal approached the bed. He had large IV's in the bend of each arm. He lay flat on his back with an oxygen mask covering his mouth and nose. Crystal walked to one side of the bed and Stephen to the other. They both looked at the man that they'd hurt so badly; tears ran down both their faces.

Crystal looked at him lying there bruised and battered, knowing that this might be the last time she saw him alive. She touched his shoulder and caressed his face. "Donnie, can you hear me?" Donnie's eyes looked directly at her. He moved his head slightly to indicate, yes.

"That's good. Don't try to speak." She took his hand in hers. "I'm so sorry for the pain I've caused you. I really am." A tear from her eye dropped onto the back of his hand. She gently wiped it off with her other hand. She could feel his grip tighten slightly.

He tried to speak through the oxygen mask. Crystal and Stephen leaned in to hear him. "I for..." He couldn't get the words out.

"Please honey, don't try to speak," Crystal told Donnie.

"I fffor---give."

Stephen instructed, "It's ok man, don't..."

Donnie cut him off once again, "you both," he finally got out. His face grimaced as he spoke. He looked determined to say more.

"He said he forgives us, Stephen." Donnie shook his head slightly in agreement.

"Thanks Don. I love you, man." Stephen touched his brother's other hand. "Do you hurt? Can you feel any of this?" Stephen looked at Donnie then over at the equipment he was connected to. Donnie moved his head slowly from side to side to say no.

He tried to speak again. The words came laboriously, and Crystal and Stephen leaned in even closer to hear what he strained to tell them. "He... loves... you... love... him... too... I'm... ok... with... it." He paused, and then swallowed. "I... must... say... this... I love both of you." Another pause. "Amanda... I... messed... up... too... Amanda... baby." His speech was breathy, and he couldn't speak anymore. Crystal and Stephen looked at each other trying to figure out what he was talking about.

"Donnie, I'm Crystal, not Amanda." *Why would he think I'm Amanda? We aren't even the same color!*

"Maybe he's delirious," said Stephen. Donnie looked at Crystal, then at Stephen. He held his glance with Stephen the longest. Stephen sandwiched Donnie's hand between his, being careful not to move the pulse oximeter that was on his index finger. He kissed his brother's hand, "Man, I love you. Don, hang in there, man." Stephen squeezed his eyes shut. "I love you, and I'm so sorry for the pain I've caused you." A tear rolled from the corner of Donnie's eye, and disappeared onto the pillow. The tears Stephen held back all rolled out of his eyes at once. "I need you man, don't leave me."

Donnie managed to get out, "Take... care... Crystal... Amanda... baby," then his eyes closed, and the machines in the room went into a frenzy. Stephen and Crystal looked at each other in horror. Hospital personnel rushed into the room, and asked them to step out into the hall. Dr. Pearson ran into the room, and rushed past the two of them.

Stephen and Crystal knew what had just happened, but neither of them wanted to say anything until the doctor came back out to confirm it. They could hear packages being ripped open, cabinet doors opening and shutting, and equipment being moved around inside the room.

They stood holding each other until Dr. Pearson walked back out. The look on his face said it all.

Chapter 37

Say It Ain't So

Melissa arrived in Charlotte shortly after midnight. She called Stephen's cell with no luck. Futilely, she tried to reach Crystal. Her voice mail picked up immediately. She decided to go to Crystal's house to see if there was a note or any indication as to what she should do. When she arrived, she saw a light on in the front of the house. *Uh oh, please let that light be on because she forgot to turn it off.* Hurriedly, she pulled into the driveway, and left the car running while she walked to the porch to see if there were any signs of life inside. When Stephen opened Crystal's door, she knew.

"Lord, no!" she cried out. Stephen nodded his head in agreement confirming that her assumption was correct. She stepped inside the house and ran to Crystal. "Oh baby, I'm so sorry." She wept loudly as she held her best friend in her arms.

"Oh Melissa…Melissa!" Overcome with grief, Crystal spoke haltingly. "Thank God…we made…it." Then, the words poured out. "We saw him and were with him when he died. He said he forgave us. What are we going to do?" she wailed. Her entire body shook with sobs forcing their way up from the pit of her stomach like molten lava erupting from a volcano.

It was too much for Stephen. He couldn't take the raw emotion any longer, and exited the front door without saying a word. Once outside, he opened Melissa's car door, and removed her keys from the ignition. He sat in the driver's seat and leaned forward resting his head on the steering wheel. He wanted to pray, but too many thoughts short-circuited his brain waves. He couldn't think of what words to say, but he knew he needed to for his own sake, as well as Crystal's. His eyes burned from the tears that cascaded down his cheeks like torrents of rain against a windowpane. His vision was blurry, and he could barely make out the purple and yellow pansies Crystal had planted in a large pot beside the garage.

"Lord, I don't know where to begin. This morning at church I prayed for forgiveness, and I forgave myself for my sins. I heard everything the Pastor said, and I received it and hid it in my heart. Today was supposed to be a day of new beginnings, right? This was the day that things would turn around for this family and me. Now something else tragic has happened. How long will these storms continue; how long is this supposed to last? Lord, I messed up. Now, my brother lies across town in the morgue, and his wife is in there mourning the loss of her marriage and husband all in the same day." He broke down and began to cry aloud again, angry and saddened at the same time. Overburdened with the pain of sorrow, he felt like he was reaching the end of his rope, and he wanted it to be over. "WHY?" he yelled out, his gaze seemingly piercing the roof of the car? He beat the dashboard with both his fists over and over. He punched harder and harder until it didn't hurt anymore. He knew he was out of control, but he couldn't stop. His mind urged him to stop, but he wouldn't. Finally, he punched so hard that he heard a cracking sound and blood oozed through his skin's surface at the same time. His brain triggered signals to remind him that he was in pain, and he stopped. Both hands throbbed as he cried and begged God to let the pain end and the healing begin for his life… and his hands.

"So how are you coping?" Melissa asked Crystal as they sat down.

"I… I don't know. We haven't been here that long," she said wiping her eyes and nose with a tissue. "One minute, he was here telling me he wanted a divorce and he wanted me out of the house, and the next he's…he's…gone." She started bawling again. "This is just too much for me to handle. God said he'd never make our burdens too heavy, but my back is breaking, you hear me? It's breaking."

"You're exhausted. Come on, let's try to get some rest; you know the next few days will be busy. Is there anyone you need to contact? Have you called Aunt Lila?" asked Melissa.

"No, we haven't called anyone. I need to call her, and probably Amanda so she can notify people at the office. Donnie said something about her before he died. It didn't make sense. I thought he was calling me Amanda. It was like he was trying to give us some kind of message. Although I couldn't decipher it, I know that he thought of her like family," said Crystal.

"Well, why don't you call Aunt Lila and tell her what happened. I called her after Stephen called me from the hospital. She said they'd be praying for you and him. She also said to keep them posted. I told her to stay put until we found out more information. Do you have Amanda's phone number? I'll call her."

Crystal told her to check with Stephen for her number. Melissa left the house in search of Stephen. She noticed that her car wasn't running anymore, and her keys were gone. Seeing a light at his house, she walked in that direction. She opened the front door without knocking and saw broken mirror glass scattered on the floor. Stephen was there—in front of the pile on his knees.

"Stephen!" cried Melissa. "What happened?"

"I broke it. I broke it. I broke it!" His lower lip quivered as he spoke and he covered his face with hands. "Just like I've broken everything, and everybody else in this family."

"OH MY GOD! Look at your hands! Stephen, you're bleeding."

"I know. I didn't do that here. I kinda took out my frustrations on your car's dashboard. I'll pay for any damages. I don't remember there being any though. I'm sorry."

She knelt beside him. "Come on. Now is not the time for this. Get up. Let's get you cleaned up." She extended her hand to help him up. Where are the washcloths? You need to clean your hands and put some antibiotic ointment on the open wounds. I'll get you some ice."

"I can't get up right now," he said wallowing in self-pity.

"Stephen, get up. This isn't about you right now. You need to get the swelling down, or you'll be in so much pain, you won't be able to help Crystal, and she really needs you right now. Come on. We need to stick together like the family we are, and we need to lean on each other. You're over here; she's over there; that's division. You need to be strong. Ask God for strength. You can and will do this. There *is* no choice in this matter. Now get up, or I'ma have to find your belt!"

He looked at her with gratefulness, his eyes puffy from all the weeping. He went upstairs to find a washcloth, antibiotic ointment and bandages.

Melissa rummaged through his kitchen cabinets in search of freezer bags to put ice in. She found them in a drawer next to the refrigerator, and filled a bag with several ice cubes. Stephen walked into the kitchen holding the items Melissa had instructed him to get. She motioned for him to sit down at the kitchen table where she cleaned and bandaged his hand for him.

"Keep this on your right hand. It's swollen pretty badly. I certainly hope you didn't break it. Oh yeah, what do you mean you took out your frustrations on my dashboard? You know what? Don't answer that right now…I came over here to ask you for Amanda's phone number. Crystal said we should call her. Do you have it?"

"Yeah, look in my Palm Pilot on the bar. Her last name is Bostwick."

"Ok, I'll just take it back over to the house. Grab a few things you'd be comfortable in and come on. You ought to stay over there with us, because you don't need to be over here alone. Do you know how to reach Pam?"

"No, not right off, but I'm sure her sister knows where she is. I have a feeling that they're in Virginia together. I have her cell phone number."

Stephen did what Melissa told him to do, and he was glad he had someone to think and to pull things together for him.

"Should I just wait until the morning to call Amanda?" Melissa asked as they crossed the street.

"No, I'll call her. I'd feel better calling her anyway," said Stephen. He opened Crystal's front door and went into the kitchen to use the phone. Crystal stood there pouring a glass of tea.

"Did you talk to Aunt Lila?" asked Melissa.

"Yeah," she said they'd be here some time tomorrow afternoon. She took it pretty hard. Dad took the phone from her and told me he'd see me as soon as they could get some things together and get on the road."

Stephen reluctantly dialed Amanda's number. She picked up on the first ring. "What the heck are you still doing there?" she asked.

"Huh? Amanda, this is Stephen."

"Oh hi, Stephen. I'm sorry. I thought you were D– I mean someone else."

"Obviously. Um, I have some terrible news, Amanda. It's Donnie..." Realizing that he couldn't control his emotions any longer, he set the phone down. Melissa heard him and ran over, taking the phone away from him.

"Hello? Amanda?"

"Who is this? What's going on? What's wrong with Donnie, what's wrong?" she screamed into the phone.

"He was killed tonight. There was a car accident," said Melissa. She began to cry as well.

"No!" Amanda screamed to the top of her lungs. "You're lying, you're lying. No! Liar! You're a liar! Why are you doing this? Huh? Why?" Amanda became hysterical, and slammed the phone down.

"Alrighty then." Melissa shook her head, and then stuck her index finger in her ear to indicate that her ears were ringing. "Well, that didn't go over well at all. She started screaming and called me a liar. She asked me why we doing this to her, and then slammed the phone down in my ear. God, please give all of us strength. Give us strength," she muttered

"She was Donnie's best buddy at the office. She's been there for a while and she practically ran the place when Donnie and Stephen were out of the office," explained Crystal.

"Yeah, Don was more chummy with her than I though. She's a trip…keeps the office alive…always talking about that darn dog of hers. She needs a man!" he said smiling and thinking about Amanda's behavior in the office.

Desperately wanting to relax, they all changed into comfortable clothes and moved into the living room. Melissa stretched out on the loveseat, and Stephen made his bed on the firm couch.

Crystal didn't feel like lying down and chose to rest on the recliner she'd purchased since Donnie took the vibrating one. Thirty minutes after they had turned out the lights and everyone had entered the early phases of sleep; there was a persistent knock at the door. Disoriented and groggy, Stephen stumbled towards the door. "What in the world?" he said looking through the peephole.

Crystal sat up in the recliner squinting her eyes. "Who is it?"

"Amanda."

"Huh?" she said quickly lifting the sheet to uncover herself. "Poor girl."

He opened the door. "Hey Amanda. You didn't have to come way over here," he said rubbing his eyes.

"Where is he? I said where is he?" she said demandingly as she pushed past him. Her face was flushed and she had mascara smeared around her eyes.

"Amanda! Well, why don't you come on in?" Stephen said curtly. He was not only frustrated by her rudeness, but also irritated that he'd been awakened from a good sleep. He didn't have the energy to deal with another person trying to come to terms with Donnie's death. As she looked around the room, she saw Melissa asleep on the couch and Crystal curled up on the reclining chair with a somber look on her face. Gripping her purse and jacket, she crossed the room and sat down opposite Crystal.

"Hi Amanda," said Crystal. "That's my sister, Melissa. She's the one you spoke to on the phone. Listen, we're sorry that we woke you up so late, but we felt you needed to know. Donnie thought of you as family."

"So, this *is* for real? You really want me to believe Donnie is dead?" Her voice became increasingly louder as she asked the questions. Melissa stirred under her covers and slowly opened her eyes. Amanda shook her head rapidly back and forth in disbelief while still mumbling the word "no". Melissa imagined that she'd done the same thing when they were on the phone.

"Why are you saying this? Why don't you just tell me where he is," she screamed. "No, I don't believe this. I just don't. I love Donnie too much. This just can't be." Inquiringly, Stephen and Melissa's eyes met across the room. However, Crystal appeared unfazed by her proclamation.

Stephen tried to offer an explanation. "He was apparently driving too fast this evening on Hwy 51 near Pineville and ran off the road. The police officer's report stated that there were witnesses who saw what happened, and no one else was involved. They airlifted him to Carolina's Medical, and he lived long enough to talk to Crystal and me. He suffered a heart attack because of the injuries he suffered in the wreck. He had a critically bruised heart and a lacerated liver. The trauma was too much for him. Don't you live off Hwy 51?"

"Yeah…" she said as if her mind were a million miles away. "Do you know where he was headed or where he was coming from?" she asked.

Crystal spoke up. Her voice was dry and raspy, "He had been here earlier. It wasn't too long after he left that the officer showed up."

Amanda put her hand over her mouth and spoke, "I'm going to be sick!" She quickly stood, looking for a place to go before her dinner and anything else that felt like making an appearance disgorged. Stephen quickly pointed to the powder room door that was beside the coat closet. Amanda ran in, and they all heard her empty her stomach.

"I knew she'd take it hard," said Crystal.

"I'll say," said Melissa, looking at Stephen. Stephen returned the gaze with raised eyebrows to imply that he knew of nothing out of the ordinary, but he did pick up on Amanda's vibes.

After a few moments Amanda re-entered the room, looking far worse than she did when she first arrived.

"You look very pale," said Melissa. "Do you need anything?"

"No, I'm getting out of here. I...I can't stay any longer. I'm sorry. I...just can't do this. I gotta go," she said walking speedily toward the door.

"Wait, did you drive yourself here?" asked Stephen. "You shouldn't leave in this condition," he said.

"I'm dealing with a lot right now, Stephen. This is too much. I'm overwhelmed. I just need to get out of here," she said.

"Be careful out there." He walked her to the door.

"Ok," said Amanda.

"Amanda, I know you probably have a lot on you right now, but I have a request. Will you please open up the office and tell everyone to assemble in the conference room? Then, call me on my cell, and I'll talk to everyone."

"Yeah, I can do that, I guess. I don't know how long I'll be able to stay, Stephen." She let go a flood of tears, which flowed like little streams all down her face. The front of her shirt was wet from tears.

"That's ok. After the conference call, record a general message about the office being closed due to the untimely death of one of the owners. After that, you should be able to leave, plus the clients can call their reps directly. Just put the phone on auto attendant."

"Good-bye, Amanda." Crystal and Melissa said in unison.

"Bye," she said softly and turned to walk out of the door.

Stephen gave her a comforting hug before she exited, and then she left. Outside they heard her empty her stomach again.

"Poor girl," said Stephen. "She's alone and has no family here. She and Donnie had a great working relationship. She's probably hurting just as much as we are right now.

Chapter 38

Ashes to Ashes

The next few days exhausted Crystal, Stephen and Melissa. Melissa tried to keep things flowing around the house while Crystal and Stephen tended to the funeral arrangements.

Crystal was at her wits end trying to figure out where Donnie had been staying the past few weeks. She searched her mind for hints in their last conversation, but couldn't remember anything. She needed access to his important papers as well as his personal items. She had no idea where he had been or where he might have kept his things. She imagined he'd put the large items into storage someplace, but she didn't know where to begin to look. No one at the office seemed to know where he'd been either. Crystal debated going down a list and calling all the storage facilities in the area to find out if he had a rental unit.

Stephen was especially grief-struck; he was distraught over the fact that he was the last living member of his family. His mother and father had been deceased for years, and now his only sibling was gone. He felt like life couldn't have dealt him a more devastating blow. He tried as best he could to maintain his composure for Crystal, but it was very difficult.

Crystal's mother and father arrived in town the next day just as they had planned. They stayed at the house with Crystal and Melissa. People with tons of food and drink, poured in all day. Donnie's friends and fraternity brothers from college came into town for the funeral, and they stayed up late the day before the funeral reminiscing about college parties and old acquaintances.

Stephen was able to reach Pam's sister in Virginia, and his instincts were right. Pam had been staying with her since she left. Pam apologized for leaving the way she did, and they talked about the separation process. Stephen apologized profusely for the way he'd mistreated her over the years; he repeatedly said that she deserved better. She forgave him, and said she wouldn't make life harder for either of them by trying to fight him in court. She explained that she just wanted a fresh start and a chance at happiness with a man who would love her the way she deserved to be loved. They ended the conversation on a positive note. Without making accusations they agreed to file for divorce at the end of the twelve-month separation period.

The funeral director came by the evening before the funeral to review the last minute details of the service. Crystal, her parents, Stephen, and Melissa, proofread the program and gave their stamp of approval.

On the day of the funeral, Stephen's aunt and uncle from his mother's side of the family arrived at the house. All of the employees from Moore Brothers piled into the living room, and each one hugged and kissed Crystal. Several of them cried as they spoke of Donnie and their memories together. A short light skinned woman, looking around as if lost, entered the room. Noticing her bewilderment, Melissa went to see if she could be of any help.

"Hi," said the woman. "Are you Misses Moore?"

"No, I'm her sister. She's over there." Melissa pointed her out.

"Thank you." She made her way through the small groups of people.

"Misses Moore, my name is Robin Jones, and I'm Sierra's foster mom. We heard about your husband's death and had to come."

Crystal began to cry. "Thank you for coming. Is Sierra here?"

243

"No, she had a project due today that her teacher wouldn't let her reschedule. They had to present their projects to the class. I know you have a hundred and one things to do, but I wanted to personally give you this. Sierra talks about you all the time and says you saved her life. I think she would have tried to kill herself if you hadn't helped her. She told me how you liked to write poetry, and she wrote this for you. She made me promise to personally put it in your hand." Robin handed Crystal a small envelope adorned with sunflowers.

"Thank you, Robin," she said and hugged the woman. "Sierra is a very special young lady."

"I know. I can see her potential, even if she can't. I pray that things will work out, and she'll be able to stay for a long time. She's going to church for the first time ever, and I'm going to try to pour blessings into her spirit."

"Me too. Thanks for coming. I'll call Sierra when things settle down."

"I'll let her know. I believe she wrote our number on the other side of the envelope. She'll be glad to hear from you."

Crystal slipped the envelope in her purse and went to the restroom to check her make-up. She hated wearing all black and wondered whose idea it was to start that tradition anyway. She checked her face, pulled the envelope from her purse, and then opened it. She smiled at the thought of Sierra writing poetry. She smiled again because in spite of all the things that had happened during the year, something positive had occurred. Moreover, she had a direct impact on the course of events in Sierra's life, and things were still going well. It was confirmation that she had done the right thing that night, regardless of her husband's feelings about it. That night, Sierra was reborn, but Crystal began to slowly die.

The only thing written on the paper was a poem entitled *Stairway to Heaven*. She could hear Sierra's voice as she read the words.

No more worries—no more pain.
He will be missed, and things won't be the same.
In a place where there's no more dying.
In a place where there's no more crying.

God is smiling on the family and sees them in mourning.
But you must know that joy comes in the morning.
He saw his name in the Book of Life,
No longer does he have to endure suffering or strife.
He has lived his life so to tell his story,
He is now gone to be with the Lord in glory.
Physically, he is gone...
But spiritually, he is in his eternal home.

"You go, girl! What a difference a few months and a positive influence can make." Crystal said out loud feeling more than proud of Sierra. She folded the paper and stuffed it back inside the envelope. Placing the envelope back inside her purse, she made a mental note to stick it inside her journal later on.

The limousine driver pulled in front of the house at 10:00 a.m. in anticipation of the 11:00 a.m. service. The funeral director gathered everyone around, and went over the procedures for entering the church, seating arrangements, and the repast slated to follow the services in the church fellowship hall.

Stephen spoke low but Melissa and Crystal could still hear him. "Why do they talk like that? Talking all soft and slow like we're complaining of the noise level or something. When they order a Big Mac combo, do they still talk like that? It bothers me. I don't want to be spoken to like I'm about to die. Talk to me with some life in your voice." Melissa tapped him on the arm to get him to hush. "I'm just sayin though..." This time Crystal hit him. "Look ladies, ain't gone be too much more of this hittin up in here." He folded his arms and continued to listen to the funeral director speak. "His voice just irritates the heck out of me," he grumbled under his breath.

When the time came to leave for the church, Crystal and Stephen rode in the limo along with Melissa, their parents, and Amanda, per Stephen's request.

During the eulogy, the Pastor spoke wonderful words about life cycles and dying young. He sensed that something had been going on with Donnie, since he hadn't been to church in a very long time. The message was very fitting and relevant. Had Donnie been there, he would have thought the same. There wasn't much weeping during the service, and the family was very grateful. Crystal had done her share of weeping over the last few days and months for that matter.

After the burial at the cemetery, the family reassembled at the church for the family meal. More people returned to the church to offer condolences and advice on how to move forward. Crystal had taken enough advice from older widowed women to last her a lifetime. She yearned for a change; she'd be so happy to get back to some sense of normalcy, whatever that was.

The ride home was long and quiet. Everyone felt drained and ready for some rest. The limo driver took everyone back to the house and placed the assorted flowers and cards inside.

"It was a lovely ceremony," said Melissa.

"Yes, it was. Donnie would have been pleased," said Crystal. "I'm so tired, and feel like I could sleep for days. Tomorrow, I must take care of some financial matters, and find a way to learn where he had been recently. Maybe I could hire someone to help me."

"Just let me know what you need honey," said Melissa.

"Right now, I need to sleep—sleep for a long time. Hopefully, when I wake up, this nightmare of a life will be over."

Her parents entered the room. "Sweetheart, your father and I are going to get on the road. I hate to leave so soon, but your father has a doctor's appointment tomorrow, and we need to get back before that big storm hits the northeast. I can come back in about two weeks to help you with whatever you need."

"That's fine, Mom. Thank you for coming. I'm going to take some time off from work, which will give me the time to do whatever needs to be done. I'm planning to go down to Charleston and stay with Melissa for a while. I have a lot of thinking and sorting out to do. My life just took a turn I would have never imagined in a million years."

"Yes, I know. Being a widow isn't easy, especially at such a young age. Looks like you have lots of people around who will be there for you. Stephen seems like a good friend too. You two need to help each other. And you're right, take Melissa up on her offer; it will be a great opportunity to spend some time away from here. Maybe both of you could take a trip somewhere." She gave Crystal a long hug, and they both cried. She told Crystal that she loved her very much; then, she and her husband gathered their things and left.

Melissa and Stephen did the same thing Crystal did. They slept, hard. They both fell asleep, one on the sofa and the other on the loveseat; All the while, Crystal slept across her bed, still completely dressed.

Some point later during the night, Crystal slipped off her clothes and got under the covers. Now, the sun shone through the blinds, and she awakened to the smell of coffee brewing. Putting on sweatpants and a t-shirt, she went down the stairs. Melissa sat at the breakfast table; she sipped a cup of coffee and read the newspaper.

"Good morning, sleepy head," she said.

"Good morning," said Crystal. "Is Stephen gone?"

"No, he's in the bathroom. Honestly, I don't think he wants to go home. We're going to go to the grocery store for you. Interestingly, of all the things people brought, no one thought to bring simple items—like sugar, trash bags, soap or eggs and bacon. I'm waiting for him to come out, and then we're leaving."

"Good morning, Crystal," said Stephen, rubbing his head with a towel as he walked into the room. "How did you sleep?"

"I slept well. Frankly, it was the best sleep I have had in a long time. I think it was from pure exhaustion though. I don't even remember dreaming about anything."

"Did Melissa tell you we were going to the store? We'll be right back," he said. "Any special requests?"

"No, you guys go ahead. Thanks for doing this for me."

"No problem," he said. "I'm going to stop by the Seafood Market and pick up some catfish. I'm in the mood for some southern fried catfish and grits. Are there any grits in there?"

"Come on, you know me. There's always at least a five pound bag here!"

"Cool. We gone hook it up!"

Melissa took her purse, and they went out the door.

Chapter 39

Closure

The telephone rang, and Crystal quickly answered.

"Crystal?" The voice was soft and faint. "Hi. It's Amanda. I didn't get a chance to talk to you yesterday. I really need to talk. Mind if I come over?" she asked.

"Yeah, come on, I'm up she said. When will you be here?"

"I'm in front of your house right now," she said.

"Okaaay, well come on in." Crystal moved over to a window on the front side of the house. Sure enough, there she sat in her car looking toward Crystal. Crystal went to the front door and opened it as Amanda walked up the driveway, towards the front door.

"Hi," said Amanda entering the house.

"Hi, Amanda. Are you stalking me?" She asked smiling.

"No… no. I'm sorry to barge in, Crystal, but I really need to talk to you. I'm sure that I have the answers to some of your unanswered questions about Donnie."

"Have a seat," Crystal said. "Is that right?" she asked sarcastically. She recalled that in recent weeks prior to Donnie's death, Amanda had flaunted a new aversion for her. Why would she believe anything this woman had to say? She pondered.

"I'm going to get straight to the point. I hate to do this, especially the day after the funeral, but I must. The truth is, I've wanted to tell you this for months now, but Donnie insisted that I stay quiet about it."

"Stay quiet?"

"Yes. Donnie had been living with me since he left you. We've been a couple ever since the night he and Stephen fought." Paused for effect, she looked at Crystal who remained unmoved by her confession. She continued. "You've been wondering what's been going on in your marriage since around April, right?"

"Mmm hmm." *So what, Donnie could have told you that.*

In April, Donnie took me out for National Administrative Assistant's Day. He took me to the Café Milano, and we had lunch. During the conversation, we began talking about our relationships. I had broken up with my boyfriend last year, and he began teasing me about not having a man. We flirted. We never had before. The conversation was kind of weird, but we both felt... Well, it was sort of like chemistry. We clicked and it was so obvious that we were attracted to each other. Candidly, he told me that although he loved you, he wasn't in love with you, and didn't know what to do about it. I encouraged him to work at his marriage, but I don't think he was really listening. I'm sure you remember the night you were out with a student. Things changed for you, right?"

Questioningly, Crystal sat staring at Amanda, not wanting to believe her but wondering how she had all of this information. Amanda continued, "He called me that night. He was furious, and it was the first time he had ever called me at home for something not work related. He said he needed someone to talk to... you were at the hospital with some girl from your class. Earlier that day I had encouraged him to make a special dinner for you. By the time he left the office, he seemed very excited and thought about the possibility that there still was hope for the marriage... Later that night, he was so mad when he called me, he just rambled on and on. Said, he couldn't believe that you had put a total stranger before him, and then he said that the two of you were not on the same page anymore. He wanted someone who understood him, and knew what made him tick—

someone like me. From then on he'd work late nights, and so would I, just so we could be together."

Crystal could feel the pulse of her heartbeat in her throat. She was sure her nose was red because she could feel her face heating up from anger. "What do you mean, 'be together'?" asked Crystal with tears streaming down her face.

"I don't mean like that, although we did kiss a few times during that time. We'd just work together as we always did. We no longer denied the attraction we felt was there. Night after night, we'd work until eight, nine or 10:00. Finally, he'd leave the office and go home, but sometimes we'd go out to dinner, just to enjoy each other's company. When he sent you on that trip, he really did want you to go and enjoy yourself in Charleston. We had no intentions of getting together while you were gone."

"Why should I believe you?" asked Crystal.

"Be real. How would I know this stuff if I didn't live it, Crystal? Other than kissing a few times, we didn't cross the line physically until he got back from Charleston. I was the one who had encouraged him to go, to find out if he could find the spark that attracted him to you in the first place. I felt myself falling for him, and I didn't want him to reciprocate unless he had given his marriage all the effort he should. He was devastated when he got back. Said that he knew something had happened, but he just couldn't put his finger on it. He came straight to the office when he got back in town. Before the McCarter meeting while we were in his office, he told me that he was going to really work on his marriage when he got back from Chicago. He felt like he'd been very unfair to you. Said he had hoped that he could reconnect with you. But he couldn't. He even told me that you had tried to pull out all the stops for him, but he just couldn't do it."

Crystal thought she'd truly be sick. "Stop lying!" Crystal shouted.

"Crystal, I'm not making this up. Why do you think I reacted the way I did when Melissa called me? I love Donnie and he loves me. Loved me." She looked down, "Like I said, we've been living together since he left you. If you don't believe me, you can come to my house. All of his things are still there, although some others are in storage. I live right off Hwy 51 in the Arbor Glen Community. He was on his way home when he died."

Livid, Crystal couldn't stand it anymore. "Home? What home? You have been in love with my husband, and now want to unnerve me. You're making this up. Why? Do you think he left you some money or something? Yeah, he and Stephen integrated you into their company, and their lives, but I don't have to. Give me one good reason why I should take anything you say to be fact? You have treated me dirty for months. You hindered me from talking to my husband when I called the office, and now the day after I bury him, here you come fabricating lies—talking about you were his lover. Where's the proof? How many other people know about this so-called relationship?"

"No one, not even Stephen. We came to the office in separate cars and didn't go to lunch or anything together during the day. You have the nerve to ask why I treated you dirty. Because I was the one at home every night trying to clean up the mess you made of him. He was devastated after he found out about you and Stephen; especially the way he found out. That's what hurt him the most. Neither of you were honest with him. He blamed himself for driving you to the arms of another man. He often told me that you'd probably leave him for someone else because he wasn't spending time with you. Not in his wildest dreams did he think it would be his brother!"

Amanda did seem sincere to Crystal, but she was having a difficult time ingesting everything she heard. Crystal paced the floor, glaring at the woman sitting in her living room. Where in the world did she come from, and why wasn't this nightmare ending for her? *Too much pain, no victory to gain. Jesus, keep me near the cross.* She felt like going back to sleep and not waking up until a year in the future. Perhaps then, the pain of the last few months and the present misery would become a distant memory. She walked over to Amanda, and Amanda stood up looking Crystal directly in the eyes.

"Crystal, I didn't come here to tarnish what you and Donnie had. I wanted to fill in the missing pieces. Let you know what he really had going on. Several times I begged him to tell you where he

251

was. Told him there shouldn't be anymore secrets. At first he didn't want to do that, but then he was supposed to tell you everything Sunday when he came over. I surmised that didn't happen when I came over Sunday night. You can't imagine how I felt having to grieve his death, alone." A tear rolled down her face… "Crystal, I'm pregnant."

Crystal felt a stinging sensation in her fingertips and saw Amanda's dark hair swish past her face as her head quickly reeled back from the impact of the slap she'd laid across the left side of her face. Before Amanda could recover, Crystal grabbed the woman by her shirt collar and then pushed her with all her might. Amanda fell back onto the couch.

"Please, please let's not do this. I told you I'm pregnant," she cried out. "Donnie knew. He said we'd be happy soon, and that he hoped it was a girl because he wanted to name her Joy. He kept saying that Joy comes in the morning. I never quite knew what that meant, but I do hope it is a girl."

"AMANDA, GET OUT OF MY HOUSE!" Crystal screamed so loud, her throat burned from the strain. "GET OUT! NOW!" As she got up to leave, the words "Amanda…baby" came back to Crystal. She understood that Donnie had tried to give her a message before he died. He tried to tell her that he had messed up, and Amanda was pregnant with his baby. In fact, the last thing he said to her was something about a baby, Amanda and Crystal. Mortified, she stood dazed, feeling like she would lose her mind right there in her living room with her husband's baby's mama watching. She collapsed on the couch and put her face in her hands. "HOW MUCH MORE LORD, HUH? HOW MUCH MORE?" She could hardly believe Amanda's revelation; the fateful twist being that her late husband left his legacy with another woman. A white woman, his assistant who was "like family." *Well, isn't this special. Even from the grave, he still got me.*

Crystal laughed out loud and held her stomach at the same time. She was sick to her stomach and felt like she would retch just like Amanda did the night Donnie died. She found the entire situation ironic as she sorted it all out. For months, maybe even for a year, she'd known something was wrong, yet he denied everything. He had fallen out of love with her and in love with Amanda. She had begged him to tell her what was wrong and prayed unceasingly that all the friction between them would end. She tried making herself believe that the pressure of growing the business and taking on new accounts was the only thing between her and her husband. When things didn't get better, she found herself in the arms and bed of another man. He chided and cast her aside because *she* had messed up. But all along, *he* was in love with another woman. *Ain't this something? Here it was that he had feelings for another woman long before she was ever with Stephen.* Instantly, it all made sense.

"Amanda, I believe you. I believe you. I'm sorry for slapping you. Are you ok?"

"Why?" she asked.

"Before he died, Donnie struggled to talk to me and Stephen, and we kept discouraging him to speak. The last thing he said was my name, your name, and baby. We didn't know what it meant, but it makes sense now. How far along are you?"

"I'm eight weeks," she said.

"So you've known for a little while then?"

"Yes. He went with me to the doctor two weeks ago, and we could see the heart beating on the ultrasound." She smiled a little as she reminisced.

"So, what do you want from me?" asked Crystal.

"I've told you, I don't want anything from you. I wanted you to know the truth, as it really happened. I realize that he wasn't divorced from you, and I know you probably think it was pretty low of me. I never meant to hurt you or your marriage. We just fell in love...it wasn't planned."

Crystal definitely understood that. She felt a calming peace encompass her. Knowing that God was showing her the power of forgiveness, she could do nothing but forgive Donnie, Amanda, and finally herself. Growing inside Amanda was Donnie's seed. She mentally prepared herself to deal with it, but knew that God would have to work yet another miracle for her to accept it and all of the implications of having a new unexpected family member.

Though oblivious to the fact, Stephen now had a niece or nephew, and her deceased husband, his brother, fathered a child by another woman. Once again she thought of the irony of the whole situation and told Amanda that she would be over soon to sort through Donnie's things. She also remembered his dying wish, which was to take care. She didn't know if he meant for her to 'take care' as a term of endearment, or to make sure that she provided for Amanda and his child. Whatever he meant, she knew that God would have to help her through it. She would be sure to take care of the little person Donnie created, and let the child know that their father was a good man. *Despite the fact that he got tired of me, wouldn't tell me, and fell in love with his assistant.*

"Thank you for being honest with me," said Crystal. "I'm glad that I finally know the truth, even if Donnie felt he couldn't tell me. It hurts me to know that he kept a secret like this from me and that he had fallen out of love with me. But you know what?" She raised her right hand as if worshipping God, "I'm going to be all right." She put her hand down and looked Amanda in the eye. "I'm going to be all right. By the grace of God, I know I will. I don't blame you."

Acting on an inkling sensed within her spirit, Crystal embraced Amanda, and Amanda reciprocated. They both cried together and apologized to each other. Then, Amanda left.

Crystal sat so she wouldn't fall down. *God says He doesn't put more on us than we can bear. But Lord...No, Crystal, no negative thoughts...I can bear this, I can bear this. With God's help, I can do anything.*

Melissa and Stephen returned home to find Amanda's car parked in front of the house, and a red-faced Amanda leaving.

"Hi Stephen, hi Melissa," she said as she passed them unloading groceries from the trunk of Melissa's car.

"You doin OK?" asked Stephen.

"Yeah, much better now. Crystal has some information to share with you. I hope you don't become too upset with me."

"Why don't you tell me what's going on," said Stephen sensing that another nightmare was taking place inside the house.

Melissa took two bags from Stephen's hands. "I told you there was more to her than meets the eye," she said under her breath. "I'm going to go check on my girl because I have a feeling girlfriend here dropped a bomb in there." She walked up the sidewalk and entered through the front door. "Crystal!" Melissa called out her name as she turned to shut the door behind her.

"Stephen, I'll give you the short version." She sighed deeply. "Donnie had been staying with me. We've been in love since the spring, and I'm eight weeks pregnant with your niece or nephew." She looked down at her feet while she waited for Stephen to say something. Since he didn't respond, she continued, "...and I hope this doesn't affect my job at the agency."

"Are you serious?" Stephen looked at her in disbelief.

"I wouldn't lie about something like this. Crystal didn't believe me at first, but she said something about Donnie trying to tell you right before he died."

Stephen thought for a moment, and then realized what she was talking about. "Yep. It was like some kind of cryptic message. So, he was trying to come clean before he died? It makes sense; he wanted us to take care of you and the baby." He leaned against the car to take everything in. He couldn't believe what he'd just learned about his younger brother. "Donnie tried to make me and Crystal feel so dirty, and like we were the scum of the earth. All while he'd been doing the same thing with you. Umph, umph, umph. Ain't this some mess?" Stephen said as if he were in a trance. He wrinkled his right eyebrow and shook his head back and forth.

"I'm sorry, Stephen. I never meant to cause you or your family any harm. I know it makes things between us uneasy, but I do hope I can keep my job, especially now."

"Well, I can't fire someone based on a poor judgment call in their personal life. If that were the case, I need to fire myself!" he said laughing, but not really knowing why. "I need you now more than ever. The three of us ran the place, remember? When is the baby due?"

"Late May, early June. The doctor isn't really sure of the date. It's a guestimate anyway. I would like to work up until the due date if possible. I never anticipated being a single mom."

"Well, I can't make any promises to you, but it is time for performance reviews, isn't it? Plus, we're family. Don't worry." He pulled her to him and embraced her for the first time ever.

"Thank you."

"You're welcome. Drive safely, and I'll be in the office tomorrow. If you need anything today, just call me on my cell."

"Will do. See you in the morning." She walked off, and Stephen took the remaining bags inside where Crystal had brought Melissa up to speed. All three of them group hugged and cried once again.

"Y'all, we got to stick together. This life thing ain't no joke is it? The twists and turns come so fast; if you ain't got God in your life, you may as well hang it up!" said Melissa.

She prepared breakfast while Crystal showered. Stephen went home to check on things and then returned to have breakfast with the ladies. They enjoyed each other's company as they reminisced about their past experiences with Donnie. It made Crystal feel better to laugh and to think about the good times. For almost a year, she'd been sad and unsure about her husband and marriage. She knew a new chapter was beginning for her.

Epilogue

December

Christmas flavor filled every room, and the day had finally arrived when Crystal didn't wake up and cry at some point during the day. It was Christmas Eve. Melissa decorated her condo so nicely that Crystal felt like she was trapped inside a Hallmark greeting card. The festive décor renewed Crystal's heart and mind. For so many months this past year, her heart had been heavy for many different reasons.

Donnie's death occurred several weeks prior to the holiday season, and Crystal decided not to return to work after her bereavement leave ended. The Principal accepted her request to extend her leave, and she took Melissa up on her offer to stay with her in Charleston until after the holidays. She was so thankful for the change in scenery, since the memories of Donnie and all that had happened during the year haunted her thoughts and weighed heavily upon her. Eagerly, she looked forward to starting off the New Year with a clean slate.

"Hey sleepy face," Melissa said while knocking and opening the guest bedroom door at the same time.

Crystal rolled over to see a smiling Melissa wearing a Santa Claus hat and a red pantsuit. She looked like one of Santa's helpers.

"Girl, where in the world are you going, dressed like that?" she asked while yawning and stretching. "What time is it anyway?"

"It's 8:45; I'm going to work for a little while."

"Work? It's Christmas Eve! What's wrong with you? What kind of company do you work for?"

"Calm down, the management team is meeting at the office, and then we're taking gifts to a family we adopted. You should see the stuff our employees brought in. People really get caught up in this kind of stuff. It's too bad they don't act lovingly toward others all year. I should be back before lunch, though. You can come along if you want to."

"No thanks. I'll stay here and enjoy the festive atmosphere!"

"Are you cracking on my decorations?"

"No, not at all. I told you it makes me feel better. It reminds me of when we were growing up, and we'd all pitch in to help Mom decorate the living room. I've just never been in a home where decorations filled every room. Go, have fun. I'll be just fine."

"Ok, come lock the door for me. I have a lot of boxes to carry out." Crystal slowly got out of bed and followed her to the front door.

After Melissa left, she decided to stay up instead of going back to bed. She sat on the futon sofa and flipped through the cable channels. Holiday programming was seemingly on every channel. She turned to the Weather Channel to see what it was like in Pittsburgh. She and Donnie visited her parents one year for Christmas, and there were twelve inches of snow on the ground. It was their first white Christmas together, and they'd stayed up cuddling in front of the fireplace after her parents went to sleep.

She waited for the northeast forecast. The weatherman said it was snowing with an expected accumulation of about six inches before the end of the day. Crystal went into the kitchen to get the cordless phone. She dialed her parents' number, expecting to hear the sound of pots and pans banging in the background from her mother's usual holiday smorgasbord.

"Hello and MERRY CHRISTMAS!" Lila said answering the phone.

"Why thank you. Merry Christmas to you too! What are you doing? No, let me guess. You're making sweet potato pies."

"No, I made those last night. I just put the turkey in the oven." Crystal could hear her mother closing the oven. She pictured her wiping her hands on a dishtowel as she spoke. "Your father needs to come in here and help me clean this kitchen."

"I wish I could be there, I'd like some homemade pie."

"I'll bring some next week when we drive down. I want you to stay put and relax. You need it. Sometimes our bodies take a while to catch up with us when we go through things. I'll be there to take care of you next week. Any other special requests?"

"You know what I want, so don't eat too much of it tomorrow because I want you to fix it here. I'll buy the ingredients for you to make some of your world famous dressing when you get here. I can't wait to taste it. No matter how many times Melissa or I have tried to make it, it just doesn't taste like yours."

"Oh, chile that is the easiest recipe," but I'll be happy to make it for my girls."

"I saw on the Weather Channel that you'll be having another white Christmas."

"Yeah. We've had a white day everyday lately. My bones are getting too old for this cold air.

"I know you probably have the heat blazin' up in there. How many do you expect to have over?"

"I think only ten this year. Everyone wants to do their own thing with their own families; it's perfectly fine with me because I'm tired anyway. Oh, we got your gifts. I'll call you tomorrow after we open them."

"Ok, thanks. I just called to hear your voice. Melissa is gone, and I haven't talked to Stephen today. Melissa went to play Santa Claus with her office staff. She's been cooking stuff all week, so I'm sure the two of us will have more than we need."

"What's Stephen doing for the holiday?"

"You know, we haven't talked about it? I have no idea. He's been very elusive this week."

"I'll bet you'll see him today or tomorrow."

"Who knows? I think he's trying to give me space, though. But anyway, I was just calling. I'll talk to you tomorrow. Be good!"

"No, you be good."

Crystal pressed the button to turn the phone off and then decided to dress for a morning run. Since she'd been in Charleston, she jogged in the mornings along the Ashley River. Her physical activity inspired Melissa to walk in the evenings. On some days, they enjoyed long walks through the condominium complex, while the December coastal air whipped their faces.

Occasionally, Crystal visited Waterfront Park to write in her journal, or walk along the Battery. Oftentimes, she remembered the time she had spent there with Stephen. He had been a wonderful friend during her sabbatical from life in North Carolina. They had continued to lean on each other while they mourned the death of Donnie. Daily, he called or e-mailed her to see how she was doing. If she hadn't heard from him by the time she went to bed, she'd send a text message to his cell phone just to say "Hi." She missed him, and he missed her. Yet, they needed the time apart. Even though her marriage had been over for months and Stephen had separated from Pam, they both were aware that a public relationship between the two of them would be objectionable to others, and they didn't want to deal with criticism or judgment from onlookers so soon after Donnie's death.

Stephen gave Crystal updates about Amanda. Although Crystal had forgiven Amanda, she still had trouble accepting the fact that her husband had a "baby momma" other than herself. She didn't want to hear any updates or have any connection with Amanda, not yet anyway.

Although Stephen was disappointed at what had happened, he was happy that his family did still have a lifeline, and he looked forward to having a new baby around. Amanda was now fourteen weeks pregnant with her abdomen beginning to show signs of the life inside. She promised Stephen that she would not reveal who the father of her baby was, as long as she was able to keep her job. Stephen didn't have a problem with Amanda or her work performance. As far as he was concerned, she still performed her job as she should have, and he wasn't concerned with what happened in her personal life. Business was just that, business.

Before leaving town, Crystal took Amanda up on her offer to collect Donnie's things from her house. She made the trip to the other side of town toward Pineville, and passed the site where Donnie wrecked. The skid marks were still visible on the road.

Crystal had felt very uncomfortable being in the place that Donnie had called home while she had been on the other side of town wondering where he'd been for weeks.

Amanda was cordial, and Crystal warm, but reserved. She did not want to chitchat with Amanda, and quickly sorted through his personal items. She left behind several items and Amanda told her that Donnie had put some larger items in Queen City Mini Storage, not far from her house. In time, Crystal knew she'd have to come to terms with Amanda and her child. But for the moment, she chose not to think about either one of them.

She usually started her day with what had become a customary jog to the downtown area. She took East Bay Street to Market, and then finished on Meeting. After her jog, she walked until she ended up at the Battery. There, she walked around while taking in the surroundings. She enjoyed the cool fifty-degree breeze on her face and hair.

Overlooking the Atlantic Ocean, she stood against the railing taking in the beautiful scenery. She imagined what Stephen might be doing back in North Carolina. She missed his company and wished they could spend the holidays together. However, he hadn't mentioned that he wanted to see her during the season, so she used the time to heal from the year's hurts. She purchased him a gift, just in case, but figured they'd spend time together once she returned to Charlotte. She turned to walk in the direction of a park bench and noticed a car similar to Stephen's parked in the distance. There was a man inside looking in her direction. For a brief moment, she imagined it was Stephen. She envisioned herself running to him as if they were in an old movie, and free of inhibition, he would embrace her.

"Girl, snap out of it," she said to herself as she walked toward the bench. She couldn't seem to take her eyes off the car. The man inside kept his eyes on her as well. As she got closer to the bench, the man inside the car opened the door and stood looking directly at her. She thought she was imagining things because the man looked exactly like Stephen. He was tall with distinguishing features. Then she saw it. The smile. The million-dollar smile. It had been Stephen watching her from afar. She ran to him, and he embraced her. *It's not a fantasy.* They were in the place where it all began. He held her tightly. Then, he picked her up off her feet and spun her around just as she had imagined.

"Boy, put me down! How long were you watching me?" she asked as she hit him on the chest.

"Boy, who you calling boy?" he asked smiling. "Not long," he said. "Merry Christmas."

"Merry Christmas to you too," she said beaming. She was happier than she'd been in months. "What are you doing here?"

"What do you think I'm doing here? I came to spend Christmas with my family. You're all I have left." He took Crystal by the hand and lead her to the park bench where they'd been just months before. They sat down and he put his arm around her shoulders. He pulled her close to him. "I've really missed you..." He looked down and took her hand in his. "I'd like to give you something, and I don't want to give it to you in front of Melissa." He reached inside his pocket and pulled out a long jewelry box. He looked at the gold wrapped box as if he were contemplating whether or not to give it to her. After a few moments, he handed the box to her. Crystal hesitated for fear of what might be inside. She assumed that inside was a watch or bracelet. Deliberately, she peeled the gold paper away from the box, and then opened it. The box held a blue sapphire ring with two diamond baguettes on either side. "Stephen!"

"What?" he asked as if he couldn't believe her response to his generous gift.

"What is this?" she asked nervously.

"It's a ring, and it's for you. I want you to wear it. I figured you wouldn't open it if it were a ring box, so I had the salesperson help me trick you."

"Stephen, I... I can't..."

"Stop. Don't ruin this moment for me. Let me explain; I want you to be the special person in my life, Crystal. I love you, and I know you love me, even if you don't say it right now. I don't want you to rush into anything. It's too soon, plus I need to straighten out my situation with Pam. But I don't want us to miss out on an opportunity to be happy in the meantime. I think you and I could be very happy together, and I want you in my life, for the rest of my earthly life, Crystal." She continued looking at the ring in the box. "I'd like for you to take the ring. Put it on." He took the ring from the box, "Allow me. I'm not asking you to marry me, but I'm asking you to commit to being with me until we feel the time is right. Are you willing?" He slipped the ring on her left ring finger that had been bare since Donnie moved his things out of the house.

She admired how it looked, and felt on her hand. Crystal was so happy to hear Stephen confess his love for her. This time, she did not feel bound by her commitment to Donnie. "I love you too, Stephen, and I am pleased to say I will be your friend, your whatever, whenever you want me to. Let's just take one day at a time and not rush, OK?"

"Thank you, Jesus!" He threw both hands in the air like his favorite football team had just made the winning touchdown. "I had hoped you wouldn't leave a brother hanging out here in the cold! I can promise you, it'll be a fun ride. I've been in love with you for a long time, and I want to spend the rest of my life proving how much I do love you."

"Ohhh, you're so sweet." She reached over and hugged him tightly. He kissed her softly on the forehead, and they melted in each other's arms. "I love you," he told her.

"I love you too," she returned.

She put her head on his shoulder. "Stephen, how did you know where to find me?"

He smiled. "I didn't know you'd be here. I was just cruising, while trying to think of the words to say when I did see you. I was just as shocked to see you standing over there. I thought I was imagining things!"

"Me too. So you've been scheming with Melissa? Umm hmm. And she told me that she was going to feed the homeless or something about a family this morning. Ya'll were up to no good!" she said playfully punching him in the side.

"She really is delivering presents to a family today. I told her I'd be in town around 10:00 this morning. She said you sometimes sleep late, so I was just killing time until I heard from her. I drove by this area because we shared something special here. Did you eat breakfast?"

"No."

"Want some? I could go for a big southern breakfast."

"Let's go to Shoney's. I saw one on the way in and they serve breakfast or brunch until around 1:00."

"That'll work. Shoney's or better yet Golden Corral. They have the best corn beef hash!"

"Girl, that stuff is nasty, and I am not stepping one foot inside of a Golden Corral any time soon. Don't you remember the drama we had trying to get that account? We're going to Shoney's because I could go for a big bowl of grits, scrambled eggs, and bacon. Then I could go back and get some of those French toast sticks."

"You want to throw down huh?"

"Yeah. I'm really hungry. I've been thinking about you, and this ring all last night and this morning. Eating was the last thing on my mind. Actually, I've been praying about this for several days.

"Really?"

"Yeah. Getting divorced from Pam is just a formality, and I'm praying that it will be uneventful. The last time, I married for the wrong reasons. Moving forward, I want to make sure that every decision I make is within the will of God."

Stephen stood, and he and Crystal walked to his car. He drove off in search of Shoney's Restaurant.

At Shoney's they enjoyed themselves and they both made two trips to the buffet. As they ate and made small talk, Crystal reflected on how her life had changed over the last year. She'd lost her husband before she actually lost him to death, and she'd committed a sin she never thought she'd be capable of. Soon her husband's mistress and their unborn child would become a part of her life. But through everything, she still had Stephen in her life, and they were happy.

They finished their Christmas brunch and headed to the mall so Stephen could get a Christmas gift for Melissa.

"I can't believe you have me out here in all of this madness. I make it a rule to never go shopping on Christmas Eve."

"I won't be long, I promise. I just need to pick something up for her. She was the strong one for us both this year, you know. I don't know what I would have done if she hadn't been around for us when Donnie died. She's my sister too."

"Ok, you don't have to convince me."

They went inside Belk Department store where Crystal showed Stephen a crystal angel that Melissa had admired just the week before. He agreed the angel would make the perfect gift for her. Finally, after standing in the checkout line for more than ten minutes, he paid the cashier, and then they headed to Melissa's condo.

Melissa had returned from spreading Christmas cheer, and the smell of cinnamon hit Crystal and Stephen in the face as they opened the front door. She let out a howl when she saw Stephen walk in behind Crystal. "Heyyy Stephen!" she said as she moved quickly towards him. She threw her arms around him, and they embraced.

"Boy, it feels good to be loved," said Stephen smiling from ear to ear.

"You know we love you, Man! I thought you were trying to surprise her. Where have y'all been?"

"Girl, I did get surprised! Look at this," Crystal said holding out her left hand."

"What? Stephen!" She looked at him, then at Crystal. "What have y'all gone and done? Crystal! I can't believe this!" She burst into tears. "I'm so happy for you!" She couldn't control herself. "God does answer prayer, doesn't He? I know there's hope for me."

"Yes, He does!" said Stephen looking as if he'd just won the lottery. "He sure does." He pulled Crystal and Melissa close to him, and they group hugged like they had so many times before; only this time, it was a joyous occasion.

"I love y'all. I want both of you to know that." He let go of the group and held Crystal only. He looked into her eyes, and she returned the gaze. "Merry Christmas, Crystal. You have made me a very happy man."

Crystal smiled, and she felt light on her feet. "Merry Christmas to you too. I am a very happy woman!

Reading Group Discussion

1. Can you identify with Crystal? If so, in what way?

2. Do you know someone like Melissa?

3. Should Lila have told Crystal about her father's affair?
   yes!! She should've told her before then.

4. Was Donnie fair to Crystal in the beginning? In the end?
   end? no he was not
   (end) no he was not.

She kept crying to fix it

5. What do you think Crystal could have done differently in her marriage and on the trip to Charleston?
   Submit to God, resist the devil

6. Pam is a minor character in the story, yet a major character, as she is what keeps Stephen from being truly happy, even if he can't have Crystal. Do you think this could happen in real life? Could someone be so withdrawn that they miss the obvious?

7. Did anyone suspect that Amanda would have a significant role in the story? *No, I kn*
   I sensed that they were messing around but the end blew my mind.

8. Could you have found it in your heart to forgive as Donnie did before it was too late? *yes, it hard but yes esp. w/ them being in the wrong as well.*

9. If you were Crystal, would you want to be a part of Amanda's child's life? *yes. He is a part of Donnie. She loved Donnie*

10. Discuss how relationships with friends of the opposite sex can stay platonic. Can married people really be "good friends" with people of the opposite sex? *according to the circumstances*

11. Were you glad to see Crystal and Stephen together in the end? Why? *yes!!*

Thank you for reading

Brotherly Love & Betrayal.

Additional copies are available at
major bookstores nationwide
Amazon.com
Barnes & Noble.com
DaphineRobinson.com

See www.myspace.com/**daphineglennrobinson**
for the latest author updates.

Email Author@DaphineRobinson.com